Keep Me

CARLIE JEAN

*For Summer, whose love for grumpy,
tattooed men made me write this story.
And to the ones looking for that 'today was
a fairytale' feeling, this is for you.*

Content Warning

Nightmares

Assault

Explicit sexual content

Past abandonment

Contents

Content Warning iv
Playlist vii
Chapter One 1
Chapter Two 10
Chapter Three 17
Chapter Four 22
Chapter Five 27
Chapter Six 34
Chapter Seven 39
Chapter Eight 52
Chapter Nine 58
Chapter Ten 68
Chapter Eleven 74
Chapter Twelve 78
Chapter Thirteen 83
Chapter Fourteen 89
Chapter Fifteen 95
Chapter Sixteen 100
Chapter Seventeen 106
Chapter Eighteen 117
Chapter Nineteen 125
Chapter Twenty 128
Chapter Twenty-One 136
Chapter Twenty-Two 144
Chapter Twenty-Three 155
Chapter Twenty-Four 163
Chapter Twenty-Five 168
Chapter Twenty-Six 174
Chapter Twenty-Seven 183

Chapter Twenty-Eight 190
Chapter Twenty-Nine 196
Chapter Thirty 200
Chapter Thirty-One 208
Chapter Thirty-Two 216
Chapter Thirty-Three 224
Chapter Thirty-Four 231
Chapter Thirty-Five 234
Chapter Thirty-Six 237
Chapter Thirty-Seven 245
Chapter Thirty-Eight 253
Chapter Thirty-Nine 259
Chapter Forty 264
Chapter Forty-One 268
Chapter Forty-Two 277
Chapter Forty-Three 284
Chapter Forty-Four 289
Chapter Forty-Five 292
Epilogue 302
Acknowledgements 306
About the Author 308

Playlist

"Hurricane" - Luke Combs

"Today Was A Fairytale (Taylor's Version)" - Taylor Swift

"Honey" - Kehlani

"Naked" - James Arthur

"Wait for Me" - Motopony

"A Part of Your World" - Jodi Benson

"The Way She Rolls" - Nate Smith

"Fall Out of Love" - Salem, Carlie Hanson

"Burning" - Sam Smith

"Don't Go Away" - Oasis

"Coffee" - Miguel

"It's Yours" - J. Holiday

"Crazy Love" - Van Morrison

"Perfectly Wrong" - Shawn Mendes

"Kiss From a Rose" - Seal

"And I Love Her" - The Beatles

"Iris" - The Goo Goo Dolls

"Feel Like Makin' Love" - Bad Company

Chapter One

Camille

OCTOBER

A pair of hands wraps around my waist, and I instantly freeze as my mind transports me back to *that* day. Suddenly, I'm not at some nightclub in America but rather in the backstreets of my home island, Lorsica, just off the coast of France.

His hands grip my ass, and I shove him away the best I can. The man snarls at me, his face going beet red as he backhands me, making my vision blur before he shoves me to the ground, my elbow thumping into the concrete. I quickly scramble to my feet. No time to cry or scream as I remember my training, and I run as fast as I fucking can.

Even though my calves scream at me in protest, the alarm bells going off in my head are louder and they propel me to keep the lead on the three men chasing me.

When the hands currently gripping me grow tighter, it pulls me back to the present and I shove the stranger off. "No, thank you," I tell him politely, not wanting to make him angry.

Where's my best friend, Jasmine? I could really use her help right about now.

He grins mischievously, and my breath hitches as I worry that he's not going to leave me alone.

My eyes dart around the room, trying to focus on anything that isn't this man. I crane my neck, looking over the man's shoulders, and that's when I see *him.*

Ryker Lewis.

The man I've had a crush on for three years but have refused to approach.

And he's making his way toward us with a scowl on his face.

"No means fucking no," Ryker grits out, shoving the other man back. "If I see you near her again, you better fucking run. If I catch you, it won't be good."

His brawny chest heaves up and down as he glares at the man. While his attention isn't on me, I take him in for the first time up close like this. My eyes snag on his tattooed sleeve down his right arm, his biceps taut against his black T-shirt.

He's tall, broad, and full of sculpted muscles from his years of training as an athlete. And my favorite trait of his, those shoulder-length, dark brown waves resting on his shoulders that contrast with his stormy blue eyes.

He's domineering, broody, and intimidating as hell.

In my peripheral vision, I see Jasmine rushing to my side, but I can't take my eyes off him. There's something about him that draws me to him, like a gravitational force I have no control over.

"Camille, are you okay?" Jasmine asks, her mocha eyes fixated on me with concern.

I nod unconvincingly.

"Let me take you home, Camille," she urges, knowing exactly why I'm internally freaking out.

Ryker takes a protective step toward me, crowding my body with his. "I got her. You can go."

The feeling of safety cloaks my entire body, and it's almost foreign. I can't remember the last time someone made me feel like that.

My lips part as my breath is sucked into the back of my throat while I gaze between Jasmine and Ryker. "I'll be okay. I just want to get some fresh air." I shrug my shoulders, trying to seem unaffected.

"I'll go with you." Ryker's deep voice cuts through the loud bass music. His tone is final, with no room for discussion.

I swing my eyes back to him, surprised. Why is he insisting on going outside with me? The part of me that still has a crush on him is thrilled, while my romantic heart is bursting at the seams at the idea of spending a fraction of time with him. But the logical part of me knows not to get my hopes up.

Jasmine looks between the two of us with hesitancy. She finally relents when I give her a small nod of approval.

Ryker's warm breath hits my ear as he whispers, "Would it be okay if I hold you in front of me while we walk out? That way no one can touch you."

A shiver skates down my body, and for once, it's not from fear.

I haven't been able to stomach being touched since the incident because every time a guy tries to get close to me, my body sets off alarms that I'm not safe.

But I find myself nodding, wanting to be embraced in the safety of his arms.

Ryker places his hands on my waist, and surprisingly, the contact makes shocks of something unnamed pop in my belly as he pulls me toward him and twists so that my back is to him. I'm rather tall at five-foot-eleven, but I fit perfectly under his chin, my body easily shielded by his as he wraps his arms gently around the middle of my stomach.

It's the first time I haven't flinched from another man's touch.

"I got you," he murmurs into my ear. With that assurance, I begin taking steps forward and he follows suit.

To my amazement, the sea of bodies seems to part for us, people getting out of the way when they see us moving toward the front door. It must be because of the scowl that takes residence on his face.

Once we break free into the cool fall breeze, I can finally breathe for the first time tonight. I take a deep inhale, close my eyes as I hold it, then let it go. I repeat it three times while I try distracting myself.

All while forgetting Ryker's still holding on to me.

Why hasn't he let go yet?

We stay silent for a moment until I start to enjoy the feeling of his arms around me a little too much.

I clear my throat and he lets his arms fall from my waist as he takes a step away from me.

I turn to face him, and I'm nearly knocked on my ass as I take him in this up close for the first time. Out of the dim lighting and flashing strobes, I can see his face more clearly.

He's beautiful.

His beard is neatly trimmed, covering a prominent jaw, with striking deep blue eyes to top it off. They're darker than mine and steal the breath from my lungs. He has this bad boy feel to him with his medium-length tousled hair and tattoos. Not to mention he plays baseball, which happens to be my favorite sport.

I like it all more than I should. He's everything I've been raised to stay away from.

I've never been more attracted to a man than I am to him. It's been that way for the last three years, ever since I first laid eyes on him.

I was on my way to cover the girls' softball team's game

that day, when I nearly ran into him on my way to get there. Words failed me at that moment when our eyes locked, but I quickly pulled it together, apologized, and kept hustling toward my destination.

But ever since that glance, he intrigued me. I heard about him around the baseball facility, but I had never had the courage to speak to him. Instead, I just crushed on him from afar. Eyeing him from the highest spot in the bleachers, making sure I went unseen.

Not that he'd notice me, but any girl with a crush gets it. I'd ogle him from afar, his signature low bun under his ball cap, his baseball pants doing nothing to hide his muscular thighs or perfect ass.

And now? He's up close and personal, looking at me with concern.

"What happened in there?" he asks. "No bullshit."

I falter, not quite sure why I want to explain what happened to a stranger, yet I find myself wanting to.

"No bullshit?" I question him back, raising a single brow to try to lighten the atmosphere surrounding us.

He doesn't budge, his scowl loyally on his face. "It means don't bullshit me. No secrets, no lies. I don't do that shit."

"Why do you even want to know? Why are you out here to begin with?" I blurt, unable to contain the questions swirling in my mind.

Ryker remains stoic, except for his sapphire eyes. They soften a smidge, just enough for me to notice it. "I feel protective of you for some reason," he grumbles like it's the last thing he wants to admit.

My heart threatens to flutter in my chest at his words, but I know not to read too much into them. He's a man, a seemingly good man, who wants to keep another person safe. It's a natural human thing, not because he feels something for me in particular.

I'd do well to keep that in mind.

Our eyes linger on one another's for a moment, the perfect fall weather wrapping around the space between us. As much as a part of me yearns to tell him, I don't. He's getting the bullshit he specifically asked not to get.

"I just don't like when people touch me without my permission. That's all," I partially lie because it's still a true statement.

Ryker scowls at me, crossing his corded forearms over his chest. "You looked like you saw a ghost in there."

"If I'd seen a ghost, I would've screamed, and that would've been interesting. I put heavy metal singers to shame," I attempt to put some humor into my words, but it falls flat.

He just stares at me, his dark blue eyes bouncing back and forth between mine, like he's trying to see through them.

"I know we don't know each other, but if something happened to you—" he starts, but I cut him off.

"Exactly. We don't know each other, so it's none of your business." My voice is curt, more than I intended it to be.

Ryker's scowl deepens, his chest heaving a deep breath as he looks up at the sky. He clearly doesn't like my answer, but it's the truth.

We don't know each other. I don't need to go spilling my demons to him.

But my heart tells me to lighten up a bit because it's not in my nature to be sassy like that. I step forward and place my hand on his forearm. "Hey, look at me," I order, using the confident and direct tone I was raised to speak in. I may be Camille Blanchette here, but Maribel De Pont is hard to get rid of.

Ryker's eyes meet mine, looking down at my manicured nails on his tattooed arm. I remove my hand, noting how the brief contact made warmth unfurl in my belly.

"I'm okay. You don't even know my name anyway, so let it go and go enjoy your night."

His brows pinch together, and it's then that I wonder if I'll ever see him doing something other than frown at me. "I know your name, Camille."

Oh.

He knows my name. But how? I was sure I remained invisible to him for the past three years.

"Must be a lucky guess," I say with a grin.

He shakes his head, his eyes roaming over my face. "The gala last year. Jasmine introduced you."

"That's right, I remember seeing you briefly. I only knew who you were because of baseball. I work for the school's paper and I cover the girls' teams. I also love baseball in general, so obviously I know of both the men's and women's team's players," I ramble, something I never, *ever* do. It's that damn crush making me talk faster than an auctioneer and spill more than I need to.

"You like baseball, princess?" His eyes lighten, but his lips remain in a tight line.

My stomach threatens to bottom out. Princess? Where did that come from? There's no way he could know…right?

"Princess?" I balk, taking a step back from him.

"You just don't seem like the kind of girl who likes baseball, that's all," he grunts, eyeing my outfit.

"And you don't seem like the kind of guy who smiles much."

"You're not wrong." He shrugs and blows out a breath. "Are you going to be okay?"

"I already was okay. I just needed a minute to clear my head outside. You can't take the sunshine out of this girl." I smile, feeling that part of myself coming back to life. Whenever I get triggered, it fades, but it always comes back.

I expect to elicit a smile out of him, but I'm rewarded with another grunt instead.

"Good." Then he digs into his jeans, and a beep sounds from behind me.

I turn to see a sport bike at the curb, an all-black beauty. Seriously? Does he also need to drive *that*? How much hotter can he get? I'm already feeling warmer than is normal in the middle of October.

He takes his key to the back end, then lifts it to retrieve his helmet. As I eye him, I find myself reeling with envy. I want the rush of riding on the back of his bike, feeling the wind around us as we drive through the winding roads near the mountains.

Ryker walks back over to me, and for a second, I think he's going to offer me a ride, but my hopes deflate the minute he opens his mouth.

"Are you good to walk back in there with your friends?"

"Yeah, go. Thank you for helping me," I say, my voice smaller than I'd like. I turn on my heel, not giving him time to see the disappointment in my eyes that shouldn't be there in the first place.

"Princess," he calls out, stopping me in my tracks.

I've never liked the title, but hearing it laced with his rough, gravelly tone has me rethinking my stance. I like it coming from him. I like it a lot.

"Ryker the biker?" I respond, looking at him over my shoulder with a small smile.

His brows narrow, nearly touching in the middle. "Absolutely not."

I giggle, unable to contain it. "Too bad." I smirk, then head back into the club, leaving Ryker on the curb, likely with a scowl on his lips. I'd bet my entire savings on it.

I find Jasmine with ease and we agree to leave. Our car ride is quiet as we're both exhausted from the night. I can tell

Jasmine's upset about something, but I won't push her to talk about it. Just like I know she's not pushing me to talk about what happened with Ryker.

Because truthfully, I don't even know what happened myself. Ryker's a lot grumpier than I imagined. I itch to find out why, but what's the point?

My upbeat attitude would annoy him, so it's best I just let go of my stupid crush. Even if it got worse tonight after looking up at him so close, feeling his muscles twitch under my palm and the way he held me in his arms.

Ugh, I need to stop. This is my last year of university, and I need to spend it investing in myself, not in feelings.

Besides, if my parents were to find me somehow, I'd be forced to move back home and live out the life they have planned for me. Finding some way to use my love for the people of my country to lure me back in.

Chapter Two

Ryker

"**R**y guy, don't do this to me," Theo whines through the phone.

Fucking Theo and his stupid nicknames.

I honestly don't know how we're such good friends. We met in kindergarten and we've been best friends ever since, despite being complete opposites. Theo's all sunshine and jokes, while I'm just not.

Don't get me wrong, my life is great. I just don't radiate sunshine like this fucking guy does.

Unless you account for my dad walking out on us when I was twelve and never looking back. That may be my issue. I have no idea where he is. Hell, I might even have siblings now. But I don't care either way.

He left and he's been dead to me since.

What kind of man walks out on his family? Because he was *bored*? I remember my parents fighting when I was little and that was always his argument. My mother had no time for him. My mother worked too much. My mother wasn't fun anymore. My mother loved me more than him.

Fuck him.

Fuck him for making my mother feel like less than she is. Fuck him for leaving us because we weren't enough for him. *Fuck* him for ruining any desire I had to ever fall in love.

If my own blood could up and leave me, who's to say someone else won't? I've been left high and dry once. I'm not going through that shit again.

"Ry guy?" Theo drawls, reminding me he's waiting for a response.

"I'm not going out tonight. Halloween is for children," I mutter, erasing a line on my iPad from a sketch I'm working for a client that I'm tattooing on Tuesday.

"We're all kids at heart really, aren't we?" Theo chuckles to himself.

"Theo," I groan, wanting to end this painful conversation. "You have lots of friends. Ask someone else."

"But I want to ask my closest friend. C'mon, Ryker, come out with me for once."

"I don't have a costume," I retort, shading in the scales on the koi fish that's wrapped around a flower.

"Wear your baseball uniform from the team for all I care, just come," he pleads. "Aurora will be there, and Cameron. Your new siblings-to-be."

Great.

They're nice, don't get me wrong. But I'm not exactly looking to add more people into my life. I'd rather it just be me, my mom, Theo, and baseball. But my mom said yes to Aurora's dad's proposal, making us soon-to-be siblings once they get married next summer.

"And her friend Jasmine, who's also my bestie now too. You'll like her. She's witty. Oh, and Camille will be there also," he continues on as if her name didn't make the digital pen fall from my hand and to the ground at the mention of it.

Camille.

The one woman in this world who stirs something in me. Annoyance for one because of her damn overly bubbly personality. But if I'm being honest, most of that annoyance comes from the fact that I think she's the most striking thing to walk the earth.

I hate it, and her, for it. What business does she have being that fucking beautiful?

She also makes me fucking stressed. The moment I saw her at the gala last year, I nearly stopped breathing, not just because of how pretty she is, but because of the primal feeling that throttled my veins.

Something inside of me yearned to protect her. From what, I don't know, yet I felt this overwhelming need to look out for her. It might be possessive and overprotective of me, but these are two things I can't feed.

Because if I have something to protect, it also means I have something to lose.

I can't control it when it comes to her, and it drives me fucking crazy. I haven't slept with anyone since the gala last year because every time I even consider it, I see her in my mind.

Then I saw her at that club a few weeks ago, and I nearly lost it when that guy put his hands on her, even more so when she reacted the way she did. The minute her eyes widened, her skin paled, and her spine went ramrod straight, I knew I had to step in.

Maybe it's the glacial, nearly silver hue of her eyes, the dimples in her cheeks, or the silky champagne hair that I want so badly to run my fingers through.

There's something vulnerable about her that I'm drawn to. She comes off like the sun radiates through her, yet I can see something more beneath the surface. And I want to dig through her barriers until I find out what it is and hurt whoever is responsible for it.

After our time outside the club, I found myself wanting things I couldn't have. Things I know I shouldn't want. Like pushing her up against a wall and kissing the hell out of her. Or spreading her thighs, lifting her skirt, and tasting what I know will be heaven. Even simply feeling her arms around my waist while she sits on the back of my bike.

I went for a long ride on my bike once I saw her walk back in to meet Jasmine, needing to clear my head.

I don't believe in that fairytale crap. And she's too good for me.

It's what I told myself over and over again on that ride, promising myself I'd let the rush of unwarranted feelings go. They're temporary. That's all.

Yeah, right, my mind chimes in.

It's been two weeks since that night, and as much as I try to ignore it, I keep thinking of her. Wondering what she's doing or if I'll run into her again. I truly don't know anything about her, other than her name, that she speaks French, and that she likes baseball.

Spring training is so damn far away, but maybe that's what I need. More time for these persistent thoughts of her to fade. Because they will. There's no reason they shouldn't.

Or maybe I need to see her again, scratch the itch, and see if it goes away.

At least, it's what I tell myself when I tell Theo I'll meet him there later.

Why the fuck I agreed to come out tonight is slowly fading from memory. There are people everywhere at Beers n Cheers, making it more overcrowded than usual. Don't even get me started on the costumes.

There's not a single original one in sight.

I lift a bottle of beer to my lips, savoring the crisp orange flavor on my tongue. Theo and I have been sitting at a high-top table for the last hour, waiting for his friends to arrive.

We've actually been having a good time, catching up on our lives and all things sports. But with each minute that passes, I get more and more agitated. Do I really need to be spending the night with her when I already can't stop thinking about her?

As if on cue, Camille enters the bar. I barely register anything around me once I see her costume. She's dressed as a mermaid— correction, she's dressed as the sexiest fucking mermaid I've ever seen.

Her bikini top is shaped like starfish, a pale pink that meshes with the iridescent blue scales on her long skirt. There are pearls wrapped around her neck, and it nearly undoes me.

Because I'd rather give her a different kind of pearl necklace.

I shoot up from the table, startling Theo before he can grab her attention. "I need to go. My mom needs help at the house."

Theo's widespread grin fades, a pout on his lips. "Dang it, Mama Lewis!"

I eye him, my eyebrow perched. "Watch it."

Theo holds his hands up in defense. "You know I'm joking. I love your mama. Go help her out and tell her that her *favorite* son says hello."

My lips twitch at his long-time running joke. "Not likely. Have fun tonight," I tell him, then escape from the bar without having her spot me.

The cool rush of October wind hits me in the face as I step outside. I only had a sip of my beer, so I'd be fine to ride my bike home, but I find myself hesitating.

Suddenly, the idea of leaving her here at the bar filled with all these fucking people makes my skin crawl. I know she'll be with her friends, but something urges me to stay.

I tilt my head toward the black sky and focus on the few stars poking out from the drifting gray clouds. I release a breath up into the air, trying to fight this goddamn pull I feel toward her.

A group of guys exit the bar and huddles in the smokers'

area, lighting up as they begin chatting. "Hey, did you guys see the blondie little mermaid in there?" one of them coughs over his exhale of smoke.

My head snaps their way instantly, knowing exactly who they're talking about.

"I call dibs," another pipes up, a disgusting smirk on his face.

My blood boils, my chest heavy as anger pumps itself in every crevice of my body. "Don't even fucking think about it," I growl, loud enough for them to hear as I near the entrance.

Looks like I'm staying now.

"You don't look like her Prince Eric." One laughs before taking a hit.

I ignore the dipshit and enter the bar. I look at where Theo and I sat but don't see them there. My eyes trail around the bar until I find Theo and Camille at a table to the far right side. So I stay on the left side and out of sight, but just enough that I can still keep an eye on their table while I nurse a beer.

Eventually, Camille and her friends make their way to the washroom. When they're gone for what feels like too long, I decide to take a trip there myself just to make sure they're all okay. I'm just rounding the corner when I see them.

My eyes instantly find Camille's, while desire fuels my veins as I look at her. Fuck, she's so pretty. Her cheeks flush as we continue to stare at one another, but Aurora interrupts the spell.

"Hey, Ryker, how's it going?" she asks hopefully. She's been trying to bond with me for a while now, and I gotta give the girl credit. She doesn't stop trying.

"Fine. You?" I respond, my tone clipped.

"Jeez, still grumpy as ever. I'll get you to smile one day."

"Don't count on it."

"Maybe you need to get laid, loosen up a bit," she suggests with that no-filter mouth of hers.

I see Camille stiffen from the corner of my eye, and I find that *interesting*. Is she as attracted to me as I am to her? Fuck, maybe we could get rid of the itch together. One time and be done.

But I knew deep down that one time wouldn't be enough for me.

I focus back on the conversation at hand, needing to get away from that line of thinking, and narrow my eyebrows at Aurora. "I'm going to forget this conversation happened," I mutter, walking past them and into the bathroom.

I grip the sink while taking deep breaths, needing to calm the hell down. Maybe that's what I need, to get laid. Aurora might be right.

But as soon as I entertain the idea, the only person my cock gets excited for is Camille. Nobody else appeals to me right now. Jesus fuck.

I splash some cold water on my face before looking at myself in the mirror.

I'm stronger than this. Physical desires can fade, and I can control them. She doesn't need me to watch out for her. She's been fine all her years here, and she'll continue to be fine without me lurking in the shadows because of some damn craving I feel to be near her.

It's then that I make the decision to abstain from any contact with her. I don't see her around as it is, but I'm not going to go out of my way to try to see her like I did tonight.

If there's one thing I've learned from watching fairytales with my mom, it's that every character has a weakness that pulls them in a different direction. And I fear she could be mine.

There's no such thing as fairytales in real life, but I'm going to stay away just to be safe. Because I've been burned once, and I'm still figuring out the remedy.

Chapter Three

Camille

MARCH

This winter has been brutal.

Not only has the weather been awful, but my class load has been insane. Working to get two degrees at once is tough, and I need a background in both business and journalism for the job I want.

I've always dreamed of becoming a part of a major baseball organization, either working in social media relations or writing behind the scenes.

As long as I can overcome the misogynistic assholes who are standing in my way. I want to break that barrier and smash it into tiny pieces to never be put back together.

I grew up with four older brothers and we all love sports. I was never allowed to play myself because it wasn't 'princess-like,' but that didn't stop me from falling in love with baseball.

Add in the fact that one of my brothers, Quentin, is a player for the Detroit Panthers baseball team.

Quentin relinquished his role in our family to pursue his

dreams, only visiting us on the holidays. It was always a tad awkward whenever he came around since my mother and father don't exactly agree with his choice, but I've always admired him for it.

Because he was able to truly be himself and do what he loves, whereas I never could. Not until I escaped, and now here I am, working on a future that feels good for *me*.

I've reached out to a few major league organizations, but I've yet to hear anything back. I could ask my brother for an interview, but I want to be the reason behind my success. Not because it was handed to me, because my parents rule a country, or because my brother is a famous baseball player.

So for now, I work for the school's newspaper, writing about the women's teams. I would love to work on the men's teams as well, but Jimmy, the other sports writer, refuses to give that up.

Men.

"Cami, you good?" Jasmine asks, her highlighter paused mid-air.

"What? Yeah, why?"

"You look like you want to put that pencil through Theo's hand," she retorts, and it's then that I notice how tense my body is.

I take a deep breath, feeling a tad lighter. Jimmy gets me riled up like nobody else.

"Please don't, Millie Moo. These hands will determine my future." Theo stares at his hand with love in his eyes. He'll be the starting quarterback this coming fall and he needs his hands more than ever.

"Sorry." I chuckle. "I was just thinking about Jimmy. He never lets me write about the men's teams and it pisses me off."

"What a prick. Do you want me to go find him and confront him?" Jasmine's mocha eyes pierce mine, her protective nature coming out. She always goes to bat for the ones she loves, and it makes me love her even more.

"No, it's fine." I wave her off, folding my legs beneath me

on the chair. We've been studying in the library for what feels like hours, and I can barely concentrate anymore. If I fail this midterm, so be it. That's the point I'm at right now.

"Pft," Theo snorts, fingers working over the fidget cube in his hand. "I'm going with you, Jas. Elio would lose it if you did that alone."

Elio is Jasmine's boyfriend, and seeing the two of them so in love has been bittersweet because although I'm happy for her, I've been dreaming of a love like that my whole life.

"There's no going anywhere. Relax, you two."

"We love you, that's all." Jasmine smiles softly.

"You're our girl. We got you," Theo adds, nudging me with his elbow as he winks at me. He's so naturally charming.

I smile at him as I pull out my phone, seeing a few emails I've missed in the last hour. Theo does the same, while Jasmine keeps her head in her book.

"Damn it," Theo groans, throwing his head back.

"What's wrong?" Jasmine and I both ask in unison.

"Ryker had to cancel our tattoo appointment tomorrow because of a mandatory baseball meeting. I've been looking forward to this for months."

"So can't you go without him?" Jasmine cocks her brow, her highlighter perched between her fingers in the air.

Theo laughs, and when he does, it's the whole body kind of laugh. "No, Jay bay bay. He's the tattoo artist. He was going to give me my first one! Fucking baseball," he mutters the last bit.

My heart seems to be beating faster at the mention of his name. It's been months since I last saw him, but my crush is still as strong as ever. I still can't forget the way my fingertips buzzed when they touched his arm at the club.

I would probably faint on the spot if he kissed me since I'm already freaking out over a graze of his fingers. Learning about him being a tattoo artist only adds to his appeal.

"How is he a tattoo artist? Isn't he like twenty-one?" Jasmine asks.

"He's actually twenty-two and started his apprenticeship as soon as he turned eighteen. Ryker's insanely talented and quickly grew his clientele," Theo explains.

I didn't know he was a tattoo artist, and the new information makes my brain swim with ideas because I've been wanting my own tattoo for a while now.

"You big baby, you'll be fine. Just reschedule it," she tells him before turning her attention back to her textbook.

Theo rolls his eyes at her, returning his focus to his phone and texting back.

I do the same, looking through the emails on my student account. It's all the same stuff, course reminders, midterm details. I'm about to close my app when I see the devil's name there.

Jimmy.

I open the email, partly intrigued, partly nervous to see what it is about.

From: Jimmy.Walt@RLU.com

To: Camille.Blanchette@RLU.com

Subject:

Hello Camille,

I hope you are having a great time studying for midterms.

Anyways, let's get to the good stuff. I have sad news. Well, sad for you, good for me. Unlike you, I got a job with a local newsprint company that features sports around the city, so I can no longer write my section on the school paper.

I know it'll be a lot for you to handle, so I already gave hockey, basketball, and swimming to my assistant. But I will need you to take over the baseball team.

Good luck. You'll need it.

Jimmy

This is what I mean when I say Jimmy is the worst, but I choose to let go of the first part of his email and focus on the end. He is giving me the men's baseball team to cover this season.

No. Freaking. Way.

I squeal and shimmy in my seat, excitement pulsing through every inch of my body.

"Whoa, what's up with you?" Theo asks.

"Jimmy just gave me the men's baseball team to cover this season. He got a job and has no time for it," I tell him, but as I say the words, my excitement quickly turns into nerves.

Because guess who I'll have to see all the time starting next week?

Ryker Lewis.

Chapter Four

Camille

"Do you want another glass of wine?" Quentin asks, his body spread across my couch. He's visiting before his spring training begins in two weeks. My brother is the star pitcher for the Detroit Panthers, and I couldn't be more proud of him as he lives out his dreams.

While Quentin and I bonded the most because we have the same personality—happy, adventurous, and caring—there was a small part of me that resented him for a few years because of how jealous I was.

"I shouldn't. It's a school night and I have my long day of classes tomorrow," I huff out, snuggling into the cozy blanket I'm currently wrapped up in on the couch.

"But we're celebrating! You finally got the role you've been wanting with the school paper. *Juste un autre, s'il te plaît?*"

I think about it for a moment, but even though I want another glass, I know I shouldn't.

"No, that's okay, Q."

Quentin sits up, eyeing me speculatively. "Look at you all

grown up and responsible. The high school version of you wouldn't have said no."

I chuckle at that because he's not wrong. I was twenty-two now, but as a teen, I was notorious for sneaking alcohol from the liquor cabinet in the bar room in the palace. Let's just say I wasn't legally drinking back then. Q and I would get drunk, giggling in the gardens as we stared up at the stars and dreamed of our lives beyond the constricting walls of the palace.

"High school me was defiant because I hated being told to be proper all the time. I wanted to let loose a little. But now that I have freedom, I like taking things at my pace, you know?"

"I'm proud of you, baby sis. You've come a long way. I still remember chasing you around the palace, never being able to keep up with your antics," he remarks, and the mention of life back home brings a bittersweet feeling over me.

There's an ache behind my ribs when I think about my country and my family, but I don't miss the pressure of being in the public eye. I always needed to look presentable or speak in a formal manner.

Let's not forget the fashion culture. I was always dressed in designer labels and while I appreciated the beauty the designers created for me, they just weren't *me*.

Now I can joke around and swear all I want, and I can dress casually without someone making a scene because a girl is in sweatpants.

And there were the countless boring meetings I had to attend. Not like the ones my parents, the king and the queen had to be a part of, but they were still boring all the same.

I did like giving back to my country. I had no problem going to events, reading stories to kids, and working in gardens at schools. But it wasn't something I wanted to do forever, not with all the other burdens being a princess came with.

"You still can't keep up with me," I tease him.

Quentin laughs. "I can't wait to tease the hell out of whatever guy you end up with. He's in trouble."

I was a bit of a wild child, getting into every trouble I possibly could. There was a time when I let all the chickens from a farm loose because I was bored at an event. Or when I started a dance off between Quentin and me during a charity event, with the entire crowd circling us at one point.

My father was *not* happy with us that day.

"Speaking of relationships, any lady I should be excited to meet soon?"

"Maybe." He smiles with a faraway look in his hazel eyes.

I sit up, the blanket pooling around my lap. "Oh my God, are you dating someone?"

"We're just having fun for now, that's all." He winks.

I let out a groan. I'm happy for him, but I don't need details about his sex life. "Ew, get out of my apartment. Go home," I tell him while pretending to gag.

Quentin laughs, the sound comforting. "Your apartment is technically mine, and I have nowhere else to go in the city."

"Ugh, I hate when you're right. Speaking of which, I'll pay you back once I can."

"As if I'd let you do that," he scoffs, running a hand through his dark brown hair.

We spend the rest of the night watching a reality TV show, the ones we all claim to hate but can't stop watching. Quentin leaves just before midnight, telling me that he'll visit as soon as he can. I teased him and said he should bring this girl he dares not to speak of, and that earned me the world's loudest sigh.

When I make my way into bed that night, I can't help but be slightly jealous that he has a sex life. I haven't been intimate with anyone ever since the incident all those years ago, not letting them get close enough to even try.

Except for Ryker. He's the first person I've willingly let touch me in a long time. And I have no clue why. I'll be seeing him tomorrow for training practice at the baseball facility for the first time since Halloween and it has my stomach churning with nerves.

We haven't run into each other since, and I'd be lying if I said I wasn't bummed about that. I have a huge crush on the man, so of course I was hoping to run into him from time to time, but he's been MIA.

Pushing the thoughts aside, I do my best to settle in for bed, but thoughts of him infiltrate my brain, making it nearly impossible as butterflies fill my stomach. I may not love being a princess, but there's something about the idea of a fairy-tale kinda love that has always intrigued me.

I want it more than anything. I love being independent and all that, but I love *love*. I want someone to be my partner in life. To experience the ups and downs, to laugh and challenge one another. Then make crazy love in between it all.

As I drift off to sleep, I dream of Ryker and me. We're on the back of his bike, riding around the back country roads, zooming past orange and yellow trees. My smile is wide as I hold on to his waist.

Then suddenly, it changes.

I awaken with a scream, my body sweating and shaking as I start to come to. Ugh, I hate when this happens. I've had nightmares on and off. Every time it's the same thing, all those men chasing me, except in the nightmare they catch me.

I wipe a palm over my sweaty forehead, then throw the blanket off my blazing body, hoping it'll help. I reach over for my reusable water bottle on my bedside table and take a long chug.

I then grab my phone and look up gardening videos online since I know it always soothes me. I love plants and miss gardening so much since living in an apartment isn't ideal for it.

After spending hours watching my favorite creator plant new wildflowers in her backyard, the idea of getting my favorite flowers tattooed pops into my head. I've always wanted to fill my body with a piece of something I found beautiful and it reminds me that we can always bloom, no matter what the roots are.

And I happen to know just the artist I trust to do it.

Chapter Five

Ryker

Today is my favorite day of the year—the start of spring training. I woke up early, got a run in before seven, and made breakfast for myself before my teammates woke up.

All the junior and senior players on the team live in a house just off campus. It's become a tradition over the years. It once started as a way for the guys on the team to bond to increase fluidity and trust within the group, and it hasn't stopped since.

After I shower, I grab my iPad, where I worked on a design for my digital art class. Once I submit it, I start on the tattoo design for Theo—a shoulder piece that features an interconnected series of lines that look pretty fucking cool if I say so myself—until it's finally time to head downstairs and round up the guys to leave for practice.

As soon as my feet hit the last step, Noah is on me. "Dude, you made pancakes this morning and didn't think to leave extra for us?" he complains.

"You can make your own food."

"Not even the first day of spring training can make this guy smile," Cuddy, a new addition to the team whom I *actually* like, chimes in.

"Get used to it, newbie," Noah huffs dramatically.

Honestly, it's kind of a game to me now. I try my best to purposely not smile because I know it drives them insane. The only time they'll catch me with a smile on my face is when we're on the diamond and kicking ass.

Then my pearly whites make a fucking statement out there.

"Practice starts in an hour. Let's go," I shout, clapping my hands and doing my best to rally the team together.

Eventually, all eight of us make it out of the house, splitting up into two cars to drive to the facility since it's cold as fuck outside. My body itches with excitement as we park a few minutes later and make our way inside. It's finally time to play ball.

There's nothing that fuels me the way this sport does. It fills my body with adrenaline and joy every time my cleats hit the field.

My goal is to go pro by the end of graduation, and my prospects are looking pretty good. My agent has been in talk with recruiters over the past three years, and every time, he's mentioned that they have their eye on the third baseman who has a wicked arm and is even better at bat.

This is my year. I can feel it. Drafting happens in July and I'm working my ass off to be a first pick.

The locker room is loud and boisterous as I come in and reunite with other teammates I haven't seen much during the winter break because of our hectic class schedules. We're like a family, and even though they all piss me off at times, our bond runs deep.

Coach Warren walks through the door, instantly quieting the group of rowdy men. He came to RLU a few years ago and has produced some of the greatest players in MLB history throughout his coaching career. He's a force to be reckoned with, hence why we all shut the hell up instantly when he walks through the door.

He gives us a spiel about the upcoming season, what he

expects from us, and what the training schedule will be like for the next two weeks.

"We leave on March eighteenth for an exhibition game against the University of New Mexico," he announces, eliciting a grumble from Noah.

"You got a problem with that, Noah?" Coach calls him out.

Noah straightens, clearing his throat. "No, sir. It's just… that's my girl's and my anniversary."

"Son, if there's something you and your girl need to learn now is that if you plan to have a career in baseball, you will be gone for important things. You'll miss birthdays, graduations—hell, maybe even the birth of your kid. It's what we do for the game."

Noah tightens his jaw but nods, not commenting back. Coach Warren isn't the sentimental type, and I agree with everything he said.

It's a sacrifice I'm more than willing to make.

"Anything else anyone wants to whine about?" Coach asks with a bushy eyebrow raised. When there's no response, he continues, "Good. One more thing before I send you guys to the weight room."

"We have a new journalist working with the team this year. They will be doing their usual duties, but this year will be a different approach. They'll also be attending away games along with doing some behind the scenes for the school's social media page."

Thank God. I fucking hated Jimmy. He always tried to get me to sit for an interview, only to stray away from baseball, which is why he never got more than a few words from me. I'm happy to see him go.

Coach's face turns serious, his arms crossing over his chest. "If any of you harass her, I will personally see to kicking your ass myself, got it? I expect all of you to make her feel comfortable and welcome to RLU baseball."

Her?

I begin to wonder who *she* could be when the door opens, answering my question.

Camille.

This has to be some kind of joke. I've successfully avoided her since Halloween—well, just her presence because she hasn't left my thoughts since—and now I'm really never going to get rid of her if she's around the team all the time.

Great.

"This is Camille," Coach says, turning his attention to her. "You have impeccable timing, Camille. I was just telling the team about you. We can chat in my office about your duties for our upcoming trip to New Mexico."

Fuck. Me.

"Sounds great," she replies, smiling brightly, scanning the room as she walks toward his office.

Her eyes land on mine and she briefly comes to a halt, her cheeks reddening before she continues on to Coach's office.

What was that about?

"All right, boys, get your asses in the weight room and see me in two hours for a tape review of last season," Coach dismisses us and follows after Camille.

The room is quiet for a beat as we all get changed into our workout gear until a freshman, Travis, opens his mouth. "I suddenly have the urge to answer all post-game interview questions," he teases, suggestively waggling his eyebrows up and down.

"She's a knockout, that's for sure," Cuddy chimes in, and I shoot him a lethal glare.

"Coach said to leave her be," I warn them. I tell myself it's because Coach is intimidating as hell and I don't want them to get in shit. But truthfully, it's driving me fucking nuts hearing them talk about her like that. Cuddy's comment wasn't bad since he's not wrong, but Travis's makes me uneasy. The guy is a loose cannon, and I heard he's been through half of the freshmen class already.

"He said not to make her uncomfortable. So don't worry, I'll make her feel real good," he drawls.

Anger ripples through me at his comment. The image of him touching her runs through my mind, making my fists clench.

Travis struts by me as a couple of guys chuckle, and I extend my foot slightly, watching in delight as he faceplants onto the floor. The room bursts into laughter as Travis shoots up to his feet, getting in my face.

"What the hell, bro? What was that for?"

I don't flinch as I tower over him, levelling him with a *I don't give a fuck* look.

"Watch yourself," I tell him, my tone clipped. I turn and walk out of the room. I don't know if he's smart enough to get my implication, but for his sake, I hope he did.

The anger pumping in my body fuels my workout session. A kind I haven't felt since I was a pissed off teenager constantly getting into fights at school. The same kind that got me in a lot of trouble and nearly got me a record at sixteen.

"Fuck," I grunt, shoving the bar with an added 200 pounds on top of it up to the rack.

"You're lifting a little heavy today. You good?" Noah remarks, tossing a towel at me.

I wipe the sweat off my face, taking deep breaths. "I'm good."

"Then why'd you trip Travis like a middle schooler would?"

I nearly smile at that. "He deserved it."

"I know we don't like the guy, but he's a part of the team. You can't be pulling shit like that."

"It won't happen again," I reassure him, despite not knowing if I truly can uphold my promise if he so much as looks at Camille the wrong way.

"Tell me the real reason why," he presses.

I've known Noah long enough to know he won't quit until he gets an answer.

"Did you hear the way he was talking about her? He needs to be taught some manners."

I leave out the fact that the image of his hands on her was like a punch to the gut. I had no goddamn right to be jealous, but I couldn't help how I felt around her. I didn't even like her and thought her bubbly personality was annoying.

Or so I tried convincing myself of.

"I like the protective macho male thing you got going on. It's a nice change from the scowl asshole thing you usually carry around," Noah chides.

"My scowl is still very much here." I scowl at him to prove my point.

"And the asshole is too." He laughs and switches spots with me on the bench.

A small smile escapes me at that, but he has his back to me so he can't see. After he's done lifting, he hits me with another question. "Do you like her?" he asks, sitting up.

"Like who?" I ask, knowing exactly who he's referring to.

"Camille."

"I don't know her, so no, I don't."

"But you're attracted to her?" he says, finally turning to face me. "No bullshit."

I curse inwardly at the use of the no bullshit rule. It's something I started saying to the people who were close to me when I needed to confide in them. No bullshit, just the truth.

"I am, and it pisses me off."

"Why?" He scrunches his face at me in confusion.

"Because number one, I should be nowhere near a girl like that. Two, I have to focus on the draft, and three, love is bullshit."

"I didn't say you needed to date her…You could just get it out of your system. Besides, you may be an asshole at times, but you're a *good* person, Ryker. You deserve good things, especially a good girl like that," Noah says, sounding very much like a captain giving me a pep talk I don't need.

"Forget it," I mutter. "And keep that shit between us. Got it?"

"Got you." He slaps my back as we exit the weight room.

Hours later, I find myself restless while I try to finish an assignment for one of my art classes. So I decide to head to the gym for a cardio session instead. But it looks like I won't be able to work out my restlessness anytime soon because of who I see in the corner of the gym as soon as I'm inside.

Her.

Chapter Six

Camille

After my night class dragged on tonight and the conversation I just had with Quentin right before it, I find myself needing a late-night session with a bag.

He called me to inform me of an update with his private investigator. It seems my parents have begun their search for me again, but he didn't get more details. I don't know why being found scares me so much. It's not like they could physically force me back home. It's the hold they have on me that is worrisome. If they spiel some sob story, I don't know that I won't crack and give in, moving back home.

Avoiding who I was born to be for the past four years has been blissful and I'm not ready to give that up.

Once I get to the gym on campus, I quickly get dressed to blow off some stress. I slip my gloves on and go to town on the punching bag in the corner of the gym.

Boxing is therapeutic for me. It makes me feel strong, like nothing or no one could hurt me if I hit it hard enough. As a member of the royal family, I was trained in self-defense at a young age, along with other sorts of training for extreme situations. It was scary at first, but after the incident, I was grateful for it because it saved my life.

Sweat drips down my back, and I glance in the mirror behind the bag, noticing a reflection of Ryker walking into the gym. The sight makes my spine straighten and butterflies flutter in my stomach.

I woke up this morning with a huge smile on my face because it was my first day working with the baseball team. I'd been thinking about what I wanted to do with my column this year and how I could stand out, until I decided that I needed to do more.

That's how I ended up suggesting to Coach Warren that I'd like to increase the team's presence on social media and give fans a deeper insight into who they are. The more people like you, the more willing they are to buy whatever you're selling. That's marketing 101, and it sold him.

You can now say hello to the new social media manager for the men's baseball team.

My duties have now doubled, but I was thrilled because I felt like this could be it. The thing that gets me noticed by a professional team if I put out good, quality content online that generates a buzz.

However, that excitement fizzled when I entered the locker room earlier today and found Ryker looking at me like I didn't belong there. I blushed, that damn crush still not allowing me to feel anything else for him despite his attitude.

And now here he is once again, eyeing me with a scowl.

I smile at him as he passes me to go up the stairs, likely to change in the men's room.

"Hey," I breathe out, waving at him with a gloved hand. My nerves ricochet as he stops in his tracks, his hair pulled in a half up half down look that makes him look even sexier than usual.

His jaw muscle ticks under his trimmed beard as he faces me. "Hey," he grunts.

This man and his grumpy responses need to go.

"Did I do something to you?" I ask, surprising myself with my bravery.

"What?" he balks, seeming shocked.

"You…I don't know. Earlier, it looked like you didn't want me there, and you always give me monosyllabic words followed by a grunt. I thought maybe I did something to upset you somehow."

"Do I need to shoot happiness out of my pores like you do?" he questions. "And that was more than one syllable if you didn't notice."

"Ah, so you do have a sense of humor. That's good." I chuckle.

He shakes his head at me, taking a step toward me. His blue eyes pierce mine, making me even more breathless as I stare at him.

God, I'm pathetic.

In the past, I've always been confident in relationships. I like to be in control and dominant, yet with Ryker, I can't even find it in me to be anything other than a girl with a silly crush, let alone take charge.

"My problem is that I *do* want you in my space, princess."

"W-what?" I draw my eyebrows together, a disbelieving laughter slipping from between my lips.

"You heard me," he says, his voice laced with tension as he takes another step closer, our chests now mere inches apart.

"How is that a problem?" I counter, my heart pounding in my ears and my eyes transfixed on his, in awe of how insanely attractive he is.

He's honestly lucky there's no drool leaking out of my mouth right now.

"Because it is," he gruffs, not answering my question.

"I'm confused. Aren't we friends? We'll need to work

together over the next few months and I don't like when people don't like me. I need this to go well."

Those dark stormy eyes bore into mine, and I swear for a moment, I see a glimmer of desire in them, but it's gone before I can be sure.

"We don't know each other," he scoffs, turning on his heel and heading toward the stairs, creating distance that does nothing to ease the growing tension between us.

I swallow as my heart beats wildly in my chest and decide to go the friendly route instead of flirty. "But we could! What's your favorite color?" I ask, hoping it'll get him to stop.

"Lavender," he calls out, walking up the stairs and out of sight.

Okay, that is definitely not the answer I anticipated. I was expecting it to be black.

I take a sip of water and mull over our conversation, feeling remnants of whiplash. One second, he said he wanted me in his space, and then the next, he walked away, telling me he didn't want to be friends. Which one is it?

As I turn my attention back to the bag I was using before he showed up, I catch a glimpse of myself in the mirror and freeze when I realize my matching sports bra and biker shorts are lavender.

My romantic heart makes my brain run wild with ideas that he said lavender because it's what I was wearing, and the color I often like to wear. But I try to bring myself back to earth and remind myself that he probably just likes the color. He's a tattoo artist, and maybe it's his mom's favorite flower?

That must be it, because there's no way a guy like Ryker would ever be into a girl like me. We're just too different. I like gardening, boxing, singing a little too loudly in the shower, and doing the occasional latte art when I have time.

Ryker seems to be built with jagged edges and no softness in sight. He has a temper from what I've seen on the field and is known as the team's asshole. Total opposite of me. Except for the night he stepped in for me at the club. He was different then.

Regardless, I need to not analyze his comment and let it go. I'll be professional and do my job, and if I can get him to like me as a friend in the process, that'll be a bonus point.

Chapter Seven

Ryker

"Owwwww!" Theo yelps, his forehead glistening with sweat as I finish up the last bit of his tattoo.

"You're fine," I tell him, wiping away the residual ink. I press the needle back into his skin, the buzzing sound providing me with a sense of peace.

"You didn't tell me this shit hurts, man." Theo half chuckles, half squeals.

"You didn't tell me you were going to be such a baby about it," I mutter.

"This is my first and last tattoo. If I come to you in two months saying differently, remind me of this, please."

"How's your nephew doing?" I ask to get his mind off the needle.

"He's good, just learning how to walk. Naturally, my sister and her husband are stressed because he's getting into everything at the farm. He also loves helping my dad feed the goats."

"If that kid is anything like you, he will try to get his hands into everything at that farm."

He rolls his eyes, his fingers working with the fidget in his hand. "I just have a lot of energy. Sue me."

Ever since we were kids, he always needed to keep his hands occupied and now uses a small fidget cube to keep for that.

"How's it going with Camille and the team?" he asks, nearly making me fuck up his tattoo.

"It's only been a few days, and there isn't much to do since it's spring training, so I haven't seen her at all." Which is true. I haven't seen her since that night in the gym where I said more than I should've.

I couldn't help it. Seeing her in that little sports bra and shorts, her skin glistening while she pounded the bag, made it hard not to. It should be a fucking crime to wear that and look that good in public. It pissed me off and made me say shit I shouldn't have, like admitting I wanted her to be in my space and that my favorite color was the exact shade of her little outfit.

"I know she's working hard on some things for y'all to do for social media."

"Yeah, I won't be doing any of that," I scoff. I play baseball. That's it.

"If you want to be drafted, you will. Organizations eat that shit up now. They want a player they can market and make money off of. Someone who will do silly videos and attract sponsors," he continues to explain my worst nightmare.

"I'll cross that bridge when I have to."

I finish up the last part, wiping it down once more before putting a layer of petroleum jelly over it. I give him the rundown on aftercare instructions when I hear the shop's bell chime. It must be the owner, Otto's, last client of the night.

"Hey there, sweetheart, what can I do for you?" Otto says, greeting whoever just walked in. I instantly know it's not the client in the books.

"I can get a tattoo here, right?" Camille's French lilt hits my ears like a freight train.

What is she doing here? Since when does she want a tattoo?

Theo bolts out of the room, and I'm right behind him.

"Millie Moo," he exclaims as he approaches and wraps her up in a one-arm hug because of his shoulder that's wrapped up.

"Hey, Theo. I forgot you were doing that today. How did it turn out?" she asks, inspecting his new tattoo as he peels back the covering to show her.

"Wow, that's beautiful," she murmurs, her eyes tracking every intricate line.

"It hurt like a bitch," he admits, putting the covering back over it.

"He whined the whole time," I speak up, making Camille's eyes dart to me. Her silvery blues lock on mine, and in that moment, I wish time could be stopped. Just so I could inspect and capture the fine details of every hue as they work together to make the color that captures me every time I look at her.

Otto breaks the moment, pulling her attention back to him. "You wanted a tattoo, sweetheart? I could probably fit you in before my next client. What are you looking for?"

She smiles shyly. "I want a bouquet of flowers."

"Sounds easy enough." Otto eyes her, making me want to gauge his eyes out.

Over my dead body is he tattooing her. Not after what I saw at the club that night.

As if luck shows up on my side, another client walks in.

"Otto, take the new one. I got her," I tell him, tilting my head toward Camille.

He glares at me, probably not wanting to start an argument in front of them, and I glare back harder. I don't give a fuck if he fires me later. He's not going anywhere near her.

"I didn't even know you wanted a tattoo. You're a badass!" Theo laughs, giving her a fist bump. "See you later, Ryker. Thanks again."

"No problem," I call out to him, then motion for Camille to follow me to my room at the back. "I just need a few minutes to clean up from Theo's session. You can sit on the chair once I wipe it down."

Camille nods, taking in the space around her with inquisitive eyes. It's a typical tattoo artist's room—a black leather chair in the middle, a station with all of my stuff, and artwork on the walls that I made.

Baseball is everything to me, but tattooing is a different kind of outlet. It's fun, soothing, and easy for me. Baseball is fun too, but there's also more pressure.

Camille sits on the chair once I'm done cleaning it while I continue to prepare my station.

"Since when did you want a tattoo, princess?" I ask her.

I don't miss the way her cheeks redden whenever I call her that. Hell, I don't even know why I'm still calling her that, to be honest.

"For a while, but I was never allowed to before." She pauses, her eyes casting a faraway look.

"And now?" I ask as I bring up my design app and begin sketching out a design for her.

"I finally found something I wanted," she answers, smiling at me.

"Why flowers?" I have no right to ask. As a professional, I know that, but I don't care much right now. She intrigues me.

"I've always loved to garden. I guess I've been missing being able to garden since I came here for school and can't exactly plant a garden in my apartment."

"I like that. You're less likely to regret a tattoo if it means something to you."

Camille eyes me cautiously. "You're oddly talkative. I thought we weren't friends?"

"And I thought you wanted to be?" I fire back at her, unsure why I *am* suddenly talkative.

"I do," she speaks slowly, unsure. "But why the sudden change on your end? Why did you insist on tattooing me?"

I groan at having to explain it. The truth is, I knew there was no stopping her being around me, nor was there any stopping the pull she has on me.

"We're going to see each other around a lot, and considering I'm about to spend the next hour tattooing you, we may as well get to know each other now."

Camille nods, then waves her hand for me to go on since I didn't tell her why I'm insisting on tattooing her.

I roll my eyes at her. "Because I saw how you reacted at the club when that guy touched you. I didn't want someone else to make you uncomfortable."

My room goes silent at my confession as her doe eyes stare at me intently.

"I don't have an aversion to people touching me in general… just unwarranted ones."

My fingers clench around the Apple pencil I'm using as images pop in my head about what happened to her, but I don't press her to tell me.

"I still appreciate you doing that for me. That's actually why I came here. I was kinda hoping you'd be the one to do it. I probably should've just called and booked an actual appointment to be safe. Sorry about that," she rambles, chuckling to herself at the realization.

I hate that I think it's cute as hell when she does that. I hate that her upbeat personality is pulling me in like a moth to a flame.

"Don't be sorry. Why me?" I ask, not looking up at her. I

keep my eyes on my iPad because I don't trust myself not to say something stupid.

"Because I somewhat know you. Theo showed me some of your work and I thought it was beautiful. I'd feel weird letting a complete stranger mark my body like that," she admits.

My lips stay sealed in a scowl as I finish off her design, unable to respond because the image of strangers touching her body is tempting to ignite the protective part of me. She also called my work beautiful. No one has ever done that. Sure, they liked their tattoos, but no one said it with as much awe as she did.

I liked it too much.

"What song is this?" Camille asks, interrupting my thoughts.

"'Crazy Love' by Van Morrison."

"I like it." Her voice is soft, the admiration in it clear. "Not what I expected you to listen to. It's so… romantic."

I shrug my shoulders. "My usual go-to is rock music, but this song has a nice melody."

"Or a secret meaning?" she counters.

"Not in the slightest," I murmur.

If she's hinting that I have some girl I'm crazy about like the artist in the song sings about, she's wrong. Sure, I've had random hookups over the years, but I never had a serious relationship. Not only did I not have time, but I was afraid of the risk that came with it.

To me, the benefits weren't worth the cost of losing it.

Camille doesn't respond, letting the silence sit comfortably in the space between us.

Once I'm done, I pass her my iPad, noting the nerves churning in my gut. "Tell me what you think. If you hate it, I'll make a new one."

Her eyes widen, her hand slamming over her mouth as she begins to nod enthusiastically. She's wearing her every thought and emotion over every inch of her face, and it turns me the fuck on. Someone being this transparent with their emotions, so freely and easily like that isn't easy.

"I love it." She beams, staring at the screen in admiration. "How'd you know I love lavender?"

I drew a bouquet of lavender mixed in with wildflowers because I had a feeling that's what she is. Someone who's trying to bloom on her own.

"Just a feeling. So you're good with it?" I ask, needing confirmation.

"Yes. The size is perfect too."

"All right, I'll print it and we can try out different placements," I tell her, sending the design to the printer system. "Where would you like it?"

"On my rib, close to my heart."

Oh, fuck me.

"Take your bra off," I order so I can have better access.

Her mouth pops open, and it's then that I realize how it could've been taken the wrong way. It's her first tattoo, and she probably didn't expect this part.

"I have to slide your shirt up to give me enough room to work with. I have to hold your skin to keep it taut for the needle. A bra is harder to slide up than a shirt is," I explain, my voice threatening to drop with lust.

I've tattooed many women before. I need to get it together. The last thing I want is to make her uncomfortable. It's with that in mind that I push the thoughts away and get ready.

She smiles, shrugging her shoulders. "Oh, okay, that makes sense." Before I can move, she moves her hands under her cropped sweatshirt and flings her lacey black bra off.

"Done, what's next?" She perks up, seemingly more excited now, but I can't take my eyes off the nipple piercings I saw poking through the fabric of her top.

God help me.

I turn and get her design out of the printer, taking a moment to gather myself before I start.

"Lie on your right side," I tell her, not looking over my shoulder as she gets situated.

Once I have the design cut out and ready, I sit on my chair and turn to face her. "Is it okay if I lift your sweater a bit more? I'll put a paper towel there so I won't see anything nor will the ink stain your clothes," I ask, my throat growing tight.

"No problem," she agrees, lifting her sweater up with one hand, a sliver of underboob showing.

I quickly avert my eyes and do my job, folding the paper towel under her sweater, careful not to touch her anywhere I shouldn't. "I have to shave the area first," I inform her, wanting her to be aware of every step.

She nods and stays still while I do that. Then I place the design on her skin, not exactly over her heart because the placement would be off, but to her side.

I grab the mirror off my station and position it so she can see. "Do you like the positioning? If not, I can wipe it off and print another one."

Camille nods. "It's perfect. I love it already."

"Good," is all I manage to say because every second near her is a test to my control.

I turn on my tattoo gun, the buzzing sound as relaxing as a wave in the ocean. I look at Camille, gun in hand, and that's when I see the excitement brimming in her eyes, but also a tinge of fear.

"Hey," I say softly, turning the gun off. "We don't have to do this. You can come back when you're ready."

"No," she says, her tone firm. "I'll be okay. I want this, please."

I learn in that moment that I would do anything this girl asked me, especially when she looks so pretty begging for it.

I turn the gun back on and set myself up, leaning my body over the side of hers to get the right angle. That's when I'm hit with a waft of something sweet, almost like cotton candy. Why does it not surprise me that this girl also smells like the sweetness she exudes?

"This may hurt. Rib tattoos are no joke."

"I can take it," she replies confidently.

I press the needle into her skin at that moment, not giving my brain enough time to expand on her words. Camille winces, her eyes shutting tightly.

"Squeeze my forearm," I order, nudging her with my arm that's holding her skin and not tattooing her.

Her dainty fingers with nails painted purple wrap around my tattooed arm, squeezing tightly.

"You okay?" I ask her, feeling sick at the fact that I'm hurting her. I've made grown men cry before in this chair and never cared. But fuck, if seeing her in pain doesn't do something else to me.

"Yes, keep going." She smiles, her eyes studying my face. I don't particularly love chatting with clients, but if it'll keep her mind off the pain, so be it.

"Where are you from?" I ask, trying to keep her attention averted.

"Paris."

Her one-word response is unlike her, but I let it go and ask her another question. "What made you want to come to America for school?"

Her nails dig into my forearm in response, but I don't flinch.

"I wanted to get away from my parents because they… they expect a lot from me. I needed to grow on my own terms. Experience life on my own for once." Her voice hitches at the end when the needle hits a tender spot.

"Sorry," I murmur.

"Don't be. Tell me something about you." Her nails release

their vice grip on my forearm as I take a second to wipe away the extra ink.

"I play baseball."

She laughs, her laughter sounding as sweet as she smells. Everything about this girl is, but something tells me that may not entirely be true.

"Something I *don't* know already."

I pick the gun back up and get to work while I think over what to say. I don't like to share things about myself, but like I've said, whatever Camille asks, I'll give to her.

"My mom and I have weekly movie nights on Tuesdays." My lips twitch, a smile threatening to take over my face. What can I say, I love my mother and whenever I think about her, it puts a smile on my face.

"It's so nice that you and your mom are close. What do you guys like to watch?" she inquires, her fingers gently caressing my forearm, her nails dusting across my skin. It sends a shiver up my spine, making me lift my hand away from her body.

What the hell is that shit about?

I shake my head and get back to work. "Whenever my mom picks, it's a Disney film. She's a sucker for them. Whereas when I get to pick, it's a thriller."

"Your mom sounds like a dreamer," she points out.

"Yeah, I guess she is," I said, continuing to draw the design on her ribs.

I never thought of it that way until now, but my mom never gave up on her dreams. She got pregnant with me during her last year of school and still managed to finish with honors.

"Do you have any siblings?" she asks next.

"What is this? An interview?" I nearly chuckle, but it comes out more like a grunt.

"We're becoming friends, remember? A friend should know these things."

"Fine," I mutter. "I don't. But when my mom gets married this summer, I'll have two step siblings, Nate and Aurora."

"Oh, right, that's exciting." She smiles widely, but it quickly fades as I press the needle into her skin. She whimpers and squeezes my arm once more.

"Almost done," I say, trying to comfort her.

"Are you excited for the trip next weekend?" she asks, switching topics.

"To play baseball for the first time since last year? Yeah, I am." My tone brightens at the thought of being able to play again so soon.

She gives me a small smile. "I'm excited too. It'll be busy for me, but fun nonetheless." She proceeds to tell me about the various social media activities she has planned for the team to do, and I grunt at each of them.

Noah and Cuddy will eat that shit up, but I'd rather be on the field doing what I do best instead of fucking around for the camera like they will take pleasure in doing.

Despite my preference in staying away from the cameras, her ideas are really good. It's going to bring a lot of attention to our team and attract sponsors that we need to keep our program running the way it does.

I enjoy listening to her come alive as she talks about baseball in general, how she wants to do this for a living.

Once I finish her tattoo, I wipe her skin one last time and admire my work. It looks pretty damn good if I say so myself.

"Let me know what you think," I tell her.

Camille stands and walks over to the mirror on the wall, holding her sweater up and turning to her side.

"Ryker the biker!" she exclaims. "It's so beautiful. Thank you so much."

I inwardly groan at the nickname she's given me, but her pure joy draws my attention more. God, she's fucking beautiful. It's then that I catch myself in the mirror, looking at her with the same adoration she's looking at her own tattoo.

Fuck.

I avert my gaze, keeping my hands and mind busy as I clean my station up.

"How much do I owe you?" she asks, but it feels wrong to take money from her. I don't know why. It just does.

"Let's do it this way. You don't owe me anything, and in return, you don't make me do stupid videos for social media," I propose, folding my arms across my chest.

Camille's eyes flash with hurt, but she covers it up quickly with a fake smile. "Oh, yeah, of course."

"I didn't mean that your ideas are stupid, Camille. I—"

"Don't, I get it," she cuts me off, her voice twinged with insecurity, and I hate that I put it there. I go to step toward her, but she straightens her spine, standing tall as she leaves my room.

"Camille," I call, following her.

"Thanks for the tattoo. Have a good night." She turns around briefly and attempts to smile, but it falls flat. She throws two bills on the counter, but before I can say something, she's already out the door.

Part of me itches to chase after her, but I already upset her enough. I don't want to make it worse. I grab the two one hundred-dollar bills she left behind, then proceed to slam my fist on the desk hard enough to rattle the pens off of it.

Not only did I hurt her with my comment, but she paid me even though I told her not to. It feels wrong to take it, but I do it anyway because if not, Otto will.

I pocket it with plans of returning it to her somehow along with apologizing to her because despite the fact that I can't give her anything more than friendship, a lousy one at that apparently, I don't want her to hate me.

It's the first time I've ever cared about the way someone feels about me, and I have a feeling it's not going anywhere, anytime soon.

Chapter Eight

Camille

"*Putain*," I curse, blowing out a breath, eyeing the purpleish bruise forming under my left eye. Last night, I got up in the middle of the night to use the washroom and tripped over a shoe I must've left out. I fell and whacked my face on my dresser as a result.

I moved here to live on my own and I love making my own choices, but it would've been nice to have someone take care of me after that incident.

I push that aside and focus on the fact that I finally get to start shooting some content with the guys today. We're doing a behind the scenes spring training feature where I'm going to interview the guys and allow fans to get to know them.

I'm also planning for them to partake in doing a partner challenge where they can't laugh at whatever the other person is telling them or else they get hit with a tortilla. I know it sounds ridiculous, but it brings in a lot of engagement on other schools' teams' videos.

As I make my way into the baseball facility, a sense of insecurity washes over me from my conversation with Ryker a few days ago.

I'm still hurt by it. His words hit a sore spot of mine.

What if my ideas are stupid? What if the team hates them? What if I fail miserably at this job and let everyone down?

Maybe I should just go home before I embarrass myself.

I pause outside the door to the weight room where I know the guys are training today and take a long, deep breath.

I got this.

I walk into the room full of men working out and realize what a bad timing this is. How in the hell am I supposed to get any work done when they're all making grunting noises, sweating, and lifting heavy things?

The answer is I'm not, especially when I see Ryker with his hair in a bun, wearing a gray T-shirt doused in sweat, clinging to his abs and muscular chest. His forearms flex as he completes his set. I've never seen a more attractive forearm before. Even more so with the tattoos decorating his right arm.

I have no idea if he has tattoos anywhere else because I've never seen him shirtless, but I'd be willing to bet there's more. I have this urge to ask him about them and study them up close, but I push the urge away, remembering that I'm mad at him and that there's no hope for us anyway.

We're far too opposite.

Some of the guys say hi to me, and I keep my head down while I smile and greet them back, hoping that my baseball cap is hiding the bruise. I begin to set up my camera and tripod in the far corner where there's good lighting and lots of space for the challenge portion when I hear a deep, rough voice coming from behind me.

"Hey."

Ugh, Ryker.

I thought we had made progress the other day, and the part of me that has a crush on him was thrilled. But then he proceeded to tell me how stupid my ideas were after I went on and on about them and telling him how excited I was.

I turn around, keeping my gaze down but my cheeriness up despite what I'm feeling. "Hey."

"Look, I wanted to apologize for the other night. I didn't mean to offend you. I felt like a jackass afterward. I just don't like social media stuff. That's all. It has nothing to do with your ideas in particular." He sounds genuinely apologetic, which makes me meet his eyes before thinking twice of it.

It takes me half of a second to realize my mistake because Ryker's on me instantly. He towers over me in a protective stance, his eyes laser focused on the bruise under my eye while his jaw clenches tightly. "What the hell happened to you?"

"It's nothing," I tell him with a smile because it's the truth. I'm just a bit clumsy.

His breath is shallow, his tone raspy from rage. "Princess, if someone hurt you, I swear *to* God, I'm going to lose it. No bullshit, tell me the truth."

A shiver skates down my spine at the protectiveness in his tone, and my romantic heart threatens to run wild with it. "No bullshit, I tripped over a shoe in the middle of the night and hit my face on my dresser." I huff out a nervous laugh, because honestly, it's silly. "I'm perfectly fine. You can relax."

Ryker's hand lifts like he's about to touch me then thinks better of it. "Be careful, okay?"

"I will do my very best." I chuckle, turning to set up the camera. I hate how easily he can draw me back in. The man has me smiling and blushing two seconds after I claimed I was annoyed with him.

"Are we okay? I saw red when I saw the bruise and lost track of my apology," he says, sounding hesitant, which is unlike him.

I think about it for a moment and turn around to him as an idea pops into my head. "I'll accept your apology under one condition."

His eyebrows narrow, his arms crossing over his chest. "What is it?"

A devious grin forms on my lips as I step in closer to him. "You have to film a *stupid* video for me."

Ryker runs a hand over his neatly-trimmed beard, those blue eyes of his burning into mine. "Fine. Only one," he mumbles.

"I won't make you go first. Don't worry. So go finish your workout." I motion to the weights and turn my attention back onto setting up.

He says nothing, but I can feel his eyes on me for a beat before he goes over to the free weight area.

Once I'm ready, I go up to Cuddy and Noah, asking them to do the challenge for me. They immediately agree, and their reaction makes my body buzz with joy.

I get them set up, positioning them so that they're in the frame just right. I catch Ryker staring as he trains, that typical scowl on his face. What's different, though, is the glare he's shooting his friends.

I ignore it and continue to explain the rules to Cuddy and Noah. They both give me a thumbs-up, indicating they're ready.

We film for the next hour and it ends up being the funniest thing I've witnessed in a while. Cuddy lost, spitting his water out all over Noah after the third hit, which then made Noah spit his water on Cuddy. While we worked, most of the team ventured over to watch. They were all laughing as well, shouting that they wanted to be next.

I filmed a few more rounds, noticing that Ryker was never on the sidelines watching like everyone else was.

He kept to his workout, showing his dedication to his training regimen. I know he's a top pick for the draft coming up this summer, and I can see why. He works harder than anyone in the room and has the skills to back it upon the field.

It's why I decide to let him get away with not filming a video for me today.

Once we're done filming, I start packing up my stuff when Travis, a freshman on the team, approaches me. "Hey, Camille," he says, smiling at me.

I smile back at him. "Hey, what's up?"

"Just wanted to invite you to a party tonight. Not sure if you heard of it. It's at the football house." His voice is kind, making me consider it. I'm not interested in Travis in the slightest, but it might be fun to get out.

"Yeah, maybe I will. Thanks for the invite," I tell him, smiling at the idea of potentially seeing Theo tonight. I should message Jasmine and see if she's free as well.

"See you there," he boasts before strutting out of the weight room.

All the guys are gone now, so I pause to send a quick text to Jasmine.

I smile at my phone as I move to text her back, when I walk into a hard chest. I startle backward, my chest thumping from the unexpectedness because I thought I was alone.

"Camille," Ryker says my name so softly, it makes my chest ache.

"Sorry." I attempt to smile at him as I will my heart to calm down, but I'm too flustered.

"I should've said something. It's my fault. Are you okay?" he asks, those blue eyes inquisitive.

"I'm good. Are you going to the party tonight?" I say, changing the subject. I walk out of the weight room and Ryker follows behind me.

"No."

"Boring." I stick my tongue out at him. "It'll be fun. It's at Theo's house. Well, the football house. Tomato, tahmato."

Ryker shakes his head, blowing out a breath in what seems like annoyance.

"Still not going."

"I'll have enough fun for both of us then." I smirk. "See you around, Ryker the biker," I call out as I walk toward the exit.

I don't know why I even want to go tonight, but something in my gut is telling me to go. Maybe I'll meet the love of my life tonight? Who knows. And that's the beauty of it all, never knowing what's around the corner waiting for you. My romantic heart hopes it's Ryker, but the logical part of me knows it's a useless thing to wish for.

Yet as I get ready, I hope he's around that corner, waiting to surprise me.

Chapter Nine

Ryker

The baseball house is quiet for a Friday night, and that's probably because all the guys are at the football house tonight for their party. Bored, I venture downstairs in search of some cookie dough Pop-Tarts, my guilty pleasure. I keep a stock of them hidden in the pantry, where no one can find them.

I tend to be protective over what's mine.

I close the pantry, a box of Pop-Tarts in tow, and head to the living room, where Cuddy, Noah, and his girlfriend, Emily, are sitting on the couch playing Mario Kart.

"Hey, Ryker," Em says, waving at me.

"Hey," I reply as I sit on the couch, needing a distraction from my thoughts that keep circling back to a certain girl who's at a party tonight.

"How come you're not at the party?" Cuddy asks.

There goes my whole not thinking about her plan.

"Didn't want to." I shrug, shoving a Pop-Tart in my mouth.

"Theo's your best friend, though," he points out as he shakes his controller.

"And?"

"As a best friend, it's your duty to attend parties thrown by your friend," Noah chimes in.

"It's true," Em adds in quietly. She's always been soft-spoken and one to keep to herself. Noah and her ended up dating after she tutored him during our freshman year.

"Meh, he's fine. Theo has lots of friends," I retort, watching as Emily knocks Noah's character off the track.

Cuddy sits up, a mischievous glint in his eye. "Did you know that Travis asked Camille to the party tonight?"

What? Is he fucking serious?

"Where did you hear that?" I sound frantic, which is unusual for me, but as of recently, there are a lot of unusual things happening to me.

Cuddy and Noah exchange a glance, but I don't have to read into what just transpired between them.

"From Travis himself. He bragged about it in the showers after our workout. He said he's pulling a move tonight," Noah finally says.

I spring up and off the couch. Not bothering to pick up the box of Pop-Tarts from the floor, I head to the entryway and grab my keys.

In no fucking universe is he touching her tonight.

"Where are you going?" Cuddy asks, his tone snarky as fuck, and I don't even care why right now.

"You guys know Travis is a pig. I'm not letting him get anywhere near her." I snarl, throwing my leather jacket on. "Why the hell did you wait this long to tell me?"

"Didn't know it was something I needed to tell you," he remarks.

"She's a grown woman, you know. She can handle herself and make her own choices. Maybe she wants Travis to make a move." Noah shrugs, playing devil's advocate, and I could throttle him for the images that pop into my head of Travis's grimy hands all over *my* princess.

"Fuck off, both of you."

I leave with that, storming out of the house, and rev up my bike as I make my way over to the football players' house. It's not far, but I want to get there as soon as fucking possible.

I park on the curb outside the house, noting the mass of people who are piled on the porch, beers spelling out "party" on the front lawn and music raging from inside.

It's a shit show here.

I storm inside, not responding to the various people who shout my name and try to call me over. I have one person I'm here for. I don't give a shit about anyone else. It's packed inside the house, and I bump into a few shoulders as I move through the crowd of people.

I check the living room and kitchen with no sighting of her. My gut churns as I think of her being upstairs with him. I have no right to be pissed off about it, but I don't trust Travis. Not for a single second.

I'm about to go upstairs when Theo spots me. His eyes widen, the cowboy hat on his head nearly tipping off as he leans forward in shock. "Ry guy, is that you?" he shouts, running over to clap me on the back.

"Hey, have you seen Camille?" I ask, skipping formalities.

"Yeah, she was downstairs playing Dance Dance Revolution with some of the guys from your team," he says.

I go to brush past him, but he grips my shoulder, halting me in place.

"What is it?" I snap at him, impatient.

"What is it with you?" he asks, raising an eyebrow at me.

"I don't trust Travis around her, okay? I'm making sure she's okay."

"You could've texted me to keep an eye on Millie Moo, but I must admit your presence here has really made my night," he tells me earnestly.

"It's a good party," I tell him, trying not to be an asshole. There are tons of people, the music's good, and laughter's constantly bouncing throughout the rooms. Telltale signs of a good party.

Theo dramatically puts a hand over his heart. "Thank you. Now go find your girl."

I don't stay to correct him, even though he's wrong. She's not mine, and she never will be.

Yeah, right, my mind mocks me.

Ignoring it, I barrel down the stairs and see a couple of guys from the team dancing. I want to laugh at the sight, but a flash of silky champagne hair redirects my focus.

I find Camille in the hall with her back against the wall, looking uncomfortable and bored as Travis leans over her while she looks away. I see fucking red as I march over to her, not stopping until I yank on Travis's shirt, pulling him away from her as I shove him against the opposite wall.

"Dude, what the hell?" Travis huffs, struggling against my arm that's over his chest.

"What did I tell you?" I seethe.

"I have no idea what you're talking about. Get off me." He attempts to move, but I hold him in place.

"That girl is off-limits and looks uncomfortable as fuck with you towering over her. If I see you near her, you'll never throw a baseball again," I threaten him.

Travis chuckles. "That sounds familiar. Isn't that how you got arrested before?"

I narrow my eyes as I shove against him harder before letting him go. I don't know how he knows about that, but it's not something I want getting out to the press. I was never charged. They made me do community service instead, but it still doesn't look good for draft prospects.

He walks away, leaving Camille and me alone in the hallway. She looks like a knockout tonight, dressed in ripped jeans, her signature high-top white Converse and a cropped sweatshirt. It's different from her usual outfits, but I like it all the same. Honestly, she could wear a paper bag and still be the most stunning girl in the world.

"Are you okay?" I ask. I was so lost in my rage while I had him against the wall that I didn't check on her.

I should have done that first.

"Yeah," she breathes out, running a hand through her hair. "You didn't need to do that. I can stand up for myself."

"I never said you couldn't." I look at her intently because something tells me she doesn't believe in herself that she could've. "But sometimes it's nice to have someone looking out for you too."

"It is," she whispers.

I take a slow step toward her, gauging her reaction. Her eyes flit back to mine, a sense of hope in them, for what, I don't know. I carefully bring my hand to her chin, and she sucks in a breath.

"Did Travis do or say anything else I should know of?"

She shakes her head, those big eyes of hers locked on mine. It takes the fucking breath out of my lungs. Her eyes dart to my lips, sending a low growl to slip past my lips as I put the other hand on her hip and bring her closer to me.

Camille closes her eyes for a beat, and when they open again, it nearly brings me to my knees. She looks so damn vulnerable, open, and trusting. Her breaths come in quicker, her eyes dipping to my lips once more.

I know she wants me to kiss her, and I fucking want it more than anything, but we can't. I need to get out of this hallway before I do something stupid. So I clear my throat and drop my hand, letting it fall away as I take a step back.

Camille looks disappointed, but quickly covers it with a smile.

"Well, thanks for…uhm, yeah, good night." Her tone is hurried and awkward as she walks away from me.

Not on my watch.

I follow her through the house, all the way out the front door. She begins walking down the sidewalk, when I cut her short as I step in front of her.

"Where do you think you're going, princess?"

"Home." She gives me a smile, but it wavers.

"You're not walking," I tell her, pointing to my bike on the curb. "I'll give you a ride."

I don't know how I expected her to respond, but the big smile and hand clap she does is not it. It's cute as fuck.

"Yes, please!" she exclaims, bouncing on her toes.

Jesus. If I knew giving her a ride on my bike would warrant this reaction, I'd have done it a lot sooner.

We walk over to my bike and I pop the back open for the second helmet. I turn and find her waiting eagerly, her eyes lit up with excitement.

"Can I put this on you?" I ask her, never wanting to cross a boundary with her. I wish she would share with me what happened to her so I could understand her more, but I want it to be on her own terms.

"Yes."

I bring my hand up to her cheek, my knuckles brushing across the soft skin there. She shivers under my touch, and it makes me refocus on the task. I brush her hair behind her ears, then carefully pull the helmet over her head.

"You okay?" I ask her.

"Mhm." She smiles at me, still looking gorgeous as ever even with the helmet on.

I tug mine on and take a seat on my bike, offering my hand to her to help her climb on the back. Camille takes it, her small hand fitting perfectly in mine. She mounts the bike, but sits further back than I'd like.

I keep my foot down on the ground for balance and reach with both of my hands behind my back, each one gripping the outer sides of her thighs. I gently pull her body forward until her chest is pressing against my back.

Having her this close to me is a bad fucking idea, but I can't seem to stop myself.

"Stay like this and hold on to me," I instruct her as I look over my shoulder to face her. "Where do you live, by the way?" I ask her, and she tells me.

Then I pull the visor down on her helmet, and it suddenly hits me that she's now my responsibility. If something happened to her while riding my bike, I wouldn't be able to handle it.

I turn forward, do the same to my visor, then begin revving the engine. Camille's hands gently rest on my hips, barely gripping me, but that won't do. So I put my hands over hers and drag them over to my front so that they're holding her close to me.

I rev the engine once more, and her grip on me tightens. "You okay, princess?" I shout over the sound of the engine.

"More than okay. Let's go," she shouts back.

It's with a smile that I kick off the curb and cruise down the road. Usually, I enjoy the sound of nothing but me and my bike, the rustle of trees in the wind. But tonight? Fuck, there's never been anything that has sounded as good as Camille's carefree laugh that swirls around us as we take off down the road.

It's infectious and endearing. I don't think driving alone will do it for me anymore after experiencing a ride with her like this.

We don't have a long ride ahead of us, but I'm going to take it slow and enjoy the fuck out of having her wrapped tightly around mine, her laughter mingling with the wind, making it the most perfect sound I've ever heard.

Camille lifts her left arm and I almost reach for it, but when I look in the side mirror, I watch her let it float in the air, her fingers moving like a wave and letting the air float through them.

I let her have her fun for a minute, then convince myself that it's because of her safety that I need her arm back around my waist.

A few minutes later, we pull up to her fancy apartment, dread settling into my body. I don't know why, but I don't want this night to end.

I shut my bike off and kick the kickstand out. "You get off first," I tell her, holding my hand out for her.

She ignores it, dismounting the bike on her own and lifting the helmet off her head. Camille shakes her hair out, running her fingers through it with the biggest smile on her face.

It's the sexiest thing I've seen in a long time.

"Thank you so much for that. I had the best time," she tells me, pure joy clear as day on her face.

I smile under my helmet, knowing I'm safe to do it there. Lifting it off, I dismount the bike and leave it on the seat. "You keep surprising me, princess." I gaze at her, trying to understand exactly who Camille is deep down.

"Let me guess, you hate surprises?" she muses, raising a brow at me.

"I don't hate anything when it relates to you."

What the hell did I just say?

I internally facepalm while Camille visibly blushes, but her eyes seem wary. I don't blame her. I keep saying one thing and doing another. I need to get my shit together.

"Good to know, Ryker the biker, good to know," she teases.

"Stop calling me that." I scowl.

"Why? It's the perfect nickname. It rhymes and it's true," she points out.

"Princess doesn't rhyme nor is it true, but it's perfect for you," I fire back, although I'm not sure that last bit is true. The more I get to unravel bits of her, the more I learn that she's less formal than I thought.

There's a quick glance of worry in her eyes, but it passes just as quickly. I wonder why, for a moment, and I'm about to ask when a man comes rushing out the lobby doors.

"*Camille, où étais-tu?*" he snaps, and I instantly take a step in front of her, but he isn't deterred in the slightest.

"*Quentin, qu'est-ce que tu fais ici?*" Camille replies to him, then looks at me when she notices how tense I am. "Ryker, this is my brother Quentin."

I take a closer look at the man, and it hits me. *Quentin Laurent?*

Holy. Fuck. He's the starting pitcher for the Detroit Panthers and the best in the league. I try to keep my cool, but the inner child in me wants to ask for his autograph.

And he's her brother? No. Fucking. Way.

"*Je suis arrivé il y a quelques heures et tu ne répondais pas à ton téléphone. Il faut qu'on parle. Tu n'es peut-être pas royal ici, mais tu dois quand même faire attention.*"

Camille and Quentin glance at me, but I don't have a clue what the hell they're saying. The word royal sticks out to me, but for all I know, he called me a royal asshole.

He wouldn't be wrong.

Camille seems fearful and upset. It bothers me and I want to do whatever I can to put that big smile back on her face.

"Hey." I lower my voice as I face her. "You good?"

"Yeah, I just need to talk to my brother."

I take in her full pink lips, down to her slender neck that I have the urge to explore with my own. "Give me your phone."

Her eyebrows narrow, but she does it anyway, giving it to me unlocked. I put my number in there, then hand it back to her.

She takes it and looks at the new contact, her eyes lighting up with the same hope I saw earlier.

"Just in case you need to reach me for social media stuff," I tell her, lying through my damn teeth. That's the last thing I want her to text me for.

Just as quickly as the hope in her eyes came, it flashes away. Camille straightens and hands me the helmet she had on as she brushes past me. "Thanks again. Have a good night," she says softly.

She walks away, her long hair bouncing in the moonlight. How many more times am I going to let her walk away while I regret every second of it? Wishing I could chase after her and wrap her in my arms where I know she'd be safe.

Unlike how my heart feels when it comes to her.

Chapter Ten

Camille

That first warm day in March after a harsh winter feels like salvation. Suddenly, everything seems brighter, everyone feels lighter. It feels like the hope of what's to come.

Winter gives you the time to rest and restore so you can bloom in the spring.

The baseball team is practicing outside today. They're more rambunctious than usual, laughter and smiles passing around the group of men.

With my camera in hand, I record the action from various angles, honing in on our star players. I capture Noah diving for ground balls at shortstop and Cuddy catching balls in the outfield.

Once I get to Ryker, I find myself in a trance as he whips precise balls over to first base from his spot on third. His forearms tighten, his shoulder muscles bunching at each throw.

His whole persona draws me in, and trust me, it's not just the tattoos and muscles. Although, *they* are insanely sexy. It's the way he stands confidently yet casually at the same time, like he knows who he is, yet isn't trying to prove it to anyone.

I'm now sitting on the fence, my legs dangling above the

red dirt as I look through footage from today while the boys wrap up practice. Today's content has already been posted—a video of "This or That" with the fan favorite, Cuddy.

Noah has the sweet *boy next door* charm, while Cuddy is all about the camera. Ryker would rather have no part in it at all, yet fans love the grumpy baseball player, but not quite as much as Cuddy.

My mind is whirling with ideas when my eyes catch on the bin of spare gloves. With a delighted hum, I hop down from the fence and pocket my phone in my crossbody bag. Then I dig out a glove that would fit me.

I've always wished I could've played professionally, but I never learned how. It wasn't allowed. Our head of security, Idris, who was more like a father to me than my own, offered to teach me, but trying to find the time to sneak away was nearly impossible, so it never happened.

Just as I find a black glove that fits perfectly, a deep voice startles me, forcing me to turn around.

"What are you doing?" Ryker asks, his arms folded across his chest, his own glove on his hand.

"Doing a quality check on the gloves, you know, making sure everything's a-okay." I wink, but internally, I want to cringe.

His eyebrows rise in curiosity as he stares at me down the brim of his RLU green-and-white baseball cap. "And did they pass inspection?"

I salute him. "With flying colors. Everything is A-plus okay, more than plain old a-okay,"

Why did I salute him?

"What were you really doing?" he prods.

I huff and swing my braid over my shoulder, fiddling with the end of it. "Don't laugh, but I wanted to try it on, maybe throw a ball or two up in the air. I've never done it before, and I've always wanted to try."

Ryker's fingers wrap around my own on my braid, stilling my nervous fidgeting. "I can teach you."

My eyes widen and my breath stops short as I take him in, the one responsible for my most severe case of whiplash.

"You'd do that?" I deadpan.

"I might be an asshole, but not enough to let you do it alone and hurt yourself," he gruffs, letting his hand fall away from my hair.

"*Ah oui*, let's go now." I tug on his arm, pulling him toward the field that's now empty since the boys have already left to shower, I guess.

"First thing, you need to show me how you plan to catch a ball." He gestures toward my glove, and I hold it up excitedly.

I put my hand inside the worn leather and do my best not to think about the various sweaty hands that have been in here before. "Open." I show him, then close my thumb and fingers together, "Closed."

"Good, now I'm going to show you how to throw a ball," he tells me, taking his glove off and placing it on the artificial grass. I do the same with my crossbody bag.

Anticipation rolls through me, wondering exactly how he plans to do that.

Ryker steps in my space, his dark blue eyes looking down at me. "I'm going to have to touch you. Is that okay?"

"Yes." I lick my lips without thinking, and his eyes darken in response.

"Turn around," he orders.

My body listens and I turn my back to him. A chill runs down my spine at his proximity. Ryker nudges his leg between mine, pushing my left leg out until my feet are shoulder width apart.

"You want to be standing like this to start, then you'll step forward when you throw it," he instructs as he moves around to face me with a ball in his hands, which he drops into my opened glove. "You're going to want to grip the ball with your middle and index fingers on top and your thumb underneath it."

I take the ball out of my glove and do as he says. "Like this?" I hold it up to show him.

"Yes, once you have your aim and are ready to throw it, you're going to want to take a step with your left leg. At the same time, your right arm will be cocked back, elbow up." He demonstrates the movement for me, and I watch attentively. "Then you want to lean your body forward as you throw it, while twisting your hips to face forward."

I go through the motions slowly with him, observing and watching each step.

I stand confidently. "Okay, I think I got it."

"All right then, throw it to me," he says as he jogs about fifteen feet away.

I do as told and adjust my stance, finding my aim and going through the motions of my throw. Except I know I messed something up because the ball goes right into the ground once I let it go.

I cover my face with my glove as laughter spills from my lips. When I take a peek at Ryker, he's jogging back toward me and scooping the ball up in the process.

"I was awful." I giggle, meeting his eyes once he's close enough.

"You're learning," he corrects, then drops his glove on the ground and puts the ball in my right hand. "Put your arm up like you're about to throw it."

I do as he says, holding my arm up and back. Ryker's body brushes against my back, his warmth searing my skin with how close he is. His hand wraps gently around my elbow, pulling it up a bit.

"Keep this elbow up higher, and"—he pauses, dragging his fingers slowly up my forearm, then wraps them around my hand—"release the ball here." He moves our hands forward, stopping just past my face. "Not here." He guides our hands further, nearly toward the ground like I just did before.

My heart beats wildly, and I'm pretty sure the sweat on my forehead has nothing to do with the oddly warm spring day.

His other hand grips my hip and twists it forward, making me gulp as I attempt to keep myself together. I wish I had the courage to take control, to turn around and press my lips to his like I would've years ago, but I don't. A part of me has this gut feeling that I could be that way with Ryker, that he'd let me take charge. But another part of me is aware of the fact that this is nothing more than a silly crush and I shouldn't let myself want more.

"Make sure you twist your hip forward when you throw, okay?" he asks, and I nod in response because he's left me with the inability to utter any words at this point. Having his hands all over me and his deep, rich voice in my ear sends heat blooming in my core when it shouldn't.

He moves back to his previous spot and I do as he says this time. The ball goes right toward Ryker, who catches it with ease. I jump up and down with the biggest smile on my face.

I did it. I finally learned how to throw a baseball. It might be a simple goal, but it's something I wasn't allowed to do before and always wanted to.

"Nice job, princess," Ryker shouts from his spot. "You ready to catch one now?"

"Yup," I shout back with my glove open, ready to catch.

Ryker winds up, but instead of the quick whips I'm accustomed to seeing him do, he throws me an easy toss. It's aimed right at me, making it easy for me to throw my glove out and close it around the ball. I throw my hands up in the air and do a little dance, shaking my hips in a circle as I twirl around.

Once I stop, I find Ryker closer now, staring at me, his arms crossed over his chest and any warmth he previously had gone.

"What?" I ask, breathless.

"Practice is done," he says harshly, a scowl on his face as he stomps away toward the dugout.

"Thank you, Ryker the biker," I call after him with a smile on my face. Not even his sudden grumpy mood could dim my high. "But what about hitting?"

He stops and looks at me over his shoulder. "Another day. I need to go."

Then he's gone, leaving me on the field with my head in the clouds.

Chapter Eleven

Camille

"It's time to pay up." I grin as I walk Ryker into an empty office in the baseball facility. It's set up with two chairs opposite each other, and my new camera, thanks to Coach Warren, is on a tripod.

"Joy," he mutters, plopping onto one of the chairs, his arms folding across his chest.

I ignore his grumpiness, keeping the cheerful smile on my face. "Correct, this is going to be so much fun."

Ryker only stares at me, unsure what he's getting himself into.

"All right, so this is how it's going to work. I'll ask questions fans sent in, and you'll answer them. If there's anything you'd rather not answer, just say *pass*."

I begin the video, then sit behind the lens so that I'm not seen but you can still hear my voice.

"Hi, everyone, today we have a fan favorite with us, Ryker Lewis. The talented third baseman and infamous team grump."

Ryker raises a single brow at that but says nothing.

"We have some burning questions here from your fans, so

are you ready to give us some answers?" I give him a thumbs-up, letting him know he can take the floor now.

"I can't wait." He raises the corners of his lips slightly, then drops them just as quickly, clearly unenthused.

But this is exactly what his fans love, so I'll take it.

"First question. If you weren't playing baseball, what else would you be doing?"

He doesn't miss a beat and answers immediately. "I'd have my own tattoo shop."

"I could see that. You're very talented," I compliment him, then realize it's supposed to be a professional interview.

I clear my throat and ask the next question. "Favorite music?"

"Anything in the rock genre from the '60s to the '90s."

"Favorite season?

"Summer."

"Are you dating anyone?"

Wait, what?

I look down at my questions and double-check that I read it correctly.

I did.

Ryker's head tilts back, thrown off by the question. He swallows once, then in his deep, rough voice, says, "No. I'm married to the game. There's no time for that."

There should be no reason why his answer affects me, but it does. It cements the fact that despite my crush on him, it'll only ever be that. A one-sided crush. He doesn't want love in his life, nor does he have the time for it.

I school my features, hoping my disappointment doesn't show as I ask my next question, not thinking twice, my voice an octave higher than normal. "What is your ideal date?"

"If you wanted to hang out, you could've just asked, princess." His lips twitch, a hint of amusement on his face.

My mouth gapes. "No, that's not what this is." I flip the paper to him, pointing at the question. "It's right here, look."

Ryker shrugs, unconvinced. "You printed them, didn't you?"

"I did, but I didn't get a chance to look them over."

He takes pity on me, relenting on his teasing as he answers the question. "If, and emphasis on the *if*, I ever took a girl out, I'd do something she likes. That would be my ideal date, seeing her in her element, happy." His voice takes on a more serious tone, his eyes locked onto mine.

My brain short-circuits and fails to compute what he just said as my body responds to his attention, wanting more of it. We stare at one another for a beat, then he clears his throat.

I sit up straight in my chair and cross my legs. "How thoughtful of you. I'm sure all the ladies listening are swooning over that."

Jealousy creeps over me and I use the paper to distract me. I read the questions and decide I want to ask him a question of my own instead. "Why are you so grumpy?"

Ryker seems surprised. "Why are you brave enough to ask me that question?"

I go to answer, then decide against it. "I asked you first."

His stormy blue eyes narrow at me, but then he does as I asked. "I don't hate the world, just some of the people in it. Also, when you're determined like I am to make it big, you need to have a one-track mind. So sure, I can come across as a grumpy asshole because I don't give anything the time of day besides my craft. Sue me." He throws his hands up in surrender, then promptly folds them back in front of his chest.

I want to poke the bear, to prod deeper into who exactly he hates and why he's so determined that baseball is the only thing that matters, but I don't. "You're a hard worker and highly motivated. It certainly shows on the field," I comment, my eyes flicking back to the paper, perusing for one final question.

"Okay, last question."

"Thank God," he mutters, his left knee bouncing up and down.

"Who's inspired you the most in your life?" I ask, genuinely curious.

Ryker unfolds his arms, leaning on his knees with his forearms as he thinks over the question. After a minute of silence, he speaks up, "My mom. She showed me at a young age that you don't need to quit on your dreams because someone quit on you. It taught me that having your own passion was important. We can't always rely on another person to fill that piece of ourselves, because when they leave, you'd have nothing."

I let out a breath, wrapping my head around his answer. "Wow, that's…deep."

"It's the truth," he retorts, coming to a stand. "Are we done here?"

"Yeah, that was great. Thank you." I stand as well, noting how he towers over me despite me being five-foot-eleven.

"Anything for you," he says under his breath, his eyes not leaving mine.

Before I can ask what he means, he turns on his heel and storms out of the room. As soon as he's gone, I plop back down onto the chair, my mind reeling with all the information I learned today.

Not only did I get to learn some fun facts about him, I also got to see a different side to Ryker. The love for his mom was evident and beyond sweet. And then his answer about the date, how he'd make it about her?

God, I wish more men were like that. Because maybe then, my dream of a fairytale of a life would actually feel like one with a love like that.

Chapter Twelve

Camille

I groan as I shove my weekender bag over my shoulder, feeling sore from the workout I had last night. I worked out my frustration with the bag, hitting it with all I had until there was nothing left inside of me but a sense of contentment.

Quentin told me that his investigator got news that my parents hired an equally effective detective to find me and that I needed to be careful not to be seen on any social media.

My new job with the team worried me at first, but it's not like I'll be seen in the videos, and with editing tools, I can always edit my voice. I don't have any personal social media, so I should be safe, but there's still an eeriness that lingers with me now, like I could be watched at any time.

I push the thoughts away, focusing on the big bus outside of the baseball facility that's taking us to New Mexico today for their first practice game of the season. I hustle out, walking a bit faster toward the bus, knowing I'm almost late. The bus is set to leave at five-thirty, and it's already five twenty-seven.

I'm not a morning person, so they're lucky I made it three

minutes early. I lift my bag off my shoulder to put it in the under compartment of the bus when a hand grabs it from me.

"I've got it," Ryker's raspy voice says, hitting me like a breath of fresh air.

The way he looks this good at this time of day is beyond me. His hair is in a low bun, pieces falling around his sharp jaw, his beard neatly trimmed. His Dri-Fit long sleeve displays his chiseled chest and taut biceps while the gray sweats he's wearing accentuate his muscular thighs and do nothing to hide the massive package he's carrying down there.

God, why does he need to look like *that*? Like the most perfect human I've ever laid eyes on. Rugged yet put-together in the sexiest way possible.

I avert my eyes and try to pull myself together. "Thanks," I say, yawning and eyeing him with slight wariness. Ryker keeps saying things that lead me to believe he's into me, and then he does something that makes me believe otherwise. Like the time when he drove me home from the party and gave me his number, then backtracked by saying to only use it if I needed something regarding my work with the team.

He may as well have thrown a bucket of ice water over me.

It's safe to say I haven't texted him, nor do I intend to. I don't chase men. Never have, never will. Despite having the world's biggest crush on him, I'll never act on it. I was raised on the notion that the world will kneel to me, and I take that quite literally with men.

"Tired, princess?" he asks, shoving his bag down first, then puts mine on top.

"The sun is sleeping, therefore so should I," I groan.

Ryker turns and nudges his head for me to follow him as we head toward the bus door. "What, you can't be a ray of sunshine unless the sun's out? Is that it?" he says, half chuckling.

I stop in my tracks, looking at him in shock. "Did you…did you just make a joke?"

Ryker glowers at me over his shoulder, narrowing his eyes at me. "I *can* be funny, you know."

My eyebrows rise at that as I approach him, a smile tugging at my lips. "Sure you can, Ryker the biker. Sky's the limit, bud."

I don't wait for his response and pass him, giggling to myself as I do. That's until Ryker grabs my hand, spinning me toward him. My chest lands against his with a thud, leaving me breathless.

"*Bud?*" He peers down at me with my hands on his chest, noting how close we are. The team and coaches are on the bus and can't see us, but the last thing I need is to get in trouble for appearing to be flirting with a player.

Yet, I can't find it in me to move.

"Yeah, we're becoming friends, remember?" My voice is strained with breathlessness.

His scowl deepens, those blue eyes scorching mine with the intensity in them. His lips part to say something when Noah interrupts him.

"You guys better get on the bus before Coach comes out looking for you two," he says, one foot on the steps and the other on the ground. His warning breaks me from the spell Ryker put me under with his proximity. I jump back immediately, not looking back as I dash past Noah and right onto the bus.

I smile and greet the team as I walk down the aisle. My heart is pounding in my ears while I make it to the empty row at the back of the bus. I take a seat and blow out a breath, resting my forehead against the seat in front of me.

Ryker is the most confusing man I've ever met.

When I finally look up, I notice that he's currently walking to the back of the bus, right toward the only empty seat left, which is right next to mine.

This should be a fun bus ride.

Ryker sits down without saying a word, throws his headphones on as he closes his eyes, and folds his arms across his chest, making sure we aren't touching.

Anytime we teeter on that line of flirting, he always does this. Retreats into himself and puts space between us. It hurts, and I'm sick of this constant back and forth thing he has going on. One second, we're somewhat flirting and he's being all protective and sweet, and the next, he's shutting down.

It's time I realize that all he'll ever be to me is a crush, or a friend at most.

I stir awake when my phone vibrates in the back pocket of my jeans. I slowly open my eyes and freeze when I notice that my head is on Ryker's shoulder, his own resting gently on top of mine.

How the hell did we end up like this?

I allow myself a moment to bask in the feel of his body against mine. He smells like vanilla and leather, his skin warm and inviting. I smile, letting myself imagine that it's real. That we're a couple who cuddle and nap together. When my imagination makes my heart ache, I stop, knowing it's not good to fantasize about it for too long.

I carefully move my head, hoping I don't wake him. I replace my head with the sweater I took off earlier and wrap it up in a ball on his shoulder. Then I pull out my phone to find Jasmine's name on the screen with an unread message.

Jas

Cami!! He's taking me to his hometown.
I have no idea what he's doing,
but I'm excited.

It's then that I remember it's their redo of Valentine's Day.

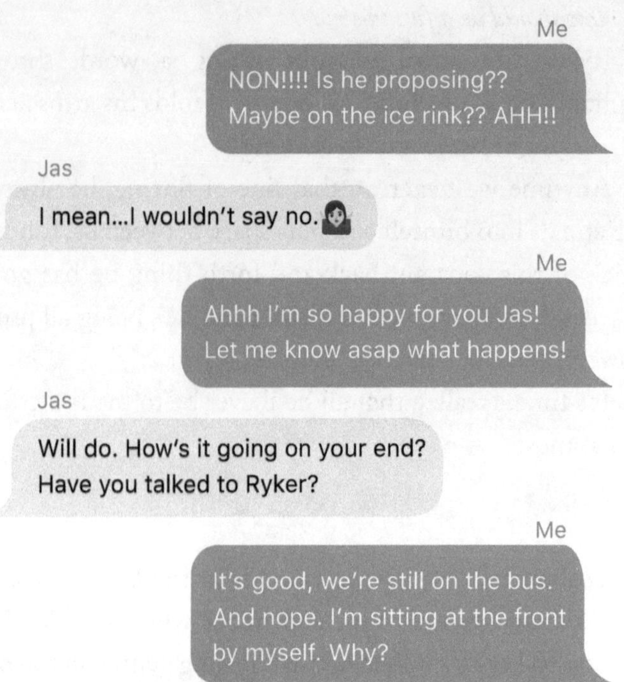

I hate to lie to her, but I don't want to tell her about what happened because she'll get excited, and it'll only raise my hopes up when I should be snuffing them out.

Ever since I started with the baseball team, Jasmine has been hoping that something will happen, insisting she saw a connection between us that night at the club all those months ago.

Maybe there was, but it doesn't matter because Ryker and I aren't meant to be together.

Chapter Thirteen

Ryker

As soon as the bus made it to our hotel in New Mexico, I all but ran off the bus, needing to put some distance between Camille and me.

During the ride, she must have passed out too because her head was resting on my shoulder, and my chin lay on top of her head. I pretended to be asleep because otherwise, I would've had to move from my position and I didn't want that.

I liked how easily she fit into the crook of my neck, her cotton candy smell that may have been too sweet if it didn't fit her perfectly.

I still pretended to be asleep when she woke up and moved, replacing her head with her sweater so I wouldn't wake up. The gesture made me feel something I never felt before. I thought I was becoming sick for a second because surely something was wrong with me.

I stayed like that until we got to the hotel, where we're now all walking into the lobby to receive our room assignments.

"Travis and Hugh, room 268," Coach calls out, passing them their keycard.

I find Camille talking with one of the female trainers on the team.

"Noah and Ryker, room 269." He passes us the card and glares at us, daring us to make a joke over the room number. In my periphery, Cuddy stifles a laugh because if anyone's going to make a joke about it, it's him.

When Coach continues down the line, Cuddy whispers in my ear, "Two can dine for sixty-nine. That's literally your room. 269, get it?"

I don't turn my head, side-eyeing him and doing my best not to laugh. It's an immature joke, but it's Cuddy, and anything he says usually makes my permanent scowl falter.

"Camille and Mackenzie, room 275." Coach passes them their respective keycard, and I don't miss the look of apprehension on Camille's face. She looks slightly frightened, and it only fuels this incessant need to protect her.

What is it that she's so afraid of?

Once Coach is done handing out room assignments, he gives us strict instructions to go drop off the stuff we don't need and to relax before we meet back in the lobby in an hour to head to a pregame practice.

But I have a different mission in mind when I spot Camille. She sits in the café off to the side of the lobby, scrolling on her phone instead of following everyone to the elevators.

With a quick check to make sure no one's left around, I approach her.

"What's wrong, princess? And no bullshit." I don't pull that card all the time, but I'm over being oblivious to what has her worrying this much.

Her head snaps up, and I immediately notice the indent on her full bottom lip from her teeth digging into it. Camille inhales deeply, her icy blue eyes trained on mine. "I don't like having a roommate, especially when it's someone I don't know. I need my own space."

I'm tempted to ask why, but I know what she just revealed to me was a lot for her. Despite her optimism, she's locked up like an unsolved Rubik's cube right now.

"Are you looking for a room?" I ask, nodding toward her phone.

"Yeah, but there's nothing left here. Everything's booked up."

I start talking before I have time to think it through. "You can stay with me. Noah's girlfriend, Emily, booked a room here for the weekend. He's sneaking out and spending his nights with her. So it'll just be me."

Camille's cheeks turn pink, her lips parting slightly. "You… what? Want me to room with you?"

"If it'll make you more comfortable, then yes. Mackenzie's hooking up with Cuddy, so I'm sure she'll be inviting him over to your room anyway," I explain.

"Did you miss the part where I said I like my own space?" One of her dark brows rises at me questionably.

"No, but I also didn't miss the part where you said everything's booked up. This is the best offer I can give you, princess."

Camille exhales in defeat, standing with her bag over her shoulder. "Okay." She smiles, but I hate the fear in her eyes. Even more so that I don't know why it's there. I don't want her to be afraid around me or *because* of me.

"Hey," I murmur, reaching out to grab her hand. It's soft and small in mine, sending a prickle of energy running through me.

She yanks her hand away a second later as she schools her face to one of indifference.

"You need to stop doing that. Especially if we're sharing a room. No mixed messages. Not anymore. Just friends." She stands her ground, staring up at me with determination.

I find myself wanting to reject her proposition, to tell her to hell with that, but she's not wrong. I've been giving her mixed messages since we met because I can't seem to stay away from her or control myself around her. It'll suddenly click that I'm not supposed to feel the way I do around her, and that's when I push her away, leaving both of us confused.

"You're right. I'm sorry. I won't do anything to make you uncomfortable, I swear," I tell her.

"I believe you," she nearly whispers. "How are we going to do this?"

"Easy, when Coach dozes off around ten, we sneak you across the hall to my room. That's what Noah does every away game and he's never been caught."

"Okay…well, I need to get the PR stuff ready before the game, so see you later." She smiles demurely, and I hate it because it's not the big smile she usually wears.

It's not the one that provides me with my personal boost of joy every time I see it.

After we finish practice, everyone from the team returns to their rooms to relax before the game tonight. Coach is big on balance and always makes sure we equally train hard and rest hard.

Noah and I are in our room, playing MarioKart on the Switch while we wait for the game.

"What are you and Em doing after the game?" I ask him.

"I'm taking her to dinner at this taco place that apparently has margaritas the size of your head. Then we'll go back to the room. It'll be late, so there's not much I can do, but tomorrow we're going to this pottery place she's been dying to go to since she's seen it online. She has no idea we're going," he explains excitedly.

"Sounds nice," is all I come back with because I can't imagine myself ever doing things like that for someone.

"What are you doing after the game?" he asks me just as his character falls off the track.

"Nothing, you know I don't go out." I press hard on the button that makes my character go faster, trying to pass the car in front of me. "But Camille is coming here for the night, so don't come back here."

Noah pauses the game as he turns to face me. "Really? How'd that happen?"

I groan, running a hand through my hair. I knew I had to tell him, but I also knew he'd ask questions I didn't want to answer.

"Mackenzie is going to invite Cuddy to her room, and Camille has nowhere else to go. It only made sense," I tell him, which is the truth. I omit the part about her not liking to share her space because that's her business.

"Those two are risky fuckers," Noah remarks. "If they get caught, it'll be the end of her career as an athletic trainer before it even starts."

He's right, it's risky as fuck, and a reminder that the same rules apply for Camille and me. If we were to get caught, it could look really bad on her and that's the absolute last thing I want.

"But," he adds, "when you know, you know. It's impossible to resist when it's the right person, even if the timing might seem wrong."

"I don't know about that. I'd never risk my career for something as silly as attraction."

Noah chuckles. "Ryker, there's more to life than baseball. You know that, right?"

"I'm sure there is, for other people, but not me. People leave, but baseball never will. It's the one thing I have control over." I instantly hate that I just opened up to him, but I couldn't help it.

I've been feeling so many things lately that I find myself wanting to open up to him.

He pauses, then says, "What if you get injured and have to retire? You can't control that, and then what?"

"I'll be a tattoo artist and coach for a living." I shrug.

"And you'll be lonely as fuck. I'm just saying, man."

I ignore him as I resume the game. Noah doesn't fight me on it. He continues playing, knowing I need time to think shit over in my head before I talk about it.

And I do. I think about how much I hate fighting this pull toward Camille. I want to kiss her and see if her lips taste as sweet as she is. I also equally want to part her legs and test my theory there too.

Being around Camille feels like being up to bat with two strikes and three balls. Do I take a chance and swing at the next pitch? Or do I play it safe and not take the chance?

I need to figure it the fuck out before it's too late to choose.

Chapter Fourteen

Camille

The baseball stadium for the New Mexico Warriors is beautiful. Maybe it's the rush of it being the team's first game or my first time covering it, but I am quite literally bouncing around with energy as I get myself set up.

I prepare to record videos of the guys walking into the stadium and to ask them what their favorite song is. It's been a hit online with other teams and should be a guaranteed viral video if the guys can come through like I know they can.

I'm still doing an article for the school paper, but I'm taking this position to another level if I want professional organizations to recognize me.

As I wait for the team to arrive, my mind drifts toward what's coming after the game tonight.

I'll be rooming with Ryker.

There's no way I can stay with Mackenzie, because not only do we not know each other well enough for me to be comfortable around her, but because of my nightmares. I'd hate to wake her up with my screams and be forced to explain what happened.

It's embarrassing. It was a long time ago, and I should be over it. I shouldn't still be afraid of something that didn't happen.

However, if I'm going to spend the night with someone, I want it to be Ryker. He makes me feel protected whenever I'm near him.

Even though I told him to stop messing with my head earlier, which, for the record, shocked the hell out of me. But I'm done. I can't do the back and forth anymore, not when I have feelings for him. It's like giving him permission to play with my heart and then put it back together whenever he pleases.

I finally spot the team bus pulling up to the curb and jump up excitedly, going to my phone to start the video.

Noah's the first one off the bus, smiling in my direction when he sees the tripod set up.

"Captain Noah of the Rockland Coyotes' baseball team, what is your favorite song?" I ask him, using the clear and graceful tone I was raised to speak in. I'll admit, it's come in handy when working in PR.

Noah tilts his head to the side in thought, then snaps his fingers. "'Jumpman' by Drake and Future gets me pumped up every time."

I give him a thumbs-up, letting him know he can keep walking. Next up is Cuddy, who is a natural in front of the camera. He lowers his sunglasses and winks.

"My favorite song," he starts, tapping his chin in thought. "I'm an open Swiftie, so I gotta go with 'Style', Taylor's version, of course. A fucking banger."

I giggle while giving him a thumbs-up, and he blows the camera a kiss before strutting on by. Ryker is next and he steals the breath out of my lungs. He's in shorts, revealing tattoos on his legs I hadn't seen before—one on his calf and the other on his thigh. My mouth waters and I drag my eyes up his body, noting how his gray T-shirt clings to his muscles, showing off the sleeve of tattoos on his right arm.

To top it off, his hair is in a half-up, half-down style that only he can pull off.

I wave him over, and he scowls as he approaches me, knowing he can't escape this.

"What's your favorite song, third baseman, Ryker Lewis?"

Ryker taps something on his phone, then takes off his headphones. His eyes drag up and down my body as if he forgot he was on camera.

I'm wearing a team jersey that Coach gave me on top of jean overalls with cut-off shorts and my Converse. I could never wear something like this back home, and it makes me love wearing it that much more.

"Whose jersey are you wearing?" he asks, a hint of annoyance in his tone.

I scrunch my nose at him and turn to show him the back with my first name on it. "My own."

Ryker just grunts in response, but I don't miss the hint of relief in his eyes.

"Favorite song, Ryker the biker?" I remind him.

That earns me a glare, but I've come to like them. I sort of enjoy bugging him, and I want to see him crack.

"'Part of Your World'."

"Like…as in from *The Little Mermaid?*" I ask, perplexed. That is not what I thought he would say. At all.

He shrugs, seeming not to care. "I like it."

My mouth hangs open, speechless, as I stare at this man who gives off bad boy vibes like no tomorrow, yet his favorite song is from a Disney movie.

The corner of his lips twists, and he grins at me, sending heat to my core and flutters to my heart.

His scowl is sexy, but that grin? Nothing could beat it.

"See you at the game, princess."

As the boys get ready for the game, doing stretches and throwing on the field, I record it all to get content for their page. I do my best not to stare at Ryker, but it's hard when his uniform looks like it was painted onto his body.

I don't talk to any of the players, careful not to disrupt their routines and focus. I'm merely here to record and stay out of the way.

Once the game starts, I sit in the stands, right behind first base. I pull my baseball cap low over my face and make sure my laptop is covering my face while keeping my eyes just above the screen to see the game.

The stadium is packed for an early spring game, filled with blue and yellow for the New Mexico Warriors. I'm the only person here in green and white. After the national anthem and the first pitch is thrown by the New Mexico coach's four-year-old daughter, the game begins.

It's electrifying watching a baseball game. I've always loved everything about it. The way a game can change in seconds, the fact that baseball has no end time, there are no timed periods to rush through.

Baseball decides when to end on its own.

I bring up my notes app and begin to take notes as the game is underway. RLU is set to hit first.

Noah is up and hits a ground ball right in between second and first base, allowing him to make it to first safely. The crowd boos heavily, but he seems to take it in stride, his years of playing baseball giving him the mental resilience needed to keep playing the game.

Cuddy is next and hits a pop fly, which their shortstop

catches. The crowd cheers and I do my best not to roll my eyes. This is their territory, so I get it, but it doesn't mean I have to like it.

Next up is Ryker. I sit up straighter in my seat as he steps up to the plate. His back foot twists twice before he plants it firmly, and he lifts his arms back and up, getting ready to swing.

It's mesmerizing to watch.

The first pitch is inside, a ball. Ryker adjusts his stance, then nods to the pitcher. This time, he swings and misses.

The crowd cheers, but I keep my eyes on him. He's oddly calm and collected, not letting the fact that he missed bother him like I suspected it might. Especially after I've heard how he's the most hotheaded player on the team.

The next pitch comes in hot, a curve ball, and Ryker swings, whipping his bat to send it flying over the center fielder and out of the park.

I stand up and cheer, making me quite literally the only person in the stands doing so. Ryker turns his head to look at me as he jogs to first base, a smile on his face. A freaking smile. With teeth and everything. It makes me suck in a sharp breath at the beauty of it, at how different he looks when he does it.

I love it.

I blush and quickly sit down to write some notes on my laptop, reminding myself to be careful. It's not a major league game with big screens and cameras, but I still need to be mindful.

The next two batters strike out, and then we're on the field.

If I thought watching Ryker swing the bat was mesmerizing, then I was not prepared to watch him catch fastballs and whip them over to first base at lightning speed.

There's a reason he's at the top of the prospect list for the draft this year. Not only can he hit, but he's one of the best third basemen in college baseball. It's a tricky position to play because it needs a quick yet precise throw to first base to get easy outs.

Fucking up a throw to first base can alter the game completely by allowing a base runner to score, and if the next person up hits a home run, then another person would just score again.

It's a crucial position, and he handles it with what seems like ease. But I've seen how hard he works. I know he's put the time in to be the best. It's admirable and hot as fuck.

The game is over a few hours later and we end up winning the game 4-1. While the team has their post-game debrief, I work on my notes for the article that the paper will need tomorrow morning. Usually, I'd interview star players from the game, but since it's the first game, I don't need to do that just yet.

As I sit on the cool concrete in the hallway near their locker room, a rush of joy and happiness like no other engulfs me. From the excitement of the game to analyzing plays and having fun with the players and making them more accessible to their fans.

It's where I'm meant to be, and I'll do my best to make sure it's where I stay.

Chapter Fifteen

Camille

It's ten o'clock, and I'm sitting on my bed, anxiously waiting for Ryker to answer my latest text message. After the game, everyone went back to their rooms, since it was nine o'clock at night and everyone was exhausted. Once I got to mine, I showered and got ready for bed, opting for joggers and a tank top, foregoing a bra.

He's seen me like this before when he did my tattoo, and quite frankly, I don't care all that much. My boobs aren't big enough for them to be super noticeable, except the piercings that occasionally make themselves known.

That was a decision I made when I was eighteen after years of begging my parents to play softball. They of course said no, so I rebelled and did something fun for myself.

My phone vibrates, pulling me from my memories. My heart races in my chest when I see Ryker's name and I pull up our text thread.

Me

Let me know when to come over.

Ryker the biker

Now.

Nerves rattle my chest when I realize we're actually doing this. I don't have much of a choice and Mackenzie told me earlier that Cuddy would be coming over. She said I was welcome to stay, but her tone lacked sincerity.

I inhale a quiet, deep breath, then stand from the bed to grab my bag filled with everything I would need for tomorrow.

"Well, have fun tonight. My cousin is out front," I lie to Mackenzie awkwardly.

"I appreciate you for this." She smiles brightly, genuine gratitude on her face.

"No problem. Have fun." I smile back, exiting the room.

I glance down the hall quickly and make sure no one's in sight. Then I tiptoe down the hall to Ryker's room.

I knock once, and before my knuckles have even left the wood, he gently pulls me inside the room and slams the door shut behind us, then locks it.

I would focus on his proximity, but my eyes instantly land on the table behind him.

"What's all this?" I ask, motioning toward the variety of snacks ranging from candies and chocolate to potato chips and popcorns.

Ryker shrugs. "I got us a few snacks, but I didn't know what you'd like, so I got everything essentially. I figured we could watch a movie."

"Popcorn with hot sauce is my favorite snack," I tell him.

"Good to know. Wait, you're not allergic to anything, are you? Shit, I should've asked first," he grumbles, looking disappointed.

I can't fight the smile that tugs on my lips. "No, I'm not. This is perfect. Thank you. And a movie sounds great."

"You can take whatever bed you want. I'll set up Netflix while you pick what snacks you want. Do you need a drink?"

He's still my grumpy guy, but there's something odd about how nice he's being. I know we said yes to being friends, so maybe he's taking that to heart and trying.

"No, I have my water," I say, holding up my emotional support water bottle that goes with me everywhere. It's huge and a lavender shade, obviously.

Ryker nods and starts setting up his Netflix account on the TV, while I lay my stuff down on the floor and drop onto the bed that is closest to the wall. Then I move to the table and browse through the snacks and decide on popcorn and sour cherry blasters.

The hum of the Netflix intro fills the room as Ryker plops down on the bed beside mine, putting space between us that I'm partly thankful for, while another part of me is not.

"Which snack do you want?" I ask him, lifting my eyes to his. I notice his are cast downward and on my chest.

He quickly averts them and shakes his head. "I already have Pop-Tarts," he says, holding up a box of cookie dough-flavored ones.

"What am I supposed to do with all of these snacks?" I giggle while looking at how much is on the table.

"You can take them home. They're all for you," he says casually.

Flurries of warmth sprinkle across my chest at the image of Ryker going to the corner store next to our hotel and buying everything just for *me*.

"What do you want to watch?" he asks, pulling me back to reality.

"Nothing scary," I immediately say because whenever I watch scary movies, I'm more likely to have a nightmare. So I do my best to avoid them.

Ryker eyes me for a beat, then exits the app to pull up a

different app instead. I don't say anything and watch with intrigue to see what he'll do next.

He settles on the animated movie section and says, "Pick one."

I smile shyly and shake my head at him. "We don't have to watch a kids movie just because I'm a big baby."

"Just pick," he grunts.

I then remember what he told me about watching animated movies with his mom. "Do you miss your mom?" I ask softly, knowing I'm prying and he usually hates it.

"I always miss her when I'm on the road," he reveals, giving me a tiny sliver of himself that firmly plants itself in my heart. A grumpy, hot baseball player misses his mom? I'm fucked with this never-ending crush.

"That's really sweet. You can pick. I'm good with any movie," I tell him, popping a couple of cherry blasters into my mouth.

Ryker settles on *Tangled*, and we both munch on our snacks as the movie begins. It's quiet for a bit because I get the feeling Ryker is not the type to talk through a movie, whereas I usually am. Whether that be reactions to things going on or asking questions out loud that no one could answer unless they've seen it before.

But as the movie goes on, I find myself unable not to make comments. I giggle and hum along to the songs, which pulls a grunt out of Ryker every time.

"Wow," I breathe, watching the lamp scene in fascination. It's beautiful and reminds me of home. The whole castle itself does. The resemblance is endearing yet a reminder of what I ran away from.

"Pretty, huh?" Ryker drawls. "Makes me wonder if actual princesses existed and stuff, would it look like this? Or would they live in a mansion?"

His rambling isn't what instantly changes my mood, even though it is odd for him to question the legitimacy of royals.

Does he know something?

A shiver runs down my spine at the idea. How different would he treat me? Would he tell everyone and expose my secret identity here? If everyone knew who I was, would men try to get to me like they did when I was back home?

"I don't know," I mutter, climbing under the covers and turning on my side and away from him.

Way to be discreet, Camille, I internally chastise myself.

"What's wrong, princess?" he asks, sounding concerned, but I choose to ignore it.

"Nothing, just tired. It's been a long day." I stage a yawn, having done it many times to get out of conversations at events back home. "Night, Ryker the biker."

Ryker doesn't respond as he continues to watch the movie, and I eventually drift off to a peaceful sleep. That is until I wake up with my throat on fire from the guttural scream that echoes out of it.

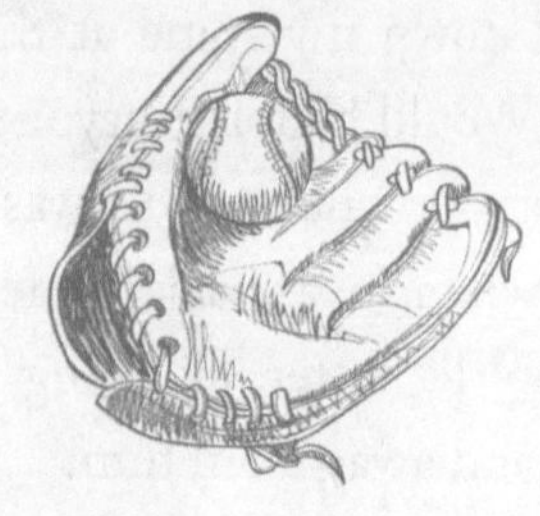

Chapter Sixteen

Ryker

I couldn't sleep after the movie ended, my thoughts unable to stop circling back to the girl in the bed next to mine. I thought everything was going well. We had snacks and were watching a good movie. She sang along to the songs, and usually it would annoy me with anyone else, but with her, I found it cute as hell.

Then suddenly she shut down on me, turned on her side, and went to sleep right in the middle of the movie. I wanted to ask her, but I found myself frozen, unsure what to do or what even went wrong.

When she fell asleep, I took the opportunity to put the money she gave me for the tattoo in her makeup bag. I meant it when I said I didn't want her to pay, and the bills have been burning a hole in my wallet from the reminder of how I hurt her feelings that night.

I turn the TV off once the movie ends and grab my iPad to work on a design for one of my art classes as the quiet hum of the air conditioning fills the room.

About an hour later, Camille gasps in her sleep. I immediately drop my iPad on the comforter and look over at her with concern. Her body writhes and her head moves back and forth as her face scrunches up in fear. Her skin turns flushed, a sheen of sweat on her forehead.

She's having a nightmare and it breaks my heart.

I'm about to wake her up when her scream pierces the previous quiet air as she thrashes underneath the blanket. Tears roll down her cheeks as she cries for help.

My fucking heart sinks and my stomach bottoms out. I hate seeing her like this, so I crouch beside her, careful not to scare her when she wakes up to my body looming over hers. I gently shake her and whisper her name, "Camille, wake up, baby. It's just a bad dream. I'm right here."

Camille's silvery eyes pop open, and before I know what's happening, she slugs me right in the jaw. I stumble back from the blow. I move my hand over to my jaw to rub at the sore spot. Fuck, the girl can throw a mean punch.

"*Ah, merde,*" Camille squeals, breathless as she clambers out of bed to join me on the floor between the two beds. "Ryker, are you okay?"

"I'm fine. Don't worry about me, though your right hook is impressive. Are *you* okay?" I ask, my hands itching to reach out to brush the matted hair plastered to her forehead. But I don't because I don't think she wants me touching her right now.

Fear flashes through her eyes, and I don't like seeing my usually happy girl like this.

"Y-yeah," she pants, swiping her hair off her forehead. "I'm sorry for that."

"That seemed like a pretty intense nightmare. Want to talk about it?" I hedge, hoping she'll open up.

Camille tucks her knees into her chest as her body shakes. Her glassy eyes meet mine and her bottom lip quivers.

"Come here." My voice is low and soft as I motion for her to come sit between my legs.

Camille's eyes waver, so I hold out my hand to her, letting her make the choice. She takes it and I gently pull her to sit on my lap. She digs her face into my neck and starts crying, her fist holding a tight grip on my sweatshirt.

My heart fucking breaks at the sound tearing through me like a saw to my insides. I carefully wrap my arms around her and run my palm up her arm while the other does the same to her back as I try to provide some sort of comfort to her.

"Princess, what happened to you?" I croak. "Please, it's killing me." I rest my chin on the top of her head, reveling in knowing she's safe here in my arms.

Camille sniffles, gathering her emotions as her breaths slowly begin to even out. After a few minutes, her head lifts from my shoulder and she peers up at me with a vulnerability I've yet to see.

She's letting me in.

She takes a deep breath and confesses, "I'm from a small island off the coast of France, called Lorsica. My parents are…" She hesitates but then continues. "My parents are the king and queen." She lets out a deep sigh. "So yeah, I'm a legit princess."

She's a princess?

Before I can say anything, she adds with a slight tremor in her voice, "I needed to get away and explore myself outside of my royal obligations and the public eye. That's how I ended up here. I ran away, changed my identity, and I've been living my own life since."

I realize I haven't said a word since her revelation when she says, "Please don't do that." Her voice breaks, a lone tear strolling down her cheek.

"Do what?" I murmur, wiping it away with my thumb.

Her lashes flutter closed for a moment as she leans into my palm, then reopen with fire in her eyes. "Treat me like I'm any different because of that. I came here to lose that part of myself, to become someone new."

"I won't. It's just a surprise, that's all," I assure her, needing time to reconcile with the new information. "Thank you for sharing your secret with me. I won't tell a soul. Is that what your nightmare was about?"

Camille's fingers loosen their hold on me, drifting up to my neck as she traces imaginary circles over my skin as that same fearful look takes over her face. "When I graduated secondary school, there was a huge celebration in the city. It's a small country, and we like to celebrate everything, any reason to throw a party."

I nod, encouraging her to continue as I listen intently.

"I snuck off, because well, I was a bit rebellious back then. I wanted to get high, and a group of guys I had no business being around offered me what I wanted. We walked away from the party to a quiet path. And then…" She pauses, her bottom lip trembling.

A grumble vibrates from my chest as I conjure in my mind where this is going.

"One of the guys got handsy, and when I told him no, he gripped my ass. So I slapped him across the face and let's just say he didn't like that. He backhanded me across the cheek and threw me to the ground. Adrenaline got me right back up and I ran as fast as I could, but they chased after me. All three of them. I made it back to the city, untouched or hurt, but in my nightmares, they catch me." She shivers at the thought, then shakes her head. "Anyways, all things considered, it wasn't that bad. They're in jail, so I shouldn't be worried, but it's like my mind doesn't remember that when I go to sleep. "

My scowl deepens while my blood boils. Somebody fucking hurt my girl. Put their hands on her. I fight the urge to ask her for their names and fly to Europe to make them pay even if she just said they're in jail.

I run a hand through my hair, trying to get my anger under control. "What do you mean it wasn't that bad? Someone put their hands on you, and there's no amount of jail that could absolve those assholes. I want to fucking bury them," I snap at the end.

Camille startles at my tone and flinches away from me.

The blood drains from my face. "Fuck," I mumble. "I didn't mean to scare you. I'm just pissed off at the image of some guy…I can't even say it."

"I know. I'm just shaken up from the nightmare, that's all." She settles back into me and brings her hand up to stroke my bearded jaw.

I cover her hand with mine, loving the feel of hers under my own. "You know I'd never hurt you, right? I'll never let anyone else ever hurt you again."

"You're the only guy I've let touch me like this in years. I feel safe with you," she whispers, staring at me with a glint in her eyes.

And this is why I'm no good for her, because some sick part of me gets off on that. Knowing I'm the only one who is allowed to be this close to her and that there's no one else in her life.

"Do you not want me not to call you princess anymore?" I ask, needing to know if she's still okay with it.

A shy smile forms on her lips, the sight making my heart jump in my chest. "I only want to be *your* princess."

Fuck.

Her words make my cock harden slightly in my pants, but I shift her so she won't notice it.

"Only mine," I murmur, tucking a strand of hair behind her ear.

Camille sucks in an audible breath at my words. I didn't mean to say it out loud, but I still meant it nonetheless.

"Let's get you back to bed." My voice is hoarse as I look at her for what she wants to do. Camille nods and attempts to lift off me, but I stand with her in my arms instead.

I carefully place her on her bed, and I'm about to pull away when Camille's voice halts my movements.

"Can you…hold me? I—"

"Anything you need," I tell her.

"Thank you." She smiles, her cheeks slightly more red.

I round the bed, then gently lower myself on it behind her, shuffling to get closer to her.

"Tell me what you want," I ask her, noting how this could sound in a very different context.

"Hold me from behind, please," she states, sounding more confident than before.

I do as she says and wrap my arm around her waist. I pull her against me while my other arm slides under her neck. Camille sighs contentedly as my arms cocoon around her, and I don't miss how perfectly her body fits against mine. If anything, I'm doing everything I can not to think about that. Otherwise, my cock won't get the message that this isn't the time.

"Sleep, princess, I'm right here," I whisper, pressing my lips lightly to the top of her head.

"Thank you," she says back, her breaths coming in slower. Then she slowly drifts off to sleep in my arms.

It's then that I realize how fucked I am, because I know that from now on, all I'll want is to wrap my arms around her every night and hope to wake up to her infectious smile every morning.

She's throwing me a curve ball, switching up the game, but I'm determined to keep playing.

Chapter Seventeen

Camille

I'm usually quite grumpy early in the morning, especially after a nightmare disturbs my sleep. But I find myself waking up with a content smile on my lips this morning as I slowly come to.

I fell back asleep with a quiet mind, everything going still except for the sound of his heartbeat against my ear. I've never experienced a peace like that in my entire life than when I was in his arms.

Ryker.

Embarrassment attempts to steal my inner peace, but I brush it away. Ryker made me feel safe enough to be vulnerable with him. I just needed him to listen, and he did.

While Ryker did make me feel safe, I know I need to continue to work on knowing *I* can keep myself safe. I can't rely on someone else to heal my demons.

The gentleness he treated me with nearly made me melt in his arms. That rugged man can be so damn sweet. It's honestly surprising to me how he's still single because what girl wouldn't be falling head over heels for a man like him?

I know it'd be all too easy for me to. Part of me feels like I'm already halfway there, and I know that sounds crazy. Yet isn't that what love is? A rush of feelings so big that they're scary, exciting, and all-consuming all at the same time?

If it isn't, then I don't want it.

While I wish I could lie like this all morning, I know we need to get up soon for their practice this morning. I attempt to move his arm off me, but it's like trying to move a block of concrete. Ryker pulls me in closer in response, nuzzling his nose in my hair. I bask in the feel of him being this close, but the rational part of my brain keeps telling me I need to stop living in this fantasy. He comforted me last night and said things he probably didn't even mean.

Like calling me his and whatnot. It was in the moment and he must have long forgotten about it by now, right?

"Don't leave," he gruffs.

I move my body to turn to face him, and he lets me, slightly loosening his hold on me.

His dark blue eyes drop to my lips, then flick up to meet my own, a shade darker than before. The same shade from the night at the football house where I thought he was going to kiss me but didn't.

"Ryker." My voice is hoarse from sleep and need as my eyes move from his lips to his eyes, noticing a storm brew within them.

"Fuck it," he growls then closes the distance between us.

His hand covers the nape of my neck as he pulls my face up to his. I tangle my fingers in his hair, tugging as his lips dip down to mine. They're so soft and careful, the opposite of this man above me.

I feel his kiss down to the tips of my toes, a jolt of joy and passion so vibrant that I could light a whole country with it. His full lips mold perfectly with mine as he kisses me deeply, longingly.

If this were a fairytale, there'd be a sweet instrumental

playing in the background and cheers from the audience. It's one of *those* kisses. One I'll never forget because of how sweet he's being. From the gentleness of his hold on me to the way his lips move so reverently over mine.

A deep rumble emanates from his chest that makes me whimper and my mouth parts. He takes the opportunity and dips his tongue into my mouth expertly, giving me the perfect amount.

I tighten my hands in his hair, pulling him closer to me. Ryker takes the hint, moving so that he's on top of me, not once breaking our kiss, and my legs wrap around his waist.

He breaks the kiss at that. "Is this okay? I don't know what you're good or not good with yet," he murmurs with his forehead against mine. He tucks a piece of my hair behind my ear while waiting for my answer.

"Everything feels good with you," I tell him. "But let's take it slow, please."

"Whatever you want, princess. You tell me to stop at any point and I will, got it?"

"Mhm, now kiss me again, please." I bite my lip to hide my smile, but fail miserably.

Ryker obliges, lowering his head down as his lips press against mine. He kisses me slowly and sensually, making me writhe underneath him.

He rocks his hips, rubbing his now hard cock against my covered pussy, then pulls back to look at me to make sure it's okay. I grab him by the back of the neck and tug him back down to me while grinding up against him in search of some friction, letting him know I'm definitely okay with this. More than okay.

Ryker's lips move down my jaw until he reaches my neck, where he plants kisses much like the ones he did on my lips.

"*Putain*," I moan, feeling the wetness between my thighs just by him kissing me in just the right spot on my neck.

Ryker's lips travel downward, kissing the skin just below my clavicle, then over the thin strap of my tank top. His teeth yank on the strap, and my core hums in excitement that he's going to take it a step further, until he doesn't.

"What are you doing? Don't stop," I breathe out, searching his eyes that have turned the darkest shade of blue I've seen on him.

"You have no idea how badly I want to see you, all of *you*, especially those fucking piercings that have been in my fantasies since I first noticed them at the tattoo shop."

I begin to shrug my strap off, when his hand covers mine, stopping me. I frown at him, suddenly feeling rejected.

"No, baby, I *do* want you." His jaw clenches as he prepares for his next words. "If I start, I won't be able to stop until your legs are shaking and your cum is soaking my beard. But I think we need to talk first."

I gasp at his words, loving how filthy yet sweet he can be. However, he's right, we should talk about what this is before we move forward.

"Okay. I know we just kissed and said some things last night, but you can take it back if you didn't mean it," I start, my romantic heart hoping for the best while also trying to remain practical at the same time.

His brows pull taut, that scowl I've come to love taking residence on his face. Ryker lies beside me, then wraps his arm around me, resting it on my lower back as he pulls me into him. I rest my palm on his chest, while I prop myself up with my other hand, resting my chin on it.

"I meant what I said," he states, his eyes roaming over my face with…I don't even know because my heart is beating too loudly in my ears for me to think.

"Then what does that mean? Only mine, as in…?" I trail off, too shy to voice it out loud.

Does he like me? Are we more than friends? What. Is. Going. On.

Ryker clears his throat. "I can't offer you anything more than something physical…I need to focus on the draft and I don't do relationships."

My romantic heart deflates into a sad puddle. I should've known, yet I always hope for the best. Sometimes that positivity stuff I have going on can make letdowns really fucking hard. The worst part is that I find myself wanting whatever he'll give me.

If my parents find me soon and I'm forced to go home, at least I can say I had this with him, with the man who makes me feel safe, wanted, and happy.

"Why's that?" I ask, needing to know why if I'm going to consider what he's offering.

I expect him to grunt and tell me to mind my business, but he doesn't.

"My dad left my mom when I was twelve. I haven't heard from him since that day." He swallows roughly, his jaw ticking. "He was always bitching at my mom about how she never had time for him, that she wasn't fun anymore. She's a veterinarian, which meant she worked long hours sometimes and he hated that even though those were the days we played ball together. That's how I grew my love for the sport."

I bring my hand up to his jaw, rubbing my thumb across it to offer some sort of comfort. "I'm sorry."

"I went off track there." He grimaces. "I've grown up with this mindset that if my own blood could leave me, who's to say someone else won't? I saw how much it hurt my mom, and I can't afford that kind of pain or distraction. Not when I have the draft looming over my head. Love is an inconvenience, to put it simply."

I want to argue with his opinion, explain why I love love and all the beautiful things about it. But I don't because it's not something that can just be explained. It needs to be felt, in all the ways it can be.

Love can be your cup of coffee in the solitude of an early morning, evening cuddles with your pet on the couch, or running around with your siblings outside in the summer sunshine. It can also be the thing that gets your heart thudding so loud you can't hear the thoughts in your head that haze your judgment and allows you just to feel.

It's electric, passionate, and consuming. Not that I would know romantic love, but from what I've seen in my life, I think my opinion would be deemed accurate.

"I'm sorry that happened to you. He lost out on knowing a great man," I murmur, my chest tightening at the image of a young Ryker wondering if and when his dad would ever come back. I can't imagine the kind of pain he's endured.

My eyes fill with tears at the thought of what he lost and how much it's affected his view on life.

"Don't waste your tears on me," he orders softly, rubbing his thumb across the small of my back while his other hand gently wipes them away.

I shake my head, keeping my thoughts to myself. "Where does that leave us?" I ask as if there's even an *us*.

"Like I said, I don't date. But I care about you, princess, and I want you to myself. We can be friends with benefits…if that's something you want," he offers, those blue eyes locked intently on mine.

"You're the only guy I've felt safe with in years…and I'd like to explore that further, for myself." I blush, instantly feeling shy.

"Me too," he whispers, his hand on my back rubbing small circles.

"You can't be with anyone else," I state because I don't like to share.

Ryker chuckles, the sound startling, yet wholesome to my ears since I don't hear that often. "Princess, I haven't even been able to look at another girl since I laid eyes on you at that gala."

Keep your cool, I repeat over and over in my head, but my heart doesn't get the same memo as it dances wildly in my chest.

"The gala…I didn't even go to last year's."

Quentin surprised me with a week-long vacation in Costa Rica for Christmas, so I skipped last year's annual Christmas Eve Gala.

"I know…that's how long you've been running rampant in my mind," he admits, and if it were possible, I'd be melting into a puddle right now. He really needs to stop saying things like this if all we're going to be is friends with benefits.

Ryker's lips tip to the right, a shy grin on his lips. "So don't worry, princess, I'm all yours."

"Good."

"And no one touches you while you're mine, got it?" His words skate over my skin, spreading warmth in their path.

"When will it end?" I bring up the lingering question that neither of us wants to talk about. I already know my heart is going to take a hit, and I'd like to know when.

Ryker's hand on my lower back pauses. "Maybe when I get drafted in July, since I'll have to move. My agent has been in talks with Detroit and New York so far, but I could be going anywhere."

I smile, running my fingers down his broad shoulders. "You'd be playing with my brother if you go to Detroit."

"I actually wanted to ask for his autograph that night outside your place, but I didn't want to bother him." He chuckles, and I find myself growing addicted to the sound.

"You wouldn't have. He's always nice to his fans."

"I imagine he wouldn't be nice to me if he knew all the dirty things I'll be doing to his sister." His voice lowers, that gravelly tone returning as his fingers brush under the waistband on my joggers.

"Please," I whisper, begging him not to stop this time.

Ryker's hand lowers and grips a part of my ass, making me inhale sharply all while our eyes stay locked. His hand then skates over my hip, down to my inner thigh, so close to where I want him, but not quite.

I grind against him, letting him know I need him to touch me. Ryker groans in response, his fingers skating upward where he runs a single digit through my soaked slit. That minimal contact causes me to moan, rolling my pussy against his hand in search of more.

One finger turns into two as they rub up and down, but neither enters me nor touches my clit. I'm just about to sigh in frustration when Ryker removes his hand, confusing me, until he puts those two fingers between his lips, sucking me off them while keeping eye contact with me.

C'est le truc le plus sexy que j'ai vu de ma vie. That's so fucking hot.

"Mmm, princess," he hums. "I knew you'd taste just as sweet as you look."

"Ryker," I whimper, needing his hands back on me.

"I'm going to be addicted to this pussy. One taste and I'm fucking done for," he growls, gently pushing me on my back as he moves to settle between my thighs.

Ryker reaches for the top of my sweats, ready to rip them off my body until we hear a knock at the door. "Ryker, it's Cuddy, open up," he yells through the door.

My head falls back on the pillow in defeat, knowing I won't be getting relief anytime soon.

Ryker curses under his breath, then looks at me with remorse. "I'm sorry, baby. Fucking Cuddy. This better be good," he grumbles as he gets off the bed and adjusts himself. Then he turns to me. "Get under the blanket for me, please?" His gaze drops to my chest, and that's when I see that my nipples are hard as rocks, poking through my shirt.

I hop under the blanket, and Ryker mouths a silent thank you before opening the door. "What do you want?" Ryker lashes out at him, crossing his arms over his chest.

Cuddy ignores him, his mouth forming an O when he sees me in the room.

Ryker yanks him into the room and shuts the door behind them.

"Dude…I knew it!" Cuddy claps his hands together, doing a little dance.

Ryker rolls his eyes. "Shut up. You better not say a word to anyone, got it?"

Cuddy halts his dancing, standing up straight as he looks Ryker in the eyes. "You got my word, unless I hear Travis talking about your girl. That would shut him up real quick."

The mention of Travis makes me want to gag. He came on way too strong for my liking at the party that night, and I've avoided him as much as I can since.

"You hear him say anything about her, you tell me," Ryker nearly growls, running a hand through his loose waves.

"Yes, sir." Cuddy nods, then turns to me. "How's it going, Cami? Enjoying road life with us so far?"

"So far, so good. I love baseball and you guys are okay, I guess." I smirk, blushing when Ryker narrows his eyes at me.

"Just okay?"

"I said what I said." I shrug, earning myself a hearty laugh from Cuddy.

Cuddy points his thumb at me with a goofy smile. "I like you. You're the only person he's not a complete grumpy asshole to."

"I like you too," I tell Cuddy while trying not to overthink the second half of what he said. I had noticed it too, but I thought I was making it up in my head.

Ryker comes around to the bed, sits, and tugs me onto his lap, then kisses the top of my head.

Cuddy chuckles. "Dude, no one was coming to steal her. Relax."

I hide my smile in his chest because I secretly like the whole possessive caveman thing he has going on right now. I like it a lot.

"Why are you even here?" Ryker asks him.

"We do have to leave for practice in twenty minutes. We're meeting in the lobby, remember?"

Shit, how late did we sleep in?

I scramble out of his lap, and Ryker jumps to his feet in search of his phone. I grab mine, reading 9:05 a.m. on the screen. We overslept.

It turns into chaos as I rush into the bathroom to get ready as soon as possible while Ryker does the same in the room with Cuddy. In my hurry to get ready, I find myself pausing when I see the stack of bills in my makeup bag.

I take them out carefully, flipping each bill as I add them up. I bite on my bottom lip as I think of where it came from until I realize it's the same amount I paid Ryker for the tattoo. For a man who's intent on keeping things casual, he sure has a funny way of showing it.

Although a part of me threw down that money out of spite because I was upset, another part also wanted to properly thank him for his work. My tattoo is beautiful and a reminder of everything that I am, a reminder of why I left.

I push the thoughts away as I finish getting ready for the day, throwing on shorts and a cropped T-shirt with our school's mascot on the back. Once we're both ready, Ryker makes Cuddy go out first to make sure no one's in the hallway to see me leaving his room.

While Cuddy is outside, Ryker's hand wraps around my hip. He turns me to face him and presses his lips to mine. He kisses me so sweetly, brushing his lips across mine, then my cheeks, my nose, and finishing with my forehead.

"See you soon," he murmurs just as Cuddy gives us the go ahead.

I give him my brightest smile, unable to contain it in that moment. As I slip into the hallway and make my way to the lobby, it dawns on me that although we just agreed to be nothing more than friends with benefits, it feels like more already.

My heart is doomed, yet I don't want to prevent myself from falling further.

What is wrong with me?

Chapter Eighteen

Ryker

Camille's been driving me fucking insane all day. In the best and worst way possible. At practice, I went harder than I needed to, knowing she was there. I always try my best, but I'd be lying if I said I wasn't doing a little extra today for her.

Being around her before was always hard because my body seems to want to gravitate toward her, but after I kissed her? It felt magnetic, making it impossible to stay away.

I found myself finding ways to be near her. I even pretended I needed to stretch out my leg just so I could have five minutes of standing next to her on the sidelines, staring at her smile that is way too fucking pretty to be real.

I never thought a smile could make me feel things, but fuck, when she does, I feel it all.

And I hate it.

The entire team is currently waiting in line for this sports bar we're trying to get into, and Camille hasn't stopped smiling this entire time as she talks with the team. I don't want to be that guy, but I can't help wishing she were smiling at me right now instead of them.

I need to get a grip.

When we're finally seated, I make sure I sit right next to her and even though it's Cuddy on her other side, I put my hand under her chair and scoot it closer to mine.

Camille bites on her lip, a smile slipping through. "What are you doing?" she whispers.

"I just want you close," I murmur, opting for blunt honesty.

A tinge of pink paints her cheeks as she ducks her head and looks at the menu in front of her. "Is that why your leg randomly needed stretching during practice?"

I grunt in response, nudging her thigh with mine.

She turns to me, her champagne curls spilling over her shoulder as she smiles shyly at me. I hold her eyes for a beat, then force myself to look away because my chest is starting to feel tight. I should probably see my doctor about that.

"You took my advice, I see," Noah mumbles beside me, sounding all too cocky.

"Shut up," I grumble, folding my arms across my chest so my hands don't travel to her thigh.

Noah chuckles, then jumps back into conversation with the guys while I stay quiet. I like to observe and listen instead, not being much of a talker.

Specifically, I like to watch Camille, but as much as I enjoy watching her like this, happy, outgoing, and smiling, I feel this deep craving within me to find out how pretty she would look coming with my name rolling off her tongue.

Although we drew a boundary this morning, I find myself already wanting to spend all my time with her.

My hand drifts underneath the table, my fingers finding her bare knee and drawing lazy circles around it. Camille doesn't seem fazed as she continues to chat with Mackenzie, who's sitting across from her.

That is until I inch my fingers higher, skating them slowly up her soft skin. Camille sucks in a sharp breath so low that I nearly miss it. The skin of her arms breaks out in gooseflesh, and I smirk knowing that I have an effect on her.

Camille turns to face me, her eyes darting from my hand on her thigh then up to mine. "Ryker."

"Yes, baby?" I say, low enough only for her to hear.

"What are you doing?" she whispers, and I don't miss the way she wets her lips with her tongue, making them look all too inviting.

I lean closer. "Well, if you were in a dress or skirt, I'd be doing you."

Her bottom lip parts, eyes glazing over. "You don't mean that, right?"

I chuckle half-heartedly. "Do I seem like the kind of person who makes jokes?"

She smiles shyly, taking a sip of her beer. "I guess not."

My fingers start back up, drawing lazy caresses over the smooth expanse of her thigh, and to my amusement, her breaths quicken.

"Stop getting me worked up. It can't lead to anything. That's not fair," she huffs out, leaning toward me.

I quirk a brow at that. "Who said it wasn't leading to anything?"

Her mouth pops open in response, and then a devious smile fills her face. "Get up in two minutes. I'll be waiting."

I go to ask her what she means, but she's already up and moving for the hallway that leads to the bathrooms.

This fucking girl. I love that she knows what she wants and asks for it.

I take a few sips of my beer and half listen to Cuddy and Noah talk about the upcoming season. As soon as the two minutes go by, I get up and make my way to her. There are only two single bathrooms and I have no fucking clue which one she went in. I'm about to knock on one of the doors when an older lady comes out.

"Jumping jalapeños, you scared the daylights out of me!" she scolds, a weathered hand over her chest.

"Sorry, ma'am," I murmur, unable to look her in the eye.

"Don't be sorry, though I wish I were the hot blonde waiting for you to razzle her insides," she scoffs, and I can't contain the roaring laughter that comes out of me.

"You can laugh all you want. I saw you two all night talking and touching. Now, get in there and rock her world like my husband did to mine." She winks and walks off, leaving me speechless.

I shake my head and knock on the other door. "Princess."

The door unlocks, and I squeeze in, then turn the lock back in place once I'm in.

I hear a snort, and my head whips up to Camille, who's doubled over in a fit of giggles. She must have heard the older woman.

My lips quirk to the side. "Yeah, I wasn't expecting that."

"I want to be her when I'm older," she says through another fit of giggles. "And then I heard this odd sound. It almost sounded like this grumpy man I know actually laughed?"

I cross my arms over my chest. "I have no idea what you're talking about."

Camille straightens and closes the distance between us, her hands wrapping around the back of my neck. "Ryker, it's okay to laugh, you know."

"I know. It's just odd I find something to laugh at. My focus is everything this year, and—"

"Right now, I want you to focus on making me come."

Her silvery eyes gaze into mine, so confident and trusting, with a sheen of desire. I don't know where this version of Camille came from, but I am fucking here for it. I waste no time and slam my lips to her as I grip the sides of her face with both of my hands. My kiss is demanding, and she's giving me everything I want, her lips parting to let me in.

One of my hands moves to the back of her head while the other grips her ass, pulling her body against mine. Our tongues work in tandem as we find our rhythm, both of our lips melding together in unison. It's crazed yet controlled and sensual. It's fucking everything.

I trail kisses down her jaw until I reach her neck. My teeth scrape against her sensitive skin, causing her body to jolt against mine.

She curses in French under her breath, her hands moving to my hair as she tugs on the strands. The slight pain turns me on even more, and my cock presses against my joggers painfully.

I suck, kiss, and lick her neck, finding out what spots make her squirm. I finally do when my lips press against the dip between her neck and her shoulder.

Camille's leg hitches around my waist, and I hold it in place. I gently press her back against the door, all while my lips work along her neck, never once breaking contact. Her body grinds against mine, a breathy moan hitting my ear and sending shivers down my spine.

Her thin yoga shorts do nothing to conceal how wet she is as she rubs her pussy against me. I adjust her slightly so that she's aligned with my cock, and I look between us, enthralled by the image of her rocking her body against mine. She slides against me, her pussy hitting my cock just right, and I nearly come in my pants like a fucking teenager.

"Where do you want me? What do you need from me?" I ask, breathless. We've barely explored each other and the feelings I'm experiencing are more intense than anything I've ever felt before.

Her hands disentangle from my hair and land on my shoulders where she begins to press. She's not strong enough to actually push me down, but I follow her order nonetheless.

My knees hit the tiled floor, my eyes not once leaving hers. "I need w—"

"You need to put your mouth on my pussy," she pants, her lust-ridden eyes gazing down into mine.

"More than happy to, baby," I say, but my voice doesn't sound like my own. It's deeper, filled with so much desire I might never escape it.

I skate my hands up her legs, stopping once I reach the waistband of her shorts. I tug them down until they reach the floor and help her get one foot out of them but leave them on the ankle of her other foot.

My eyes immediately fixate on the lacy lavender thong. Correction, *soaked* thong.

Christ, she's so wet I can see it coating the inside of her thighs, and the sight makes me fucking feral for this girl. I lean forward, running my nose up and down her slit and breathing her in.

Camille's hands find my hair and a soft little mewl leaves her lips.

"I'm sorry," I apologize, balling her panties up in one fist.

"Don't even…"

Me shredding her panties cuts her off, and I discard them in my pocket.

Camille mutters something in French, but I don't hear it because the sight of her bare pussy for the first time has me speechless. She's glistening with arousal, and it's because of me. On top of that, her pussy is fucking perfect.

I lift her leg off the ground and set it over my shoulder, opening her up to me. Then my fingers reach up to her slit and I part her, flicking my tongue against her clit.

Camille bucks off the door, her nails digging into my scalp.

"Mmm," I groan against her, blowing a breath on her clit.

"How is everything about you so pretty? Your face, your heart, and even your drenched pussy."

"Why don't you put your tongue on it, see if it tastes just as pretty as it looks?"

I lean back slightly to look at her in fucking awe, because her demanding exactly what she wants is the sexiest thing. I spread her once more, then dive in, sealing my lips around her clit and tugging on it. Camille moans loudly, then slaps a hand over her mouth. Under normal circumstances, I'd take her hand off, because there's nothing hotter than hearing her, but I'll let it pass since we're in public and anyone could hear.

I switch up the pressure, sucking harder and then gentler on her clit. Her hips roll against my face in response and my tongue comes into play, licking her slit from top to bottom, savoring every inch of her arousal as it soaks my face.

I flick my tongue against her clit, my eyes on her, drinking in the way her body reacts to each and every move I make. It's by far the best thing I've seen.

Sliding two fingers inside her tight cunt has me moaning against her. Her pussy grips me so well, and if she's already tight like this, fucking her is going to be even better.

Camille's thighs begin to shake, and I smile against her.

"That's it," I praise, pulling back to look up at her. My chin is soaked, her arousal dripping down from it. She sees it, her eyes widening when she realizes how turned on she is. "Don't even apologize. I fucking love this." I keep my eyes on her so that she knows not to be embarrassed.

She nods and throws her head back against the door when I return my mouth to her clit. I tug on it roughly as my fingers slide in and out, fucking her. I curl them inside, earning myself a gasp followed by her thighs shaking around my head.

"Ryker," she moans before throwing a hand over her mouth and screams as she comes.

I don't ease up and continue sucking and fucking her and as she rides it out, admiring how she comes undone for me. Once she comes down from her high, I carefully set her foot on the floor, a smile on my lips.

"You okay?" I ask.

Camille bends over, hands on her thighs. "Yes, no. I don't freaking know. That was…intense."

I stand, pulling her into me, wrapping my arms around her waist. "Have you never been given an orgasm?" I ask, my fingers brushing away the strands that are sticking to her forehead.

"Yes, but nothing like this, *ever*."

"Good," I murmur, kissing her forehead while ignoring the fact that this is not good. Not even fucking close. We've just scratched the surface, yet she already consumes me.

And so help me God, I didn't want it to stop.

Chapter Nineteen

Ryker

I let Camille out of the bathroom first, after insisting that I didn't want her to take care of me. If we were anywhere else, I would've let her like she begged me to. Hell, I've been fucking my hand with the thought of my cock in her mouth for weeks. Okay, maybe more like a year or two.

But we were already flirting with the boundary, and if we were gone any longer, it would've been suspicious.

I check my phone to see that three minutes have passed, which seems like a good amount of time between her returning and me, so I swing the door open, only to come face to face with Travis.

"Why are you so close to the door?" I bark at him.

"I was just about to knock. After Cami returned to the table, I assumed this one was empty." He smirks. "Apparently not."

"That's what happens when there's a line. I went in after her. Now you'll go in after me," I explain to him in a stone-cold voice, tired of this conversation already.

"You think Coach would like to hear that you're messing around with our social media manager? What about her boss? I'm sure that would get her fired real quick."

I bite my tongue and grind my molars together. "Nothing's going on, so tell them whatever you want."

"Or I could talk to them about your arrest when you were sixteen." He cocks his head to the side, knocking the air out of my lungs.

I take a step toward him, anger simmering in my blood. "What did you just say?"

Travis stands straight, trying to intimidate me, but he's off by a few inches. "An old friend of mine and I reconnected over the summer. We had some beers, nachos, you know, guy stuff."

My face is blank, giving him nothing as I impatiently wait for him to get the fuck on with it.

"Baseball naturally came up, and my poor friend, you see, he used to play. Used to be great. But the key phrase is *used to*. Wanna know why?"

Fuck, he knows.

"Turns out a guy named Ryker Lewis broke his pitching arm. He was never able to pitch the same way after it healed." He sighs, dramatics clearly being his thing. "Sad story, isn't it?"

I cross my arms over my chest. "It's not the full story either."

"The media won't care. All they will talk about is the up-and-coming rookie who's a hothead with a record. Good luck making it big after that."

I *was* hot-headed, but I didn't have a record. That's where he's wrong. Since I was under eighteen, I wasn't charged and got let off with community service and anger management classes instead. There was nothing there, yet the fear of him exposing this to the press has my chest feeling tight with pressure.

"What do you want, Travis?"

His smile is saccharine. "Nothing, for now." Then he walks past me into the bathroom.

I hate that he's rattling me. If he tells the media about my past, who's to say they won't believe it? What happens then? I won't get drafted because no team will want to sign the hotheaded kid who almost got charged with assault.

It doesn't matter that I don't have a record. They'll focus on what did happen.

That after a high school baseball game I got into it with the other team's pitcher. We were all at an after-party at someone's house when I saw him trying to corner Theo's sister. She kept saying no, and he pushed forward anyway. Theo wasn't there, so I did what needed to be done.

I didn't mean to break his arm. It was an accident, but that fucker deserved it nonetheless.

On top of that, Travis has a suspicion about my relationship with Camille. He has no solid proof, so I'm not going to worry about it for now, but it's a reminder that we need to be careful. Especially if he's gunning for something to pin me with.

But if he even tries to fuck with Camille's career or anything that has to do with her, I will gladly break his arm too.

But this time, it won't be an accident.

Chapter Twenty

Camille

One week has passed since that weekend in New Mexico, a weekend I won't be able to forget. I don't think the connections I made with Ryker will ever be broken. I was not only able to share with him my secrets, but also a side I haven't been able to share with anyone else in years.

The dominant, confident, and sexy side.

God, it's been years since a man touched me like that. Actually, scratch that. No man has ever touched me the way Ryker did, making it a new experience in and of itself.

Every brush of his lips against mine made my chest ache. Every caress of his rough hands across my skin made me shiver, and every time his mouth connected with my pussy, I saw stars. I don't know if it's because I was raised as a royal, with the mindset that *I* have the power, but I've always been this way sexually.

Unabashed and in control, knowing exactly what I want and not being afraid to ask for it.

That night after dinner, we went back to Ryker's room, and while I was anticipating more happening, Ryker and I stayed up late, talking about anything and everything while a Disney movie played in the background.

We decided to stray away from our childhoods, neither of us wanting to go down that solemn path, and instead, the topics stayed light and playful. Well, mostly I was playful and spent the majority of the night trying to make Ryker laugh. Every time I succeeded, I felt like I was on top of the world.

I feel the same way now as practice comes to a close because Ryker promised to teach me how to hit a baseball after. The team is slowly trickling out as Ryker walks to home plate and dumps a black duffel bag on top of it, causing red dirt to swirl in the air.

He takes out a baseball tee, along with a bat that looks like it's made for children.

"Going back to the basics there, Ryker?" Cuddy calls out as he slows his jog down to a stop between Ryker and me.

"Shut up." Ryker shakes his head, not taking his focus off his task.

Cuddy turns to face me then, his eyes lighting up. "Is this for you?"

My eyebrow arches from intrigue. "Apparently so. I've never swung a bat before."

"I can stay and help," Cuddy offers, but Ryker cuts in.

"We don't need your help," Ryker says bluntly as he stands.

"Oh, I get it now. You wanna wrap your arms around her, press your body ag—"

"Leave, *now*." Ryker glares at Cuddy, arms folded across his chest.

Cuddy's lips curl devilishly before he wraps me in his arms for a hug that I know is platonic because of his secret relationship with Mackenzie, but it doesn't stop Ryker from sighing and muttering something under his breath.

"If you leave right now, I will make you breakfast tomorrow," he proposes.

Cuddy releases me instantly and turns to walk backward, smiling victoriously. "Not only did I get to witness Ryker turn possessive over something other than baseball, but I got a breakfast out of it. *Sa-weet.*" He throws a fist in the air, then jogs to the dugout.

Ryker's lips remain in a scowl while his brows pinch inward at his friend. "You okay there, Ryker the biker?" I inject playfulness into my tone, hoping it takes the grumpiness out of him.

"I will if you stop calling me that," he mutters, but the slight crook of his lips tells me he likes it when I call him that.

"Never." I smile, tucking my hair behind my ear as I change track. "Is all of this really necessary?"

"It is if you want to actually learn proper swinging techniques," he counters, setting a foam ball on the top of the tee. "I have a steel bat and softballs in the bag for when I think you're ready to advance."

I clap my hands together, all too excited to swing my very first bat. Even if it's a foam one. "All right then, let's get to work."

With his arm outstretched toward me with the bat in his hand, he orders, "Show me how you plan on gripping it."

"Well, it depends on what we're working with. If you're packing, then two hands might be needed."

Ryker closes his eyes briefly, then opens them, letting me see the war he's fighting within himself. "Let me teach you how to hit a ball first before you make my cock harder than the bat in my bag."

I pout my lips at him. "Fine." I take the bat from him and put my left hand near the bottom, my right hand above it. "Is this the right way?"

Ryker takes a step toward me, his hand landing on top of my left one and he twists it slightly. "You want to make sure your knuckles are lined up. Now, let's see a swing."

"Just give it a whack?" I ask as I step into the batter's box, digging my Converse into the dirt for traction.

"Bring the bat up and behind you while keeping your right elbow at a ninety-degree angle, nice and high. Then keep your eye on the ball and swing."

"Like this?" I purposely do the opposite of what he says, letting my elbow hang downward, the bat resting on my shoulder.

"You're trouble," he mutters as he moves to stand behind me.

The hair on my arms stands when he presses his front to my back, while his right hand trails gently up my hip, over my ribs and under my bicep where he lifts it higher into the air.

"Lift the bat off your shoulder and leave it like this." His gravelly voice brushes over my neck, making me shiver as my body instinctively grinds back against his.

Surprising me, his lips press against my pulse point, his tongue hot making me gasp while pleasure unfurls in my belly.

"God, you just have to smell so fucking sweet, don't you, princess?" he groans painfully, rolling his hard cock against my ass. "Do you enjoy making me want to say fuck it and take you right here on this field?"

I know he has to work at the shop after this, so I'm halfway tempted to take him up on his offer since we haven't had the chance to be alone since New Mexico.

"Someone could be watching," I remind him, coming to my senses amidst the rush of lust.

Ryker steps back instantly, his voice hoarse. "Show me what you've got."

After I take a moment to refocus and calm my erratic breathing, I do as he says, imagining the stance he takes when he goes up to bat. I have it memorized because…well, I can't keep my eyes off him, okay? Sue me.

Digging my right foot into the dirt, I bend my knees slightly and shift left to right on the balls of my feet before settling in. Then, with a deep breath and my eyes on the ball, I swing the bat forward and send it flying toward second base.

Pride swoops over me, and I can't do anything but stare at the foam ball on the dirt, knowing I did that. It's so simple, something kids experience at a young age with a parent or a coach. But for someone like me who's always wanted to but never had the chance, and is finally doing things for *me*, it's everything.

Ryker remains silent as he jogs to get the ball, then sets it back on the tee. We do this a couple times, letting me get used to the motion of swinging the bat until I grow tired of it.

"I want the real deal now, please," I plead, turning to Ryker, whose hard gaze is unrelenting on mine. "What is it?" I start blushing, wondering why he's staring at me like that.

"Just wondering how it happened that I'd do anything you asked me to when you look at me like that," he answers, bewildered and confused.

Meanwhile, my heart is fluttering so hard I fear it's going to leap right out of my chest. I'm so used to Ryker's grumpiness, but every time he shows me the softer parts of him, it makes me fall a little more and more in lov—I mean, like. In like with him.

Ryker clears his throat and wordlessly takes the foam bat from me, replacing it with a steel one.

"I'm going to pitch you some balls, so you have to remember to swing through fully and use your hips. It'll give you more power," he instructs before jogging to a spot a few feet in front of the pitching mound and dropping his bag of balls on the grass.

While he gets set up, I practice swinging with the heavier bat. It's not so heavy that I'm unable to do it, but it is different from swinging a foam bat.

"You ready?" Ryker calls out, ball in his glove as he twists his ball cap backward with his free hand.

Well, now I'm not ready. How am I supposed to focus when he looks like my wildest fantasies right now?

His dark green long-sleeved RLU shirt hugs his arms and the black shorts he's wearing show off his thigh tattoo that's peeking through the hemline of said shorts. To top it off, his hat is now flipped backward, those long brown locks free in the wind.

It's a sight to behold.

It's my turn to clear my throat, which is drier than normal. "Yeah, of course," I say excitedly, making it known that I want to let him have his way with me, right here, right now.

I go through my ritual, digging my right foot in before bending my knees and swaying lightly from side to side. My chin dips as I nod, letting him know he's good to go. Ryker nods back, then underhandedly throws a lob to me.

I swing and miss, which makes me want to curl up in embarrassment. "You didn't see that," I yell. "Erase it from your memory."

"Just keep your eye on the ball. You got this," he encourages me.

The next one, I make contact with, but my swing is pathetic and only allows the ball to land a few feet in front of me.

"Again," I tell him. I'm not leaving this field until I have one good hit.

The same thing happens with the next few balls, not going very far when I hit them.

"You're swinging too slow," he comments, then shifts his body to pretend like he's swinging a bat. He swings slowly and says, "This is what you look like, when it should look like this." He does it again, this time swinging much faster.

I take a practice swing, whipping the bat faster this time. At least, I think.

"How's that?" I huff, wiping a bead of sweat from my forehead.

"Good, but I think you can do better," he challenges me while casually tossing the ball into his glove over and over. "Swing the bat with purpose. I know someone's pissed you off before. Get that anger out right now."

I mull his words over, my mind filling with images of my parents, of the people who attacked me. And for once, rather than fear filling my head, it's anger for what they did to me and what they took from me. A normal childhood, a chance to be myself, and those men who took my sense of safety.

When I get into my stance, I dig my foot in a little harder, gripping the bat with a determination I've never experienced. And this time, when my bat hits the ball, there's a piercing thud before the ball is soaring rapidly into the outfield.

"Holy fuck," Ryker says in astonishment, but I don't acknowledge it. I want more.

"Keep going," I shout, enjoying this release.

The next few balls are the same, crushed balls into varying parts of the outfield. Each time I hit the mark, I feel lighter than before. It's therapeutic for some reason. I smash the last ball into left field, hitting the fence right under the sign that reads two hundred feet.

Dropping the bat to the ground, a mixture of emotions hit me all at once. Happiness and frustration mix together, and tears stream down my cheeks as I smile widely.

Ryker rushes over to me, a concerned look on his face. He pulls me into his arms and I rest my head under his chin while his hand presses against my lower back.

"I don't know what's happening." I sniffle against his chest.

"Shhh, it's okay. I got you," he murmurs, kissing my forehead.

Once my body settles from the height of my emotions, I pull back from him and attempt to wipe the tears from my cheeks.

With a gentle push, Ryker ushers my hands away and does

it himself. We stare into each other's eyes, and I can't help but wonder, how is this only a hookup for him?

Is this how people act with their friends with benefits?

His eyes light up with pride, breaking the intimate gesture. "You fucking crushed those balls. You should play for our school's team. Hell, maybe even our team."

I smile up at him, loving his praise. "Thank you, but I don't think so. While I love the sport, I don't want to play it professionally."

"Understandable."

"Thank you for taking time out of your schedule to teach me," I tell him, hating how easily my cheeks seem to heat up around him.

Ryker's lips twitch into a side smirk. "No problem."

I'm about to ask him to come over later so we can finish what we started earlier, but we're interrupted. "The girl can hit! What can't she do, honestly." Cuddy claps, revealing himself in the dugout.

While I don't love that he saw me break down, I know he's not the type to make fun of me for it.

"Cuddy, why the fuck are you still here? Actually, since you're here, you're going to help me collect the balls in the outfield."

"I can help," I chime in.

"No," Ryker says quickly. "Let me take care of it."

I hear the undercurrent of his words loud and clear, even if he doesn't say it.

I let him and Cuddy collect the balls while I lean against the fence, face tipped up to the slowly sinking sun in the sky. There's a hue of purple mixed in with the orange and blue, and it hits me then how grateful I am.

To be here, in Colorado. To have met the people I have.

Even if one of them is a man who has no room for me in his future, no matter how much I envision him in mine.

Chapter Twenty-One

Camille

I think girls' nights should be planned for and coveted just as much as date nights are. There's nothing like getting together with the people who know you like the back of their hand to gossip, eat, and laugh.

You can't ask for anything better. Especially when Aurora is in town for a visit.

"I'm so sore." Aurora sighs, shifting her body in the booth.

"Conditioning been tough?" I ask over the rim of my beer can, taking a sip. Aurora is on the USA Volleyball Team, which means her body is always being tested and challenged.

Aurora snickers, shaking her head slightly. "Yes, but that's not why. Let's just say Cam really missed me when I went away to San Francisco with the team."

Jasmine jumps in, sharing her own story. "Oh, I know exactly what that's like. Every time Elio comes back home from traveling with the hockey team, I'm very much reminded of how much he missed me. Hell, just last week he fucked me so hard my legs were still like jello in the morning."

Don't get me wrong, I couldn't be happier for my friends,

but I have to ignore the heavy weight of jealousy that sits on my chest because I very much want to be getting the kind of sex they both are.

The bone-chilling, earth-shattering, makes you forget your own name kind of sex. I've never had it before and didn't know it truly existed until Aurora and Jasmine shared their experiences.

"The virgin no more," Aurora teases, earning a playful shove from Jasmine and a giggle from me.

"What about you?" Aurora asks, turning her attention to me.

"Oh, I'm no virgin. I had a few hookups when I was back home, but that's it." I blush, but not from embarrassment. More so from the fact that I haven't been interested in sex since the incident, and now all I want to do is fuck her almost-stepbrother.

"Get it, girl," Aurora says with a smile.

"Agreed." I tip my beer to her water cup, and Jasmine joins in with her glass of wine as we cheers.

I shift the conversation to Jasmine. "Are you excited for your European vacation?"

Her face lifts into pure joy. "I cannot wait, even if Elio spoils me way too much."

"I still can't believe he bought you a damn bakery." Aurora swoons, hugging her water to her chest.

Jasmine blushes and rolls her eyes. "Ugh, I know. He's turned me into a softy and I hate it."

"That's what happens when you're in love." I wink, taking a sip from my beer. "Where are Cam and Elio tonight anyway?"

"They're at our apartment, along with Theo," Jasmine fills in.

"Theo's pissed we're not there, but my girls come first." Aurora smiles, and I can't help but be proud of her.

I didn't know her all that well despite my friendship with Jasmine because Aurora was that secluded when she came to school here. She went to class, studied, and played volleyball. That was it.

She reminds me of Ryker in some ways, and the thoughts carry me away to images of him on his knees for me. My core starts to ache so I cross my legs and shake my head, doing my best to refocus on the conversation going on.

"What about you, Millie?" Aurora asks.

"Uhhh, what about me?"

"What's going on with you?" Jasmine clarifies, inspecting me closely.

I sigh. "Nothing, yet everything. Midterms drained the life out of me, and I've been working so hard on creating and organizing content for the baseball team."

"No, no, it's not that. You have this glint in your eyes, and your smile looks more… radiant." Her eyes narrow, staring me down as if she can see through me.

"And now you're blushing!"

I chug my beer, trying to avoid this conversation.

"All right, what's his name? I can look him up and find out more than you probably know." Aurora grabs her phone, far too excited to be stalking someone.

"You actually might already know him," I mumble, slinking down in my seat.

"What?" they both shout, drawing the eyes of everyone in the bar.

Before I can respond, Jasmine being the people reader she is, calls me out, "It's Ryker, isn't it?" she questions, but where I expected sass, her tone is nothing but soft and sweet.

I sit back up, a smile blooming on my face despite how much I fight it. "Yes, but it's nothing really. We're just messing around." There's a ripple in my heart as I say the words, but I ignore it.

"I actually don't know much about him. He's locked up better than Area 51," Aurora says, tucking her dark blonde locks over her shoulder.

I know why he is the way he is now. It breaks my heart knowing what he's gone through, but if he hasn't told Aurora himself, then I won't either. It's not my place to share his past.

Jasmine claps her hands together. "I knew it! Ever since that night in the club, I knew this would happen!"

"How *did* this happen? Spill the deets." Aurora snaps her fingers, looking like a kid on Christmas morning as she and Jasmine lean in closer to me.

Aurora has no idea about my past, so I can't get into exact details. Instead, I give them a shortened version.

"We've been seeing each other more since I started working with the team, so that didn't help the crush I've always had on him." I lift up my T-shirt to show them, and their eyes widen. "He even tattooed me."

"Oh, that's beautiful," Jasmine marvels.

"Agreed. He's very talented. But go on." Aurora rolls her hands in a circular motion so as to say *get on with it*.

So I tell them everything. I recount how he came to the party and took me home on his bike, our flirty conversations, our baseball lessons. I tell them a bit of a white lie when I explain the whole weekend in New Mexico and say that it was just a regular nightmare he comforted me after. I explain how we opened up to each other *and* our little trip to the bathroom.

"Okay, that's hot." Jasmine takes a sip of her rosé while pretending to fan herself.

"He's my stepbrother-to-be, so ew," Aurora mock gags. "*But* if he were a different guy, I'd agree and say that was very hot."

"Hey, some people are into the whole stepbrother thing. There's a whole channel on it online if you know what I mean." Jasmine raises her brows.

I snicker at that and signal our waitress, Marcela, because I need another drink.

"Hi," she says, attempting to smile, but it doesn't reach her eyes. "What can I get you?" Her voice wobbles, instantly raising alarm bells. Marcela has always been on the shyer side, even though she's a waitress, but this is different.

"Marcela, are you okay?" Aurora is the first to ask, since she was her old coworker for a few months.

"Oh, yeah, just great." She tries to smile again while a tear escapes the corner of her eye. "Shit," she curses, swiping at it quickly.

"Sit, please." I pat the open spot beside me in the booth, my eyes pleading with hers. I don't know anything about her, but girls support girls. Always.

Marcela looks around her, but Aurora is quick to jump in. "My brother owns the place, and it's slow in here. Don't worry."

Her resolve crumbles and she slides into the spot next to me, her hand slightly shaking.

"What's going on? How can we help?" I offer softly, my fingers itching to offer her comfort, but we're not exactly friends yet.

"I-I don't know why I want to tell a bunch of strangers everything, but I do."

"We're technically not strangers. You and I used to work together," Aurora reminds her.

"Yeah, but it's not like we talked outside of work. I don't really *know* you," Marcela says quietly.

Aurora nods, knowing she's not wrong.

"We're still here for you if you'd like to talk," Jasmine chimes in, giving her a sweet smile, but I can see the worry in her eyes. Jasmine's always been the protective one, and right now she wants to go into protection mode.

"I've only had one close friend, but she transferred schools this semester." Marcela's voice tightens, her throat bobbing as she swallows.

"That's hard to deal with. You know Cami and I are on campus for the next few months. We'd love to hang out with you if you're feeling lonely," Jasmine offers, and I nod in agreement.

Marcela smiles while a tear strolls down her cheek. "I appreciate that, but that's not why I'm upset."

She takes a moment, then releases a breath. "I'm upset because said friend moved to the same school as the boyfriend I've had since sophomore year in high school, and I just received a video of them making out."

My jaw drops open while my heart breaks for her. I could never imagine dealing with the sort of betrayal she is right now.

No one says a word because I think we're all a little in shock.

Marcela chuckles, but it lacks any humor. "You know what the worst part is? It was someone who was supposed to be my best friend. Getting cheated on hurts, but with my *best friend*? It's like getting screwed two times over."

"I'm so sorry you're dealing with this," I say, whispering *screw it* in my head as I pull her into a hug.

Marcela's body slumps in my arms as she starts crying. I rub my hand on her back, trying to soothe her while I let her get it all out. Jasmine and Aurora look equally as heartbroken as I am for her.

A few moments later, once she quiets down and we break apart, Marcela wipes at her eyes and says, "I'm so sorry I dumped all of that on you guys and had a meltdown like that." She cringes, as if embarrassed.

"Nope, none of that," Aurora remarks. "Don't ever apologize for having a feeling other than happiness. It's what makes you human."

"Can I say something a little blunt?" Jasmine presses her arms against the table, slightly leaning forward.

"She's sensitive right now, Minnie," I warn, not that Jasmine is ever rude, but I don't know if what she's about to say is what Marcela needs to hear right now.

"No, it's okay, say it," Marcela replies, giving her the go-ahead.

"I'm not saying you can't be upset, because you have every right to be. I just want to say, fuck both of them. You don't need a friend like that, and as for Hunter, I hope he—"

"Wait, how did you know that was my boyfriend's name?"

Jasmine's lips form an O. "Well, you see…"

"Theo has a big mouth, okay?" Aurora explains. I mean, he was the reason Jasmine's dad even found out about her and Elio.

Marcela shakes her head, but I don't miss the small smile his name brought on her face. "I know in time I'll realize I'm better off, but I found out a few minutes ago and it just hurts so much," she sniffles.

"Jasmine's offer still stands. Actually, no. From here on out, you just gained three new besties." I pretend to slam a gavel for the full effect.

"I'm not in town much anymore, but I'll give you my number," Aurora adds.

Marcela looks overwhelmed, her honey-brown eyes pooling with appreciation. "Why are you all being so nice to me? I don't get it."

"Because girls have to have each other's backs. I'm sorry you've maybe grown up not believing that, but in this friend group, we'd go to the ends of the earth for each other. And now you're included in that." I nudge her shoulder with mine, earning myself a small smile.

"Thank you all so much." She blows out a breath. "My mind feels like such a mess."

"Understandable. You've been through a lot in the last few minutes. Do you want to get out of here? We're all going back to my apartment, and we have an extra room if you want to spend the night," Jasmine says.

"Oh no, that's okay," she begins to protest, but Aurora is having none of that.

"You don't need to sleep over, but I refuse to let you go back to work in this state of mind. I'll go talk to the manager tonight, which so happens to be my brother, and you'll be good to go."

That's how we all end up piling into Aurora's car, heading toward the luxurious apartment building Jasmine and I call home. But it's funny because even as we say hello to the doorman, Colin, and enter the elevator, it still doesn't feel like home.

It's not until we enter Jasmine's place and my eyes lock with dark blue ones that I feel it. He may not be where I'm from, but he's the only thing that's felt like home in a long time. And that right there is a big freaking issue when all we're supposed to be is fuck buddies… who have yet to even have sex.

Despite knowing that, my soul recognizes his for whatever reason, categorizing him as my safe place, even though I'm almost certain he's going to break my heart when all of this is over.

Chapter Twenty-Two

Ryker

When Theo asked me to hang out tonight, I thought he meant just the two of us. I'd agreed because truthfully, I've missed him since baseball season was gearing up, and soon, I won't see much of him anymore.

It also helped that Camille was out with her friends, which meant I needed something to do tonight other than hope that she wanted to come over. We haven't seen each other since the day I taught her how to hit a ball because we've both been busy, but I'm going to fucking combust soon if I can't see her.

The number of times I've replayed eating her sweet pussy while I've jacked off is concerning.

I try to keep my mind off of her and pay attention to what the boys are saying. On our way back from getting dinner, Theo made a pit stop, and by pit stop, I mean he dragged me up to Elio fucking Mazzo's apartment. The guy's a retired hockey legend and also happens to be dating Jasmine Park, a friend of Camille's.

Cameron also happened to be here, who I guess will be my stepbrother too if he marries Aurora one day. Which reminds me that Aurora's dad and my mom are getting married this summer. Great.

We're now all sitting in the apartment's open space living room with Theo, Elio, and Cameron, and I hate to admit it's not that bad.

"I'm just saying, there's strong, and then there's country boy strong," Theo argues.

"Dude, you're not stronger than Elio. Drop it." Cameron tries to reason with Theo, but he's not having it.

"Listen, I know you're a legend and an ex-professional athlete, but manual labor creates muscles in places you don't even know about," Theo counters, pointing a finger at Elio.

"You want to bet?" Elio raises a brow in challenge. "Let's arm wrestle, right here, right now."

"Are you two seriously going to arm wrestle like a bunch of teenagers?" I scoff.

"I think they are," Cameron mutters as we watch Theo and Elio roll up their sleeves, drop to their knees on the floor, and rest their elbows on the table.

"Ry guy, give us the official countdown," Theo calls out as he and Elio lock hands.

"No."

"Ronnie boy?"

Cameron shakes his head, but gets up nonetheless. He's too damn nice. "All right, on three. One, two, three!"

They're instantly battling it out in the center, their arms not favoring in one direction or the other. Elio looks like he's about to break a sweat, but when I look at Theo, I see nothing but pure amusement dancing in his eyes.

"That's all you got, Eli Oldi?" Theo huffs out sarcastically.

Elio grunts and his arm gains some traction on Theo, taking

the lead. Theo chuckles, and then suddenly, he's smashing Elio's hand down.

We're all silent for a beat, then Theo erupts. He jumps up and down, screaming, "I did it! I beat a hockey legend at an arm wrestle. Oh my God."

Cameron and I laugh at the spectacle, but I can't deny I'm impressed. Theo's always been bulky, after he gained some weight in high school, and now that he's in a D1 sport, the guy looks insane.

Elio shakes his head as he takes a seat on the couch once again. "Settle down, kid."

Theo smiles happily as he too sits back down beside Cameron. "This is going down as the best night of my life."

"That's the saddest thing ever if that's true," I comment.

"Be happy for him. He hasn't been laid in a long time, so he needs to get his hits somewhere," Elio remarks, reaching for one of the apple crumble mini pies Jasmine left out.

"Psssh." Theo waves him off. "At least I don't get my hits from fucking my friend's daughter."

My eyes widen, as do Cameron's. Did he just say that? Then again, it's Theo. The shit that comes out of his mouth is usually out of pocket.

"Point taken," Elio agrees, but then his tone turns icy. "But talk about Jasmine in that way again and I *will* kick your ass."

Theo throws his hands up in defense. "Sorry, Eli Oldi, didn't mean it that way. I thought we could joke about it now since the two of you are public. You know Jasmine's my girl. I'd never disrespect her."

"She's not *your* girl either. Maybe just stop talking," Elio says, but there's humor in his voice. "And that nickname fucking sucks."

"What? It's genius. It's a mix of your name and you being the oldest in the friend group!"

"We're not a friend group," I retort.

"As if. Elio is dating Jasmine, who is best friends with Aurora, who is dating Cameron. I'm best friends with both Aurora and Jasmine, meaning I got the in. And since you're *my* best friend, Ry guy, you are in the group too."

"What a joy." I smirk, but it's half-assed. The last thing I need is more friends. The team is enough, and in a few months, I probably won't see any of them ever again anyway once I go pro.

"I miss her." Cameron sighs, staring at the background on his phone that has a picture of my soon-to-be stepsister.

"Same," Elio agrees, staring at a picture frame on the coffee table with a photo of him and Jasmine in it.

"How does it feel to be in love? Seriously, I've never felt it before," Theo asks, his voice devoid of his usual joking manner.

Cameron, being the quiet one, looks at Elio to take this on. "It makes everything feel more intense. You feel more *alive* than ever before. It makes you wonder how you went through life without them and terrifies you to imagine a day when you do," Elio answers.

My brain conjures up an image of me saying goodbye to Camille, and it makes my entire body go rigid.

"It fills something inside of you too, like a permanent warmth in your chest that never seems to go away," Cameron adds, his dimples popping out as he smiles.

Before anyone can say anything, we hear the keypad whirring. Elio jumps up in confusion, but stops halfway to the door when it swings open and four girls enter the apartment. Jasmine leads the pack, followed by Aurora and Marcela. Then Camille walks in, her eyes latching onto mine instantly.

I suck in a breath at the sight of her. She's wearing a tight white T-shirt and light-colored ripped jeans that I would love to take off despite how good they look on her. Her hair is up in a sleek ponytail, and I have to curb the urge to close the space between us and yank on it as I devour her mouth with mine.

Cameron stands and scoops Aurora up into a hug, whispering into her ear as they sway.

"Babe!" Jasmine jumps up and into Elio's arms. "We brought Marcela home with us. She needs some girl time."

Are couples in love always this nauseating? Jesus Christ.

At the mention of Marcela, I swing my head to Theo, who has his eyes locked on her, his face filled with concern. It's no secret he has a thing for her, despite her having a boyfriend.

Theo charges toward her. "Who hurt you?"

Marcela shakes her head. "I don't want to talk about it. I just want to have fun."

"Yes, more drinking, less talking!" Jasmine links her arm through Marcela's as she drags her to the minibar.

I avert my eyes back to Camille, who's making small talk with Cameron, Aurora, and Elio, while Theo just stares longingly at Marcela. Should I go over there and just talk to her?

I sound like a fucking teenage boy.

Camille makes the decision for me when she walks over to where I'm sitting and plops down beside me.

She smiles, disarming me. "Hi."

I smile back at her, unable to control it when I've been missing her and she's this goddamn stunning. "Hi."

"A smile? Wow, what did I do to earn such a thing?" she teases, getting comfortable on the couch.

"Existing."

Camille's pink lips part at my confession, then close as her eyes flit all around my face until they finally land on my lips.

Fuck it.

I lean in and give her a sweet, yet chaste kiss. To my luck, no one says anything, all too absorbed in their partners or the conversation going on around them.

"Thank you," she whispers.

"For what?"

"Kissing me."

"You never have to thank me for that. I should be thanking you, baby. Anytime I get to touch you is a privilege."

"Is that what friends with benefits say to each other?" Her words are like a bucket of cold water, dousing the intimate moment. It's a reminder that my brain and heart are two different organs, and I need to stop speaking without fucking thinking first.

"They are when their friend is as beautiful as you are," I say, doing my best to back myself up.

Camille either thinks I'm full of shit or doesn't care, because she just smiles and turns to face our friends, who are now all lounging on the couch with various drinks in their hands. Save for Cameron and Aurora, who don't drink.

We play some drinking games, and it's surprisingly a lot of fun. Marcela is a bit quiet as she observes and sips on her drink, while Theo can't seem to take his eyes off her. He doesn't pry, though, merely keeping watch to make sure she's okay.

Within an hour, Jasmine and Camille are drunk, so Elio calls it for the night. "All right, I need to get her to bed," he says, standing with Jasmine, who's locked around his body like a koala bear.

"Mmmm, yes, take me to bed." She drunk giggles.

"I mean to sleep, *dolcezza*."

She pouts at him, then cranes her neck at us. "He's no fun, but I hope you all had fun. Marcela, are you staying the night? Aurora and Cameron are. You're more than welcome."

"No, I need to get home, but thank you," she says, standing and grabbing her purse.

"I'll give you a ride," Theo offers. "You don't mind, right, Ryker?"

"Actually, I'm going to walk Camille up to her apartment and make sure she's good, then I'll Uber home."

"I can just wait a few minutes. It's no big deal," he says matter-of-factly.

The guy can't read the room, can he?

I tilt my head and glare at him, hoping he'll get the hint this time.

Theo's head tilts in response and then he straightens. "Oh. Oh, OH! Yeah, totally, you stay and make sure she's good."

"You don't have to drive me home," Marcela protests, but Theo's already walking with her to the door.

"You're right, I don't have to. I *need* to make sure you get home safely," he responds, and she doesn't argue.

"Bye, AV baby! Bye, Jay bay bay! Bye, Millie Moo!" Theo shouts, waving at the girls. "Bye, Ry guy! Bye, Ronnie boy! Bye, Eli Oldi!"

Jesus Christ, Theo and his nicknames.

Marcela smiles for the first time tonight and then says goodbye to everyone as she and Theo leave.

"It was so nice to see you all," Aurora says, pulling Camille into a hug. "I'll try to come back soon, but with my volleyball schedule, it can be tough."

"Keep making us proud out there, Rora. You're crushing it," Camille tells her once they've parted.

"Right? Aurora Vallacourt is a fucking badass!" Jasmine slurs.

Camille and I say goodbye, thanking Elio and Jasmine for having us over even though I didn't want to be here in the slightest when I first showed up.

As soon as we get into the hallway, Camille jumps onto my back.

"What the hell are you doing, princess?" I ask, gripping her thighs to keep her secure.

"Going for a ride. It's fun up here." She giggles and begins doing a lasso with one hand. "Giddy up, cowboy!"

"I can think of something else for you to ride."

She slaps my shoulder. "Ryker the biker, how dare you talk to a lady like that?"

"I'll talk to a lady like that when I know it gets her panties wet, or am I wrong?" I ask, hitting the button for the elevator.

"*Une femme ne révèle pas ses secrets*," she sing-songs.

"For all I know that was French for *my pussy is soaked*," I tease her, right as the elevator doors open and I step inside.

"I said that a lady doesn't reveal her secrets." Camille giggles. "Is that so?"

I spin her around my body so that her chest is to mine and press her gently against the elevator wall as my lips meet hers. I keep it sweet since she's tipsy and I'm not trying to be that guy.

Camille's fingers tangle in my long hair, tugging as I deepen the kiss. A little sigh escapes her, making me pull away.

"Nooooo," she whines.

"Your sounds are going to drive me fucking wild, and I can't go there with you right now. Not when you're drunk," I tell her, tucking a loose strand of her ponytail behind her ear.

Camille's mouth twists, silvery eyes narrowed at me. "Boo you for being such a gentleman."

I stifle a laugh and ask for her floor number, which I realize is just the next one up. Once we get into her place, I set her on her feet and take in the space around me. The layout looks similar to Elio's, but this screams Camille with all the pops of bright colors everywhere.

"Do you want anything to drink? Maybe coffee or tea?" she asks, practically skipping into her kitchen.

"No, thank you," I say, coming up behind her as she preps her French press.

"I need a coffee and a croissant before bed. They'll help me sober up a bit," she explains and begins making herself a coffee.

She does her thing, munching on a croissant she pulls from a bakery container, intriguing me when she starts making latte art that she's oddly good at doing. She puts the finishing touch on the flower she's made.

"Pretty interesting talent you got there," I murmur, resting my chin on her shoulder as I admire her artwork.

Camille leans into me, resting her head against mine. "My nanny taught it to me. It's pretty useless honestly, but it's my MJ."

"What's an MJ?"

She turns to face me, jumping onto her countertop and taking her baseball mug into her hand. "A mini joy, little things that bring me a spark. So for me, that's latte art, gardening, boxing…"

"What about a BJ?"

"I would consider blow jobs a mini joy…"

I bark out a laugh at that, which causes her to smile so damn brightly that I want to laugh more just for her to smile at me like that again.

"I like where your mind went, but that's not what I meant. What's a big joy for you?"

Camille ponders my question, taking a few sips of her coffee before answering.

"Connecting with people. It's something I didn't get much of growing up. Of course, we had public relations events like balls and fundraisers where I got to meet people. But none of it was real. It was all for show or for some other purpose than just for getting to know someone for who they were. I think that's why I enjoy doing content for the team so much because it combines my love of baseball and connecting with people. It's fun and refreshing, two things I missed out on a lot at the palace," she tells me.

"That's beautiful," I reply honestly.

"Thanks, now tell me what's your MJ and BJ?" She waggles her brows at me with a seductive smile on her lips.

I can't help it. I lean in and kiss her, but pull away just as quickly. Camille leaves her arms wrapped around my neck, and I step in closer so that I'm now between her legs.

"My big joy is baseball. It's the one place where I feel centered and at peace. My mini joys would be tattooing, riding my bike, and movie nights with my mom."

"I love those." Her fingers trail down my chest, making me shiver. "Speaking of tattoos, can I look at yours?"

I should say no, but I can't do that when it comes to this girl. I lift the bottom of my sweater and tug it over my head since most of my tattoos are on my upper body.

"Wow," she breathes as her fingers trace the designs going up my arm.

Silence falls over us as her fingers skate up to my shoulder and down to my chest where there's a large piece across it. It's filled with intricate line designs, with small things I love woven in between. There's a pair of Mickey Mouse ears for my mom, a paw print of the dog I had when I was a kid, and right over my heart is a baseball.

Camille's fingers run across each one, her gaze focused and undeterred. "This is beautiful," she whispers as her thumb strokes over my heart, and then she peers up at me. "*You're* beautiful."

Her words make my stomach flutter, raising my concerns that I must be getting sick because what the hell is that shit?

I tug my lips up to the right, then toss my sweater back over my head. "Thank you."

"I want more tattoos. Can we go to the studio now?" Her eyes sparkle as her fingers run up and down my stomach. If I had keys to the shop, I might've actually said yes.

"Not today, princess," I tell her, stopping her fingers when they get to the waistband of my jeans. "Finish your coffee and let's get you to bed."

She oddly does as I say, finishing up her cup and placing the mug in the sink. Grabbing my hand, she leads me to her room where she heads to the en suite bathroom to change and wash her face.

After a few minutes, Camille steps out in a long T-shirt, with God knows what *or* what not underneath.

"Bed," I say, pointing to her king-sized bed.

She jumps into bed and tucks herself under the covers. I placed a fresh glass of water on her nightstand while she changed, in case she might need it in the middle of the night. I don't think she'll be hungover by any means, but just in case.

"So I'll head out. Text me if you need anything."

"Would you…would you mind staying over?" she asks shyly.

"You sure?"

"I'm sure. Stay, please."

"Okay."

I kick off my boots and hang my sweater on her doorknob, then climb into bed with her. It's uncomfortable as fuck in my jeans, but I ignore it because I get to stay the night with her.

She turns over to face me, a yawn escaping her. "Cuddle time?"

I smirk. I'm not one fond of cuddling, but I'm learning I love it too when it's with her.

"Come here."

I reach for her under the covers and slide my hand under her shoulders as she wraps her arm around my neck to pull her body flush to mine as our legs intertwine.

"Sweet dreams, princess," I whisper, pressing my lips to her forehead.

"Sleep well, Ryker the biker."

Chapter Twenty-Three

Camille

’m still half asleep when I attempt to roll over to my other side to try to fall back asleep. I already know it’s too early for me to be up, especially on a Sunday. But my body’s trapped underneath another warm body, preventing me from moving the way I want.

I crack open one eye to see that Ryker’s sprawled on top of me. Well, half of him. His leg is strewn over my hips and his head is nestled on my breasts while his inked-up forearm is resting under them.

Giddiness bubbles up inside of me, knowing he’s here and mine. For now.

I had the best sleep I’ve ever had last night. There’s just something about him that has me wanting to cling to. My fingers run softly through his hair and I massage his scalp.

He emits a contented sigh. “Mmm,” he hums, sounding so unlike the grump I know.

“Shh, sleep,” I whisper, repeating the motions with my fingers. Minutes go by without a word from either of us, so I assume he fell asleep until a groan leaves his mouth and suddenly his lips are on the mound of my breast, peppering the area with kisses over my T-shirt.

"Ryker." The word is breathy as each press of his lips heats my entire body.

"I've been dying to look at them. Can I?" he gruffs, sounding strained.

"Yes."

Ryker grunts in approval, lifting his head as he cups me through my T-shirt, weighing them in his hands. "Fuck, baby. Your shirt needs to go, *now*," he rasps, moving his hands to the hem. He lifts it up and over my body, leaving me bare save for the cheeky pink underwear I have on.

"You're a dream, you know that?" he says as his eyes roam hungrily over every square inch of my body. Once they land on my breasts, his eyes darken.

I'll take it he's a boob guy.

The thought is swept away when his mouth wraps around my nipple while his hand pays attention to my other nipple, twisting and pulling.

My back arches off the bed and I let out a low moan.

My piercings make it feel more intense, and Ryker's tongue around the barbell is making me see stars. His breath is warm against the cool bar, and the contrast is dizzying. "These are so fucking hot."

"So good. Keep going," I moan, wrapping my legs around his waist as he settles between my thighs.

Ryker doesn't respond. Instead, he just keeps going as he moves between my breasts, bringing me closer and closer to the edge of my looming orgasm. I've never come this way, but I guess there's a first time for everything, right?

Suddenly, his hard length grinds against my soaked panties, so slowly, I can feel every inch of him, which nearly makes me lose it.

"Ryker," I gasp, my entire body on fire.

"You like that?" he grunts, grinding into me with more force this time.

I rub back against him and revel in watching his forearms flex in response. "I'd like it more if it were inside of me." I tug on his hair, forcing his mouth off my nipple.

"Fuck." He throws his head back. "I don't have any condoms."

"I have an IUD, and I've been tested. I'm clear."

"I'm good too, but it's up to you. It's always whatever you want," he tells me.

I smirk. "I know it is, and I want your cock in my mouth first. Then I want you inside me."

"Baby, you're going to make me come before any of that happens if you keep talking like that."

"Then strip, lie down, and let me suck you," I order him, loving how strong it makes me feel to be in control.

Ryker does exactly as I say, standing up from the bed, where he discards his clothes, and my mouth waters at the sight.

"You're gorgeous," I breathe, in awe at the sight in front of me.

Ryker shakes his head and lies down on the bed. "I thought you were using that mouth to suck my cock. Don't tell me you're a liar, princess."

"Oh, I will." I smirk devilishly.

On all fours, I crawl over to him and grip his cock, humming in appreciation as I stroke his length. His cock is thick and long, the perfect size. I've never seen anything I've wanted to put my mouth on more.

"Your cock is amazing, Ryker." I kiss the tip, the saltiness from his pre-cum hitting my tongue.

"Fuck," he mutters.

I lean down and spit on his cock, using my hand to coat his entire length. Ryker's muscles tense in anticipation, and I grin, knowing how much power I have over him. With my hand holding his base in a firm grip, I suck his tip into my mouth. His thighs tremble underneath me and it spurs me on. I suck more of his length into my mouth, swirling my tongue as I do.

"You're so good at sucking my cock, baby," Ryker moans, his dirty words making my clit throb.

I attempt to put all of him in my mouth but fail, my gag reflex making me have to pull back.

"Fuck, that sound, do it again."

So I do, shoving him as far as I can go until my gag reflex kicks in once again. It turns me on knowing he loves it rather than being annoyed that I can't take all of him.

Ryker's breathing becomes erratic, his hands fisting the sheets. *God, that's so hot.*

I settle in a rhythm, sucking and licking him while my other hand comes up to squeeze lightly on his balls.

"Okay, you need to stop," he grits out, putting a hand on my shoulder.

I let him go with a pop. "But I'm having so much fun." I pout, then flick my tongue over his slit.

Ryker's body jolts at the contact, but before I can go back to toying with him, he has me on my back. He pulls my panties to the side and starts eating my pussy.

"Fuck," I moan as his tongue flicks over my clit rapidly. I was already close just from sucking him off, and the unexpectedness of this is so hot it's bringing me even closer to the edge. While I love to be in control, I also like to give it up and trust that he can take care of me.

Ryker's tongue and mouth ravish me, like I'm his first and last meal. A moan vibrates from his chest as he does and my hips buck wildly at that, my back arching, trying to both get away from the insane pleasure but also get back closer.

My body clearly is at a loss, battling between needs.

My hips come up when his tongue spears into me, and this time he lifts them higher, my back fully off the bed as he brings my pussy closer to his face.

My orgasm slams into me at the passion with which he devours me. "Ryker!" I scream, my voice unknown to me as the throes of lust distort it.

Ryker doesn't let up, only pushes my legs further apart and continues to lap at my clit, sucking it into his mouth. I scream his name again as another unexpected orgasm hits me, filling my body with a buzzing warmth that has me spent by the time he sets me back down. Ryker stands from the bed, his cock throbbing with the need for release.

"Where are you going?" I pant.

"I was going to take care of it in the bathroom. You seem exhausted."

I perk up at that, shaking my head. "Ryker, if you don't get inside me, I will—"

"What?" He smirks.

"Will be very sad." I jut my bottom lip, giving him puppy eyes.

Ryker crawls back on the bed, his body hovering over mine and cloaking me in a sense of protection, yet there's a hint of danger lurking. His eyes are darker than I've ever seen them, and his jaw is set so tightly I fear he's going to chip a tooth.

It's clear Ryker wants me, but I know he's going to be doing everything he can to rein in his self-control.

His lips dip down to taste mine. The combination of my cum on his tongue mixed with his scent makes me whimper against him. His cock rubs up against my slit, causing my hips to jolt upward.

My move makes his tip prod my entrance, and we both still. It's eerily quiet, the sound of our heavy breathing filling the air.

"More," I whisper as a sudden wave of emotions passes

through me. I'll never have more than *this* with him, so I'm going to enjoy every fleeting moment that I can.

"Are you sure?" he asks, his body wound tightly as he stays perfectly still with his tip nudged against my entrance.

"Yes, please," I beg.

Ryker lowers his lips to my forehead, then whispers in my ear, "Tell me if anything's wrong, promise?"

I nod, feeling so damn happy I'm doing this with him. He not only makes me feel wanted and sexy, but more importantly, safe and cared for.

Ryker pushes my knees further apart, his eyes glued to my pussy as he watches his cock slide up and down my slit, coating in my arousal. I look down and the sight turns me on more than I ever thought possible.

"I know, baby, I've got you," he rasps, lining himself up with my entrance. Then, in one thrust, he slides all the way in.

Strangled gasps leave us, followed by a string of French curse words leaving my lips while Ryker breathes heavily above me.

Once the sting subsides due to his size, pleasure settles over me and has me attempting to rock my hips against his for some friction.

"Fuck me," I urge him. "And come inside me when you're done."

Ryker's eyes flit between mine, a small smile forming on his chiseled face. "I love that you look like a princess but talk so fucking dirty."

My response is stolen out of my lungs when he rocks in and out of me for the first time. It turns my brain to mush as my sole focus becomes the sparks of pleasure all over my body.

He feels incredible, better than I could've ever imagined.

Ryker brings my hands above my head, intertwining our fingers as he sets the perfect rhythm. I feel all of him while he rocks into me at just the right angle and pace, making me moan and call out his name.

"You're doing such a good job, Ryker. Your cock is fucking me so well," I tell him, my voice low and seductive.

"Fuck," he moans. "Best pussy ever. So tight, so wet, so *mine*." His thrusts then turn primal, his hips jutting against mine more rapidly.

"This okay?" he grits out, knowing I told him I didn't want anything rough yet.

"You're perfect. Don't stop."

And he doesn't. He continues to fuck me like that. Our hands intertwined, his balls slapping against my ass as our eyes stay locked on one another the entire time. Taking in every single reaction as we lose ourselves to our bodies, letting them take over.

I lift my head up in search of his lips and he dips down, kissing me with just as much fervor as he's fucking me with.

"Now it's my turn to fuck you," I say when we pull apart, more than ready to get on top.

My favorite position.

Ryker rolls us over so that he's lying down and I'm on top. His eyes roam up and down my body before focusing in on where we're joined. "You're so sexy, especially with my cock inside you."

I lift up slowly, feeling every inch, and then slam back down, stealing my own breath at the feeling. "Oh God," I moan, swiveling my hips as I begin to ride him. I slightly lift my hips while rocking against him to brush over my clit with every thrust.

"You're so good at riding my cock, naughty thing, aren't you?" he rasps, his eyes dark and full of need as his hands come up to cup my breasts.

"Just for you," I whimper as his hands start playing with my piercings. My lower belly pools with warmth, my pending orgasm lingering, but I need more.

Bending forward, I lean over him to bring my breasts right in his face. "Suck."

Ryker smirks, then obliges, his lips wrapping tightly around one of my nipples as his hand tugs at the other. My orgasm hits me then, shooting up my spine and making my fucking world shake. I don't know how long I scream his name, but I don't register anything until Ryker has me back on my back and is pounding into me as he finds his own release.

"You want me to fill this pussy up, baby? Coat you in *my* cum?" he grunts as sweat drips from his forehead.

"Oh God, Ryker, yes, please," I whimper, feeling sensitive from my orgasm and possibly the lingering feelings I don't want to think about right now.

That's all it takes, and suddenly, he stills inside me, his cock jerking as he fills me up, warmth coating my walls.

Instead of flopping on me in exhaustion, Ryker sucks in a breath and leans down to kiss me. I expect it to be hot and wild, just like the sex we had, but it's the opposite. His lips are soft and gentle as they meld with mine. He then moves his lips across my face, pressing kisses all over me.

I blush and start to giggle, rubbing my nose against his. We both breathe in deeply, our foreheads touching while we stay silent.

But my mind keeps running rampant with four little words.

I am so fucked.

Chapter Twenty-Four

Ryker

It's game day.

The second half of our baseball season is finally starting and this is my version of Christmas morning.

Baseball usually runs from late August to October, then picks up again in April and May. We're sitting at the top of our division, and my stats have never looked better. My agent informed me that the Detroit Panthers are heavily interested and willing to sign me if all goes well for the rest of our season.

Instead of crumbling under the pressure, it pushes me forward to work harder. I've been lifting heavy, sticking to my nutrition plans, and getting extra cardio with Camille any chance we get.

The game is tonight at seven, on the first Friday of April. The grounds are solid after thawing from a cold winter, and the sun's been peeking out over the mountains longer and longer every night.

I couldn't be fucking happier.

I arrive at the baseball facility early to get some extra stretching in for my shoulder, making sure it's in perfect condition to whip balls over to first base. As I walk through the building,

I find myself smiling more than usual and it's not just because tonight's our season opener.

It might also have to do with a certain blonde I can't seem to keep my hands off. Ever since Sunday night, I've found myself at her apartment nearly every day this week, finding excuses to leave with her after practice.

And each night ended up with me inside of her.

I can't get enough of her, and I fear I never fucking will. I think I've finally met someone more insatiable than me. Knowing how much she craves me makes me want her all the more, a rabid cycle we can't seem to get out of.

Pushing through the door to the locker room, I find most of the team hanging out in groups as they get fired up for tonight. I'm about to pass them without a word when Noah spots me.

"Ryker, where are you going?" he asks, falling in step with me.

"To find Mackenzie and go through some stretching exercises for my shoulder."

"Good idea." He nods. "But you should come hang out with us after, join the pregame party."

I raise a brow at him. He must be fucking joking because he knows me better than that.

Noah chuckles. "Dude, I'm just kidding. You should've seen the look on your face. I know you like your peace and quiet before a game."

I don't reply and move to the back room. For the next twenty minutes, I stretch out my shoulder with Mackenzie and go through my pregame preparation before we have to hit the field to warm up together.

In the meantime, I like to sit at my cubby in the locker room with classic rock playing in my headphones to get me ready and in the zone.

It's almost game time, which means we need to get our asses on the field. We're all walking down the tunnel to our dugout when I see Camille, who never fails to make my heart want to beat straight out of my chest.

She's got her camera set up, with the question 'What's your guilty pleasure movie?' on her whiteboard for us to answer as we walk by. Noah's leading the group and gets the luxury of answering first.

"*Marley and Me* makes me cry every time," he says without an ounce of shame.

Cuddy's next, and I already know his answer because he never shuts up about these movies. "The Twilight Saga, and yes, I'm team Edward, duh." He winks, oozing confidence as he struts by the camera while a few of the guys snicker.

I do my best not to stare at Camille now that I'm next, but I fucking fail.

What else is new?

She's wearing her personalized jersey, with cut-off jean shorts and her signature Converse. Her long blonde locks are falling in waves around her shoulders, almost in a freshly-fucked look.

I find myself wanting to wrap it around my fist while I pound her from behind, just like I did last night.

Camille's gotten more and more confident in bed with me, asking for things to be a little rougher. I always go by what she needs, never taking things too far even if my control threatens to slip away sometimes.

"*The Little Mermaid*," I tell her, doing my best to rein in the smile on my face as hers expands at my answer.

Camille bends over and then stands with a reusable mug in her hand, thrusting it toward me. "Here, this is for you. Good luck today, Ryker the Biker."

She handed me a cup of coffee with a baseball designed foam on the top.

"What's this?" I ask her, doing my best to sound unaffected.

She shrugs. "It's a good luck coffee. You told me you like having one just to hold for comfort in between innings, and I thought the design was cute."

She's fucking cute. I told her how coffee reminds me of my mom and how it helps center me if I start to get stressed. The urge to kiss her is strong, but I remember where we are and it's snuffed in an instant.

"Thank you." I nod, making my way to the dugout, my heart feeling weird as fuck in my chest. I've never experienced this until I met her.

When I get there, I place the cup in my usual spot, and then we're gearing up for game time. Cuddy and I toss the ball across the field, slowly backing up and creating more distance.

During stretches, I do a quick scan of the stadium, looking for her. She's been busy since the game started, running around to do various things for our social media accounts. That girl works so damn hard, and I admire the hell out of it.

I spot her right above our dugout, our team's hat on her head, covering her face to stay inconspicuous to any cameras. Our games are often shown on sports networks, and she told me she needs to hide the best she can.

Not wanting to stare too long, I continue to trail my gaze across the stands. The crowd is already electric, the seats filled with green and white for our opening night. It generates a buzz in the stadium, one that fuels me from the inside out.

We're the home team, which gives us the advantage of having the last at bat. I feel good as I jog out to third base, the leather encasing my left hand adding to the excitement pumping in my body.

I've never felt more at home than I do on a field with a glove on one hand and a ball in the other. My mind ventures to images of Camille's body wrapped around mine, and that same feeling of home hits me.

Before I get to dwell on that notion, the umpire yells, "It's time to play ball!"

As the opposing team's batter sets up in the box, the cheers become deafening, our RLU fans really showing up today. Enough that by the fifth inning, we're up by two runs and the opposing team has yet to score.

Aspen's team is getting amped up, especially with their best hitter walking up to bat. I'm on the balls of my feet, ready to move any way possible in case it comes my way. The batter swings and misses on the first pitch, but on the second one, he crushes it to the far left, sending the ball into foul territory, right where Camille is sitting.

Chapter Twenty-Five

Ryker

Time comes to a stop, and I watch in what feels like slow-motion the ball hit the top of the dugout and come right at her at full speed.

I scream her name to get her attention, but when she looks up, her eyes widen right before the ball hits her in the jaw.

Fuck.

Before I think it through, my legs are taking me toward her, sprinting and then jumping up and into the stands to get to her. There's a crowd formed around her, but people part ways for me when I barrel my way through, telling them to get the hell out of the way.

I drop to my knees once I get to her. "Cami, baby, it's Ryker," I say softly. "Let me see."

Camille's eyes peek through her fingers. They're filled with tears that's breaking my fucking heart to see, but then I see her smile peeking through too.

My brows pinch inward. "Are you laughing?"

"Yes," she says, the sound muffled by her hands. "Everyone is making such a fuss when I'm fine, only mortified."

"Let me see, please," I urge her, knowing my team is going to give me shit for going off the field, but I needed to check on her.

Camille's hands fall away, showcasing the red marks on the right side of her jaw, along with a few scratches. The visual makes me want to fucking end that guy.

"I'm fine. Get back on the field." She brushes me off with a smile.

My jaw tightens. "You're not sitting here anymore. Come with me."

She doesn't argue and follows me down the stands. She waits as I hop the fence and lift her over it, eliciting a chorus of cheers from the crowd.

Fuck me.

I point to a spot on the bench in the dugout, and she sits, setting herself up there.

Coach Warren's voice filters in through the chaos of the crowd. "You saved the girl, now go play some fucking baseball. The medic team will check on her."

I nod curtly and jog back to the field, getting myself into position. It hits me then that when it came down to it, I chose to check on Camille instead of keeping my head in the game. I don't like that one damn bit.

Baseball is the dream. It's everything. I should be focused on it, not her.

That same hitter who fouled the ball that hit Camille sets back up and hits a fucking bullet of a ball, giving our outfielders a run for their money. He's rounding second base when the center fielder whips it over to me. Judging by the speed of his throw and the guy running, it's going to be close. I adjust my stance, putting one foot on the bag, and bend my knees for the ball that's coming in low, just as the runner slides into me.

Somehow, I manage to make the catch, but the impact of

being kicked in the leg causes me to fall off the bag, losing the potential out. Part of me wonders if he kicked me intentionally or he just slid the wrong way, but I already lost focus once tonight. I can't lose my cool too.

The crowd's boos echo around the stadium as the next batter comes up, taking a few practice swings outside the box.

That's when the dumbass on the bag next to me decides to chat. "Sorry about hitting your girl," he apologizes, and I nod in response, keeping my eyes on home plate. "I just thought girls loved balls in their face. Guess it's not these balls, huh?" He chuckles as if he's a fucking comedian.

I don't laugh. It's taking everything in me not to react, to keep my eyes on the game and my fists at my sides and not at his mouth as I smash his teeth in.

The new batter swings and misses, and the dumbass decides to talk again. "She's pretty. Maybe I should take her out to dinner to apologize."

A wave of possessiveness ravages my body, so fierce that I fear I might actually knock this dumbass out. But I have no right to the feeling. She's not technically mine and she'll most likely go out on dates with guys once I'm drafted.

The thought alone enrages me more, and I'm about to tell him to get lost when the ball is hit on the ground right next to me. The dumbass makes a mistake by stepping off the bag, assuming I'll be throwing it to first base, but I tag up on the bag to get him out. I wind up and whip the ball over to first base and get that out too.

"Don't even fucking think about it," I bark as I jog past the dumbass.

I'm suddenly shoved from behind, and knowing exactly who it was, I waste no time turning around and shoving my fist right into his nose. He remains upright and swings back, getting me good in the jaw. It's the only one I'm allowing him to get so it doesn't seem one-sided. Now, though, he's done. I yank his jersey and rear my fist back, hitting him repeatedly until our teams are shoving their way between us.

Noah has his arms wrapped around me, preventing me from doing any more damage. "Ryker, stop. You can't get suspended," he yells at me, using the one thing he knows will get through to me. Usually, it does, but this asshole pissed me off talking about my girl like that.

It has me attempting to break through the barricade of people separating us until I hear Camille's voice from not too far away.

"Ryker," her voice is full of panic, and my eyes instantly find hers. She stands off to the side of the two groups keeping the fight at bay, which is way too close for my liking.

"Let me go," I snarl while nodding in her direction. Noah must get the hint because he lets go of me, but he walks beside me to ensure neither the dumbass nor I do anything stupid.

As soon as I'm close enough to her, I see the fear swirling in her eyes, and fuck me if that isn't a punch to the gut. "Camille." My voice is strained with the need to touch and comfort her.

"I…I…" Her voice is choppy as she attempts to calm her breathing. "Are you okay?"

I press my forehead to hers, letting out a shaky breath. "I don't give a shit about me right now. Are *you* good? I'm sorry if I'm scaring you, and if that brought up bad memories for you, but that fucker deserved it. "

A thought appears in my mind, noting how easily my body went from blood-boiling anger to calm within seconds of being around her, but I don't let myself think too much about it.

Camille inhales deeply. "I'm not afraid of you, just of losing you. I didn't like seeing him hit you."

I'm about to respond, when Coach Warren's booming voice

interrupts, jolting us apart. "Lewis, get your ass on the bench. You'll be there for the rest of the game."

I knew it was coming, and I know it'll be the same punishment for dumbass, but I oddly find myself okay with the decision. The viewers will see that I was provoked first, so it's not a bad look on me and now I get to sit on the sidelines and make sure Camille's okay.

I call that a win-win if you ask me.

I plop down next to Camille on the bench as the game gets back underway, noting the way she's eyeing my bloodied knuckles. "They're fine," I assure her, flicking my gaze to hers.

"What happened?" she asks as she stands and heads to our cooler where the ice packs are.

I blow out a breath, lift my hat, and rake a hand through my hair. "He shoved me."

Camille sits down back beside me, a look of *that's bullshit* on her face as she brings the ice pack to my knuckles.

"It's nothing you need to hear," I murmur, wincing at the sting of the ice on my split open knuckles.

She seems to understand what I'm saying, her eyes on her hand that's keeping the ice pack on mine. "You don't need to defend my honor, especially not when your career is concerned."

"Fighting isn't against the law in baseball, so it happens. The Panthers know I'm hotheaded, and sometimes, agencies look for players like that. It draws in views and fans more than you'd imagine."

While that *is* true, they don't go looking for draft picks that have been arrested before for breaking someone's arm. Which is why I still need to figure out how to go about the whole issue with Travis, but that's a concern for another day.

Right now all I care about is Camille.

"And for the record, I'd defend you in any situation."

Camille's eyes dart up to mine, a whirl of appreciation in her silvery hues. "Thank you," she says softly. "And I'd do the same for you."

I chuckle, but it lacks humor. "Not needed, just make sure you get my good side in your videos," I tease, lightening the conversation.

"That's no problem when all sides are your good side." She winks, and the sight makes me want to take her back to the locker room and lose myself inside of her.

Our conversation from there on is easy, commenting on the game as we beat them 4-0. As the stadium begins to empty out, along with our dugout, I make sure to find Camille.

"Don't leave yet. Wait for me," I ask, brushing my fingers faintly against hers.

Camille nods, and I rush back to the locker room, hoping our post-game meeting goes quicker than normal. Because I need Camille like I need a ball in my glove.

And I'm not going to last until we get back to her place tonight.

Chapter Twenty-Six

Camille

Since I already edited all of the content I shot tonight and scheduled posts to go live for the next few days, I'm left alone with too much time to think as I wait for him, specifically about what happened tonight. Getting hit by the ball wasn't a big deal to me. It happens and I'm okay. I was just left with a nice bruise and a couple scratch marks.

What's running over and over in my mind is what happened when I was focused on Ryker running to come check on me. Were there cameras on me? Did my parents catch wind of it and are already on their way here?

Not to mention, the worry I felt when the fight broke between Ryker and that other player because the idea of anyone hurting him made me want to scream.

The anxiety in my stomach intensifies from all of it, so I text my brother Quentin and ask him to have his PI team look into things for me.

Needing to move my body and clear my mind, I make my way to the locker room. I already have access to the room, so no one will question why I'm in here and I don't want to be by myself with my worries.

I want Ryker by my side and the peace that settles over me whenever I'm with him.

The room's empty when I push through the doors, all of the dirty jerseys in the hampers, the smell making my nose twitch. Ryker's cubby is the only one with stuff in it, meaning he's alone. But where is he?

I'm about to turn around and look elsewhere when I hear the shower running. I quietly walk back toward the showers. "Ryker?" I call out from the archway that leads to the shower stalls.

"Cami?" he calls back.

I step into the shower area, and my eyes instantly find him in the second stall from the end, a billow of steam rising atop of it.

"What's wrong?" he asks.

"Nothing." I shake my head and force a smile. "I was bored waiting for you, that's all."

I know he wants to call bullshit, but for whatever reason, he doesn't.

Instead, he exits the shower with a towel wrapped around his waist, and my mouth waters at the sight of him. From his sinewy muscles, mixed with the droplets of water on his skin that I want to lick off, I'm debating doing something really bad in a place I shouldn't.

"You're so hot," I blurt out, my cheeks heating instantly. I wasn't supposed to say that out loud.

Ryker smirks as he saunters over to me. "Look who's talking." His eyes scorch my skin as they roam my body hungrily, but when they land on my jaw, his eyes harden and he grimaces. "Are you okay?"

"I'll be honest. It hurt when it happened. But I'm fine now, no pain." I shrug.

"You have no idea how badly I still want to kick his ass." He scowls.

I don't want him to get upset, nor do I want to be reminded of my worries, so I change the topic. "And you have no idea how badly I want to kiss you."

Ryker wastes no time and presses his lips gently to mine while holding me around my waist. Every brush of his lips against mine melts my worries away and everything around me begins to fade.

Before I get lost in it, I break away from him. "Ryker, we can't do this here."

"Everyone's gone home. I had to stay late to talk to Coach about what happened, and I know he won't come in here," he says, then drops his lips to my neck, eliciting a gasp from me. "Where's that rebellious girl at? Be bad for *me* this time."

Excitement shivers down my spine, making my toes curl in my sneakers. "Okay."

Ryker's deep blue eyes darken, and then he's lifting me up. I wrap my legs around his waist and pull him to me until our lips meet in a searing kiss as he walks us into the shower he was in. One of his hands lets go of my body and he turns the water back on.

I throw my head back as giggles overtake me, feeling so safe with this man. I shriek as my clothes begin to dampen. "Why are you turning the water on? I still have my clothes on."

"I need it to drown out how loud I'm going to make you scream." He smirks as his fingers tug the button and pull on the zipper of my shorts, yanking them down my legs.

I step out of them, along with my shoes, socks, and underwear, and set them on the bench where the spray of the water won't soak them more than they already are. My hands reach for the hem of my top, but Ryker stills them with his hand on mine.

"Let me," he rasps as he slowly peels my top off, leaving me in my white lacy bralette. His eyes darken as he looks me over and suddenly, he's ripping that off my body too, tossing it on the bench behind us.

"I want to come on your tits one day," Ryker hums, then latches his lips onto one of my nipples, sucking it into his mouth.

"Yes, please," I murmur as I lean my head against the tile, letting the water trickle down my body.

"I need to make you come on my tongue first, and then I'll be dying to slide into you, so I'll paint you in my cum another time."

"Mhm." I nod incoherently, lost in the pleasure of his lips on me while his hand trails down my stomach and finally right where I want him.

Ryker runs a single digit through my slit, and I jolt in response, my body attuned to his touch. His finger moves down toward my center, dipping inside the slightest bit. "More, Ryker." I pant as my body heats despite being under cool water.

He obliges, his finger sliding in deeper as his mouth continues to lavish my breasts. He adds another finger, filling me as he begins to pump them inside of me. My hips rock against his hand, chasing my orgasm.

While it feels good, the mention of me coming on his tongue has me hyper-fixated on doing just that.

"I need your tongue," I tell him, pulling on his wet strands to get his mouth off me.

Ryker licks his lips and kneels. He lifts my leg on his shoulder, presses soft kisses to my mound, and inhales deeply. "I love everything about your pussy, you know that? The way it smells and tastes. It's fucking perfect."

Then his tongue is on my clit, flicking and licking as his fingers continue to pump in and out of me. My knees buckle but he doesn't stop. If anything, he picks up his pace, flicking rapidly my clit with his tongue.

The sensation makes my entire body heat as a buzz begins

to unfurl in my stomach. I'm not quiet as moans escape my lips, my fingers digging into his scalp. Ryker's lips wrap around my clit and suck as his fingers curl inside of me, making me black out as an orgasm rips through me.

"Ryker!" I scream as waves of pleasure course throughout me.

"That's it, baby, give it to me," he rasps, lapping up everything I give him as my body settles from the intense orgasm.

I rest my head on the cool tile, taking a moment to breathe as he continues to lick my slit up and down.

"Do you have any idea how good you taste?" he asks, making me lift my head to look down at him. His beard is covered in my arousal, and the sight makes my pussy ache.

"No…" I trail, unsure where he's going with this.

"Want me to show you?"

"Yes," I answer without a doubt, willing to try anything with him.

Ryker's tongue returns to my pussy for a few strokes, then he stands and grips my chin. "Open up."

I do as he says and stick my tongue out, making him hum in approval. Ryker's mouth hovers above mine, and then he opens it, spitting my cum out of his mouth and into mine. With my mouth still open, my cum on my tongue, he licks the seam of my lips, spreading any remaining proof of my orgasm onto them.

"Taste yourself, princess, see how sweet you are."

I close my lips as I swallow, then lick them clean. That is the hottest thing I've ever experienced.

My thighs shake, and if he weren't holding me like this, I'd have buckled to the ground.

I grab his face in my hands and pull his lips to mine, kissing him fiercely. Ryker kisses me back just as hard, his tongue entering my mouth. He tastes like me and I find myself even more turned on over that fact. Our hands explore each other's bodies as our lips work together.

Reaching between us, I yank on his towel and throw it onto the wet tiles. My fist wraps around his cock, twisting and working his hard length, eliciting a rugged moan from his lips.

"Fuck me," I tell him as his lips descend on my neck, making my core heat up once

again.

"How?" he asks, and the question makes my stomach flip. Ryker always makes sure I have a say, and the small gesture makes me question how deep this has gotten for me.

I ignore it and turn my body around, then bend over, my hands on the wall. Ryker groans, and his hand cups my pussy, making me shiver. With his thigh wedged between mine, he nudges them farther apart as his fingers begin to play with my clit.

"You want to be fucked from behind like the naughty girl you are, is that it?" he rasps as the head of his cock replaces his fingers, the tip rubbing against my clit, making me gasp.

"Yes, and I want it hard. Be rough with me."

I trust Ryker more than anyone else in my life. I know he'd never actually hurt me.

He presses a sweet kiss on my shoulder, his words tickling my ear. "Whatever my princess wants, she gets."

Ryker grips my chin and turns my head back, pulling my lips up to his for a searing kiss as he fully thrusts inside me. I moan into the kiss, my hips moving in tandem with his as he slowly rocks in and out of me.

He lets go of my face, placing one hand on my hip, while the other fists in my hair. "You ready to take my cock how I want it?"

"Use me, take what you need."

Ryker grunts, the sound so masculine and rough that it makes my clit throb. He rocks out of me, leaving only the tip in, and I swear you could hear a pin drop from the anticipation of what's to follow.

With a pull of my hair, Ryker pushes inside of me, deep and hard. Shocks of pleasure erupt all over my body at how deep he is.

"Fuck," I moan, hands gripping the tile for dear life as he begins to use his hold on my hips to move me up and down his cock. Our bodies slap together under the spray of the water, the sound echoing off the walls.

"Cami, baby, this pussy, fuck," he moans low, his deep timbre adding fuel to the fire brewing in my core. "I wish you could see how perfectly you stretch around my cock. Prettiest damn thing I've ever seen."

My entire body shakes as his words skate over me, leaving me a convulsing mess as he continues to pound into me without pause. "I want to come on your cock," I whine, the pleasure too much yet not enough.

Ryker grips my hip, keeping his pace, and his other hand travels up my stomach, stopping at my breasts where he plays with my piercings. He knows they're sensitive and a guaranteed way to help make me come.

I bite down my lip to avoid screaming, only allowing moans and whimpers to escape as he builds me closer and closer to that peak. His lips blaze a path from my shoulder to my neck as he continues to fuck me, his hips rocking rapidly while his fingers toy with my nipple piercings.

I'm so close, my entire body is tight with the need for release.

"My naughty little thing, huh," he huffs. "Show me what a bad girl you are by coming on my cock."

His words set me off as my orgasm hits me, spreading an unworldly burst of pleasure throughout my body as I tighten around him.

"Fuck," he shouts, his thrusts increasing in speed as he chases his release.

"Ry, come for me," I tell him as I continue to ride out the aftershocks of my orgasm.

Ryker stills inside me, doing just that as he comes, grunting and whispering my name into my neck as I shake from the aftermath of my release.

He pulls back, the tip of his cock still inside of me. "I thought this was pretty before, but I was wrong. Seeing our cum on my cock as I slide it back inside of you is better," he husks, sliding his cock in and out of me slowly, prolonging our highs.

Once we've collected our bearings, he pulls out of me and I wince.

Ryker gently turns me in his arms, concern pooling in his eyes. "Hey, you okay? Did I hurt you?"

"I'm great," I tell him sincerely. "It's expected to be sore after that."

He kisses my forehead, making my heart beat twice as fast. "Let me clean you up," he murmurs, guiding me so that my hair is under the spray of the showerhead. I've never let someone do this for me, and it feels more intimate than what we agreed on.

But I don't have it in me to stop him either, so I remain quiet as he lathers his shampoo in my hair and rinses it out. I love the fact that I'll smell like him after. A peaceful silence surrounds us, our bodies taking the lead instead through gentle touches and caresses as he washes my body.

Home, safety, love, my mind screams at me while he takes the utmost care in drying me off, making sure no inch of skin has a single droplet on it.

I know, I whisper back to my brain.

I need to make sure he never knows, or this will all end sooner than I want it to.

I know I'm fooling myself, because either way, there will be an end to this, but I want him in any capacity for as long as I can have him. Which means my feelings need to stay locked up for now until it's time to part. Only then can those feelings break free while breaking me in the process.

Dans quoi est-ce que je me suis embarquée?

Chapter Twenty-Seven

Ryker

"What kind of popcorn do you want tonight? Cinnamon sugar, dill pickle, hot chili…" my mom lists off different flavors as she prepares for our weekly movie night.

During the baseball season, it becomes more like once every two weeks or so, but we do our best to make it work. We're all we've ever had. Well, until now, I guess, considering she's getting married soon.

I'll be standing as her man of honor, while Aurora will be the flower girl, with Nate as the best man. She and Paul want a small wedding consisting of immediate family and a few friends, which is why they're forgoing traditional bridal parties.

I can hardly wait, just ecstatic at the idea of someone else being able to hurt my mom and turn their backs on us.

Can you sense my sarcasm?

"Ryker." My mom raises her voice, taking me out of my head.

"Hot chili please. Do you need help?" I ask, getting off the couch and heading to the kitchen to help her regardless of her answer.

When I enter the open kitchen space, I find her setting spices and oils on the counter while the kernels start to pop on the wok.

Her brown eyes roll at the sight of me, but her lips are fighting a smile. "I don't need any help. Get out of here." She attempts to usher me away, but I remain planted.

"I'll watch the popcorn while you mix the dressing."

I never let my mom do anything alone and always try to help in any capacity I can.

"You played great last night. Your arm is looking stronger than ever," she comments while adding chili oil to a mixing bowl. She's never missed a home game, always in the stands cheering me on ever since I picked up a glove and a ball.

"Thanks, Mom. I feel great, probably the best season start for me to date."

She picks up some cayenne pepper and adds it into the bowl. As she mixes the spice and oil, she glances at me with a perched brow. "You seem lighter out there too."

The kernels are popping one after the other, filling the space between her comment and my response because I'm not sure what she's alluding to.

"Coach says I've put on ten pounds of muscle—"

"No, Bear." She chuckles, using the nickname she gave me as a child. "I mean, you look happier than I've ever seen you before. Is there something else or…someone perhaps?"

I shake the wok, ensuring all the kernels are being popped as I think of what to say. She's not wrong. This is the happiest I've been.

"Nope, just excited for the draft and to be done with school," I tell her as I transfer the popcorn into a large bowl. *And* being around the girl who radiates sunshine might be a plausible clause as well. But I'll never admit that out loud, for fear that it'll make whatever I'm feeling become real.

"I'm so proud of you. Draft or no draft, you're my greatest accomplishment."

I look away, blinking at the sudden swell of emotion her

words bring. Something must seriously be wrong with me. Now I'm tearing up at sentimental shit? She squeezes my shoulder, knowing what I'm not voicing. That I love her and clearly can't handle this conversation right now.

My mom remains quiet as she coats the popcorn in her infamous hot chili seasoning. I grab us sodas from the fridge while she takes the popcorn to the couch. We pull up her favorite streaming service since it's her night to pick the movie.

"Pick our poison," I say as I flick through the options on the screen.

My mom throws popcorn at my head for that. "You love Disney movies. Don't be smart with me."

"Yes, Mama." I chuckle, eating the popcorn that fell on my chest.

She settles on *Monsters, Inc.*, and as the film plays, we find a rhythm where we talk for spurts or remain quiet as we focus on the movie.

Moments like these are my favorites. I love spending time with her, more so now because I know once I get drafted and she gets married, I won't be able to see her as often.

So I cherish these moments, just her and me.

But about halfway through the movie, Aurora knocks on the door to pick up allergy meds for her dog, Pickles. I thought it was about to be a quick stop, but she and my mom haven't stopped talking in the doorway. Aurora fills her in on how playing for Team USA is going and that she's visiting for the weekend since it's Cameron's cousin Finn's birthday.

I didn't mind the interruption until my mom gets a call from her work and tells Aurora to come on in to talk to me. Aurora walks into the living room, a bright smile on her face.

"Hey, Ryker, how's it going?" she asks, sitting on the couch a seat over from mine.

"Good. You?"

Her demeanor deflates at my clipped response, blowing out a breath. "What did I do to make you hate me?" she asks, throwing me off.

I know she has a knack for saying what's on her mind, but I wasn't expecting her to say that at all.

I sit up now, putting the bowl of popcorn on the coffee table in front of us. "Aurora, I don't hate you." I look her in the eyes, hoping she can see the honesty in mine.

"Then why can't you talk to me like a normal person? Hell, we're about to be brother and sister, but you treat me like I'm an inconvenience."

"I'm sorry. I tend to be an asshole," I admit.

Her lips quirk at that. "You got that right, but it's not all you are. I only learned one piece of a puzzle. I'd like to get to know the others."

The ones I keep hidden beneath that defense mechanism, she means. The ones I've begun to show Camille.

"Why?"

Aurora leans over, scooping some popcorn into her mouth before she speaks again. "Wow, this is good." She sighs. "Why what?"

Slightly irritated, I repeat my question. "Why do you want to get to know me?"

"Because we're going to be a family, Ryker. Whether you like it or not, it's happening." She pauses, her hazel eyes softening. "You know, it was hard for me too to accept my dad dating your mom at first."

My eyebrow arches at that, intrigued. "How come?"

"You're aware that my mom isn't here anymore, and I was worried that my dad was trying to replace her. Force me to call someone else *'Mom'* and move on. But that wasn't the case at all, and I love your mom. She's the sweetest person and I'm happy they found each other." She smiles, and something inside me loosens hearing how much she adores my mom.

"Yeah, your dad makes her happy too. I've never seen her like this before," I comment, thinking about how she started singing in the shower after they met, something she hadn't done since my dad left her.

"Our parents deserve to be happy, Ryker. I think we sometimes forget that this is their first time living too, you know?"

I never thought of it that way, that our parents are experiencing this thing we call life one day at a time just like us. It doesn't erase the fear and the reason why I'm not exactly thrilled about this marriage.

"They do, but I'm scared." The words fall out of my mouth before I can catch them, and I can't take them back. I don't know what it is about Aurora, but I find myself wanting to vent to her.

Aurora's face contorts into confusion for a beat, then softens as if she gets it. "It's okay to be scared. It means you have something you care about. Be grateful it's there to be cared for."

"What if I don't want more things to care about? Adding more people into my life who can leave sounds like setting myself up for pain," I scoff, raking my fingers through my hair, hating how vulnerable I sound.

It's like that kid who's hurting over his dad is still there deep down, protecting present me from experiencing that shit again. I wish I could tell him to scram. It'd make shit a lot easier, but it's also gotten me to where I am today.

Her cautious voice pulls my focus back to her. "You know there's a chance every time you step on that baseball field, it could be your last. All it takes is the right injury, and poof, everything's gone." She snaps her fingers for the full effect.

"That chance is always there. The same applies to relationships in all forms: family, friends, and lovers. The risk of losing them will always be there, but it's a heck of a lot more fun to enjoy whatever it is you have with them while you can, instead of isolating yourself in fear."

Sadly, she's not wrong. Thinking I can live a pain-free life is a delusional way of living. I simply don't want to increase my odds of getting hurt. While I know what she's saying is true, it'll take some time for me to accept it. It's not to say I'll make a total one-eighty degree change, but I could start by offering her the friendship she's been seeking from me.

My lips lift to the right in a smirk. "When did you get so wise?"

"Therapy."

We both chuckle at that, but I cut it short. "I'm sorry for being distant when all you've been is kind."

"Would we be true siblings if we got along at all times?" she teases, eating another handful of popcorn.

I smile at that, which causes her to perk up. "I don't have any siblings, at least that I know of, but I'd like to be yours and Nate's." I extend the olive branch, feeling like I might pass out.

"Of course. You already are." She smiles, then asks, "Have you talked to your dad at all?"

"No." My answer is curt. Knowing it's not the way I want to keep doing things, I explain, "Neither my mom nor I have heard from or seen him since the day he left when I was twelve. We could look him up online, but what's the point? He doesn't give a fuck about me, and the feeling is mutual."

She places her hand on mine, giving it a quick squeeze before removing it. "I'm so sorry, Ryker. I'm grateful you get to be a part of my family, and even if there's a day we're legally not, you'll *always* be my brother."

"All right, enough with the emotional stuff. I can't take it." I look up at the ceiling, blinking away the emotions coming to the surface.

Before I know what's happening, Aurora's hugging me, and fuck, I can't hold it in anymore. Tears leak down my cheeks as I let out years of emotions onto her shoulder. When you bottle shit up, it'll make you break when you least expect it.

All that fear and pain slowly drift away as I let it out. Aurora doesn't say anything, rubbing my back in a comforting way. It feels good to be chosen for once. It may not be by my own blood, but somehow that makes it better, knowing they don't have to but are anyways.

Once I've calmed down, I pull away from her, feeling slightly embarrassed as I wipe at my cheeks.

"It's okay to cry. You can still be a badass who drives a motorcycle and has tattoos." She grins, then pulls the bowl of popcorn on her lap. "I'm finishing this. I hope that's okay."

"Thank you, Ro, I appreciate it." I smile, then slide over to grab the bowl of popcorn. "I'll take this back, though. Get your own popcorn."

"See, you got this brother thing down pat already."

Chapter Twenty-Eight

Camille

I think I might pass out.

After my rendezvous with Ryker in the showers the other night and again in my bed later on, I momentarily forgot what I was worried about when I went looking for him in the change room.

Until Quentin texted me this morning.

Quentin

I'm flying in today. Will be at your place at 9 am.

Seeing that after having his detective look into the repercussions of my getting hit in the face at the game last night has me on edge. Quentin's in the middle of his own baseball season, so if he's flying here, it can't be good.

Putain, je suis foutue.

It looks like I'll be missing classes today, so I pull up my text thread with Jasmine and send her a text.

It's not a total lie. Quentin is visiting. But am I okay? I guess only time will tell.

I glance at the time, seeing I have about two hours until he gets here. To pass the time, I do my best to reduce the anxiety brewing in my stomach. I meditate, shower, eat, and even watch some gardening videos, but nothing seems to help.

A knock at my door has me bolting off the couch, my phone falling to the ground as I race to look into the peephole. I breathe a sigh of relief when I see it's Quentin.

I slide the lock and let him in, doing my best to smile when I see him. "Aren't you supposed to be playing a game with a bat and a ball?" I attempt for some humor, but he ignores me.

"Let's sit," he says, gesturing toward the couch.

That makes my nerves triple. I was being a tad dramatic earlier, but now I might actually puke. "Q, what's going on? You're scaring me. What did he find?" I ask frantically, twisting my fingers as I sit.

Quentin's hazel eyes look so apologetic, and that alone scares me. "The video went viral," he informs me, making my eyes bug out of my head. I don't go on social media during the weekend. Besides, the only account I have is the team's.

"*Ugh, tu te fous de moi*," I whisper, putting my head in my hands. "How bad is it?"

"You can't see your face that clearly with the hat you were wearing, and the dyed hair helps. But those only keep the unknown eyes away."

I inhale sharply. "What does that mean?"

"My PI guy did some investigating, and he was able to find out that Mom and Dad know. They know you're here."

Time stands still, everything frozen as my world changes. Just like that.

When I blink, it's as if it's a different place entirely. "How sure is he?"

Quentin removes his ball cap, running a hand through his hair that's longer than it was before. "He was able to hack into their PI's computer. He had the video, but that's it."

My breaths begin to come in quicker, my skin turning icy as I struggle to breathe.

"Hey, *regarde-moi, Camille*," he says calmly, holding my face between his palms, forcing me to stare into his hazel eyes. "You're going to be okay. I swear it. They have no plans of coming here. My guy would see it. And if he ever does see that, we'll handle it. Together."

I nod frantically while tears spill down my cheeks. "O-okay." My voice shakes. "What now?"

He sighs at that, and I already know I'm not going to like the answer. "No more baseball games for you. You need to lie low and stay out of public as much as possible. School's wrapping up this week thankfully—"

"No," I cut him off, finding my voice, surprising him and myself. While I'm still scared at what's to potentially come, I refuse to bend to their will anymore. "I'm not hiding. If they want to come here, let them. They can't physically force me back home."

Quentin smirks. Then I remember my brother knows me better than anyone. He knew I'd freak out at first, and by telling me what would happen if I clung to that fear, *hiding*, he knew I'd come to my senses.

Smart play, brother, smart play.

"There she is. Now, you do need to be careful. I wasn't kidding. Stay off of any videos and don't end up on social media again. Be aware when you go out, in fact, I should get a bodyguard—"

"Not happening. I came here to escape that. I'll stick to my friends and won't go out alone, ever. I promise."

Don't get me wrong, fear is coursing through my veins at the news, and my world *is* different now, but I'm choosing to find a way to live with it. I have to. It's the only way.

I could hide and sit here, scared, waiting for the day they choose to come here. Or I could do it my way. I'll still live my life, but I'll be more aware and strategic going forward.

"Good," he says as he lies back on the couch. "You should move in with me, though. We're constantly on the road for baseball right now. They'd never know where you are."

"Going to you is the first thing they'll do if they don't find me here. Sorry, but no. I'm not dragging you into this," I retort as my body begins to itch with the need for someone I know it shouldn't.

Ryker. He makes me feel safe, and I'm craving that now more than ever.

"Always so stubborn," he chides, shaking his head. "I'm not giving you a bodyguard, but I am going to be having one of my PIs stick around. They'll start tomorrow to keep an eye on things from a distance, *d'accord?*"

I want to argue, but I know it's for the best. If they're sending out someone not meant to be noticed by me, it's a good idea if I have someone looking out for the things I can't see.

"Fine. When are you leaving? Don't you have a game in New York tonight?" I ask, needing him to leave so I can see Ryker.

Quentin splays a hand over his chest. "Ouch, baby sis. Trying to get rid of me so soon?"

I roll my eyes as a smile tugs at my lips. "Yes, I have things to do. I miss you, but I also need you to leave."

"I know, I was teasing you. I do need to get going. I'm probably going to pay a fine for being late, but I don't give a shit. I needed to come see you, and if you ever need me, I'll be here as quickly as possible. It's you and me, baby sis, till the end."

Q pulls me into a hug, making me instantly feel better. He's the reason I got out, and I'll forever be grateful for the gift he's given me.

"What about the girl you're seeing?" I tease as I pull back.

His face scrunches in confusion. "What are you talking about?"

"The cheerleader? I see the way you look over at her when the camera pans to you."

"You have to swear to keep your mouth shut." His voice is stern, devoid of joking.

"I promise."

"I didn't know she was a part of the dancing team. We hooked up before the season started, a one—"

"Skip those details, please." I grimace.

"Anyways, when the season started, not only did I realize she works for the organization, which means she's off-limits, but that she's also the little sister of that one teammate I can't stand. So nothing's going on between us, as much as I wish it would."

"No!" I squeal, all too excited about this. "You did not sleep with your enemy's little sister! This is *so* juicy. You clearly still want her, and I'm sure she wants you but is too scared."

"Are you done making my life sound like a novel?" he huffs in annoyance.

"No. Maybe it'll be like the one book Jasmine was telling me about—a surprise pregnancy that induces forced proximity, then love. Or a marriage of convenience somehow..." I trail off, thinking of all the fun ways this could play out for him.

His face pales, devoid of the sun-kissed hue that normally exists. "Not a chance. I'd like to say this was fun, but it wasn't. Remember what we talked about. I need to get going. Bye, baby sis, love you."

"Thank you, Q, love you too."

Once he's gone, I run back to my room and retrieve my phone off the floor, needing to escape for the day before I know someone's always watching me.

Me

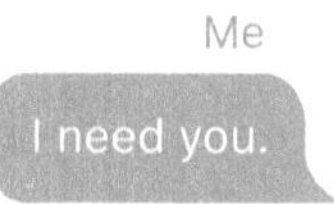

Instead of a text back, he calls.

"Hi." My voice is quiet.

"Princess, what's wrong?" His deep timbre wraps around me, making me feel safer already.

"I want to go somewhere far from here for the day."

"I'll be there within the hour to get you. Don't wear a dress. We're taking my bike," he complies, no questions asked.

I try not to overthink that small tidbit but fail. Part of me believes he likes me, more than he intended to because he's much kinder and caring toward me than anyone else. Who else would drop their plans for the day in a second because I said I needed them?

Chapter Twenty-Nine

Ryker

I'm ditching classes today, which is a first for me. All because Camille said she needed me, and when paired with the desperation in her voice, it was a no-brainer.

I opted for joggers and a black T-shirt, forgoing my leather jacket since it was a rather warm day. On the drive over to her place, I plan out our day to make sure it includes things I know would make her happy.

A first for me too.

I'm taking Aurora's advice and appreciating what we have before our time's up. I still can't offer Camille more than this, not when I have my career to figure out in the next few months, but I'll enjoy all the time we have together to the fullest.

I send her a text to let her know I'm waiting outside, and minutes later, she comes out the lobby doors, a wide smile on her face as she waves to the doorman.

My eyes trail up and down her body as she approaches me, making me tighten my grip on the handlebar. She's wearing those ripped jeans I love so much, the ones her ass looks phenomenal in, with a Beatles graphic tee and our school's ball cap on her head.

When she's close enough, I lift off the bike and pull her into me, kissing her hard.

Camille falls right into it, her hands resting around my neck as I palm her ass with both hands.

"Hi," she says once we part, silvery eyes sparkling.

"Hi, you ready to get out of here?"

"That's kind of my thing, running away. So yes, more than ready." Camille giggles at herself, making me smirk as I shake my head.

She's too fucking cute.

I help her with the helmet, making sure it's secure and safe. Once I'm seated on the bike, I hold out my hand for her to get on, and she takes it as she lifts her leg and straddles the back of the bike with ease.

This time, she scoots closer of her own accord, her front nestled to my back as her arms wrap tightly around me.

"Hold on, princess," I yell over the rev of the engine.

"Always," she yells back.

We pull up to my mom's house, a small cottage-style home. It's all my mom and I ever needed, enough space for the two of us and a backyard I could practice throwing a baseball in. I'm going to miss this place once she moves in with Paul, Aurora's dad.

She bought it after my dad left because she wanted to start our lives anew, and that meant a new house. One she loved, unlike our previous one that she had no say in. My dad was a dictator, always wanting things to go his way, never meeting my mom halfway.

We made a lot of memories in this house, and I'm grateful he's never tainted the walls with his harsh remarks.

I kill the engine and we dismount, removing our helmets.

Camille's brows pinch, looking at the house in curiosity. "Where are we?"

"This is my house." I guide her toward the steps and unlock the front door.

"Wait." She stops. "Am I meeting your mom? I would've worn something more presentable."

I pull her toward me and slide my hand up her waist, stopping with my fingers under her chin. "She's not home, but even if she were, you look amazing. You always do."

"Thank you," she whispers.

I lean forward, pressing my lips to her forehead, then pull away with her hand in mine as I lead her toward the backyard.

"What are we doing here? I thought we were escaping?"

"We will, but there's something I thought you might like to do first," I say, surprised at the nerves ratcheting inside me. I stop once we're in front of a bed of dirt, with various packets of flower seeds beside it.

Camille stills, her eyes bouncing from the flower bed to the unplanted seeds. "Ryker, what is this?" She chokes on the end of her words.

I wrap my arms around her from behind, resting my chin on the top of her head. "It's your own garden. You mentioned missing gardening, so I thought this would make you feel better today."

Her body vibrates underneath mine, and I worry I did something wrong as she turns in my arms with tears strolling down her cheeks. "This is the sweetest thing anyone has ever done for me."

"Better than your brother breaking you out of your own country?" I joke, trying to make her smile while I wipe away her tears.

It works and fuck, the rush of joy I get from seeing it should be bottled up and sold as a top tier drug.

"Yes, this is amazing. But you seriously want me to garden

here?" she asks, looking for the reassurance I'm more than willing to give.

"I wouldn't have brought you here if I didn't mean it. My mom is too busy to get one started and I know she'd love it. You're more than welcome to come over and take care of it whenever you want."

"Okay." She sniffles. "What are you going to do for the next hour or so, though?"

I shrug, pulling away from her. "I'll probably get some sketches done for clients, maybe start studying for finals. Don't rush, take your time. Once you're done, we'll escape somewhere else."

Camille's eyes bounce around my face, her pillowy lips parting into that smile that makes me smile in return.

"Thank you for this, for knowing exactly what I needed."

I tuck a loose strand of hair behind her ear, my thumb grazing her jaw gently. "No problem. Now, go get started so we can get out of here. Our day isn't over yet."

Camille squeals, wraps her arms around me, then darts off to the dirt and sink her knees in the grass as she gets started.

I find myself staring in admiration for too long and shake my head as I retrieve my iPad to do some work. Grabbing the nearest lounger, I plop down in it and attempt to work on the sketch for a dainty birth flower tattoo.

More often than not, I find myself distracted by the pretty girl in my backyard, on her hands and knees as she gardens.

As much as my mind wants to trail off in *that* direction, I don't. While I think fucking her in my room all day would make her smile, she wants to escape, and I have the perfect place to do just that.

Lottie's Place.

Chapter Thirty

Camille

I love this man.

I know I shouldn't love him. But I do. How can I not after he brought me to his house to garden because I mentioned *one* time how I missed it?

Unraveling the softer parts of Ryker has been one of the greatest adventures I've been on, one I never want to end. Just like this day, it's been absolutely perfect so far.

After I finished up in the garden, we had brunch. I taught Ryker how to make crêpes, my favorite, and topped them off with strawberries and a drizzle of chocolate sauce. We made a huge mess, but we laughed a lot as Ryker followed my instructions, yet his crêpe still fell apart miserably when he tried to flip it. But that didn't matter to me. What mattered was that he was trying and doing something new for me.

Once we cleaned up, he threw a couple of snacks in his backpack along with two water jugs, and then we were on the road to the unknown.

Thirty minutes or so go by, and I still have no clue where we're going. Truthfully, in all my time here, I haven't gone too far out of the city limits. Until today, it looks like. Pine trees pass by in a blur of differing shades of green and brown as we cruise along a back road. I can see the mountains more clearly, their jagged edges more pronounced and beautiful this close.

It's quiet this far out, the only sound being the bike's engine and the few cars we've passed. I like the solitude of it, something I didn't have much of growing up.

Eventually, we pull into a nearly empty red-dirt lot that's caged in with a haywire fence, with the words *Lottie's Place* hanging up high on a post.

"What is this place?" I ask Ryker as I fluff out my hair after removing my helmet.

He takes it from me and stores it underneath my seat. "You'll see, c'mon." He looks giddy as he takes my hand, and that alone makes me more excited.

There's a cabin made out of logs with the words *Lottie's Place* in purple on a banner hanging over the door, with two rocking chairs on the wraparound porch and a golden retriever eagerly waiting for us.

As soon as our feet hit the steps, the dog jumps up, its tail wagging rapidly back and forth. "Hi there, sweet…boy," I confirm, giving him cuddles. I look for his name on his collar and burst out into laughter when I do.

"What is it?" Ryker asks.

"Sebastian."

"Maybe his owners also realize *The Little Mermaid* is a great film." He smirks, giving the dog head scratches.

"I see you've met, Bash," an older man croaks, causing us both to stand upright.

"He's adorable." I swoon as Bash licks my hand.

"That he is, and a damn good dog too. Even gets me a beer when I ask him to." The man chuckles, making both of us laugh.

"I'm assuming y'all are here to take the gondola up to the see the field?"

Field?

"Yes," Ryker interjects quickly. "She's never been, and I wanted to surprise her."

The older man's eyes crinkle, a knowing look in his eyes. "Say no more. I've been there. Why do you think I built this place? My wife wanted a place to look at the stars surrounded by her favorite flowers. God bless her soul, she left me last June."

And now I'm going to cry. "I'm so sorry," I offer my condolences.

"Thank you." He coughs. "Lottie was everything and still is. She's here with me, in the flowers and stars. And, of course, in our kids. But anyways, you two go have fun. This ride's on me."

"No, I—" Ryker attempts to protest, but the owner stops him.

"Don't worry about it, son, go on up there and just be. Enjoy it and each other's presence."

We both thank him and proceed toward the gondola lift, my heart heavier yet lighter with each step. That old man just made my heart break and mended it back together in two seconds. He deserves all the best in life.

As we make our way to the top of the mountain, we're both quiet and take in the stunning scenery around us. There's a silent buzz brewing between us in the cabin, the same one I feel in my stomach every time I'm with him.

Ryker slides up next to me, his pinky interlocking with mine. I exhale deeply at the comfort of the contact, and he inhales sharply.

The top of the mountain becomes visible, and the sight before me steals the breath out of my lungs.

It's a field of lavender.

Nothing feels real as Ryker ushers me off the gondola with a hand on my lower back. My eyes flit around the expansive field, full of differing shades of purple, all surrounded by a metal fence. There's a rocking bench made out of wood, wrapped in fairy lights that I imagine would look breathtaking at night.

I turn on the spot, taking in the view from being this high up. I can see a mass of green trees in the distance, as well as other mountains. It's like the city is gone, the only thing around us being nature.

It's beautiful and perfect.

Taking a step forward, I bend down and run my hands through the flowers, feeling a sense of contentment wash over me like never before.

"Wow," Ryker breathes, taking in our surroundings.

"It's stunning. I can't believe this is real," I murmur, sitting on the grass, careful not to sit on any flowers.

"I know," he says, looking right at me.

My heart swells, overcome with the love I feel for him. Staring into his eyes causes my chest to fill with warmth, while my mind whirls at the fact that he exists, and I get to be in his orbit by some lucky chance.

"Come here," I tell him, my voice hazy and filled with a desire so strong that I might burn this field down if he doesn't give me what I need, which is his body next to mine.

Ryker sits alongside me, pulling me in between his legs, my back to his front as we look out at the field in front of us.

"Thank you so much for this, for today. You were there for me with no questions asked. I appreciate you for it," I tell him, stroking the hair on his forearms.

"You're welcome." He kisses the top of my head. "But if you want to talk about it, I'm here to listen."

I debate it in my head, quickly deciding that it's best if he knows what's going on. My voice threatens to shake, but I maintain my composure. If Ryker knows I'm scared, he'll be on guard more than he already is. "The clip of me getting hit by that ball went viral, and my parents saw it. They know I'm here."

His hold on me tightens. "What? How do you know?"

"Quentin has a PI on his payroll, and they hacked my parents' PI guy…yeah, it's shady work, I know," I joke. "But yeah, they found the video on their laptop. Meaning my parents have seen it."

He's silent for a beat as a light breeze washes over us, wafting the scent of lavender.

"So what happens now?" he asks carefully.

I shrug in his arms, looking out into the differing lavenders planted amongst the grass. "Nothing really, not until we know what they plan to do with that information. My brother's team is on high alert now, watching my parents' every move. I won't know anything until they see movement, like travel plans to come here or something."

Ryker releases a harsh breath against my neck, nuzzling his nose against it. "What about you? Are you safe?"

"Nothing's any different. Quentin's social media team made sure nothing came up about connecting me as the long-lost princess of Lorsica, so we're good there. He also hired a bodyguard of sorts to tail me discreetly, to look for things I don't know how to be aware of," I explain, those feelings of fear beginning to trickle in at how serious this could get.

"I don't like this, Cami," he grumbles. "What if your parents come here? What then?"

I shrug once more because I have no idea. "Pretend I have amnesia. Forgot who they are. Move to Canada. Ask them to leave," I deadpan, throwing out ridiculous solutions.

"No, we need an actual plan." He shakes his head on my shoulder.

We?

I like the sound of that.

"Can we brainstorm later? I wanted to escape it for today," I remind him, not wanting the talk of all of this to ruin my perfect day with him.

"Okay." He kisses my head once more. "Tell me something."

"I'm wearing black lace panties."

Ryker groans, a pained laugh leaving him. "Jesus Christ, Cami."

I feel him harden against my ass.

"You're hard from that?" I say, astonished.

"Baby, I can get hard from watching you breathe. Knowing you're real and mine is all it takes to get me going." He grins, his deep blue eyes swimming with something I don't dare to name.

I adjust my body, turning to throw my legs over his hips. I straddle him as he leans back on his arms. My fingers thread in his long hair and pull his face toward me as our lips meet in a soft, sweet kiss.

Our lips move together in perfect harmony, memorizing each other as we kiss slowly, longingly. It feels like appreciation for one another, mixed with desire and something deeper than we care to admit.

Our hips start to grind together, seeking friction to ease the fire that's blazing between us now. The kiss turns heated, our tongues seeking and taking, teeth biting and pulling as moans fill the air between us.

Before I know it, I'm on my back in a field of lavender as Ryker peels off my jeans and panties and slides into me with something other than just lust in his gaze. Our bodies move together sensually. It's slow and gentle, and our eyes stay locked on one another's the whole time.

My arms wrap around his neck, while he leans on one forearm with his other hand framing my cheek with gentle swipes. It's bliss and ecstasy wrapped into one fluid motion that I never want to end.

"Ryker," I breathe.

"Camille." He sighs, resting his forehead on mine as he continues to rock in and out of me.

"I feel complete like this," I whisper, staring into his deep blue eyes.

"Me too," he groans, sounding pained.

"What's wrong?" I frown.

"I don't want this to end. This moment, it's perfect. But my cock fucking aches to come." He chuckles at the end.

I giggle at that and press my lips to his. "It's okay. All good things pause, then resume once again."

"Isn't the saying *all good things must come to an end?*" He stills inside of me.

I shake my head. "Nope. I like this better because then no good things have to end. Instead, they pause, and then happen again."

"I like that." He grins, kissing me once more as he pulses inside of me. "You gonna come for me too, princess?"

"Yes," I moan as he hits that spot inside of me, the one that makes me dizzy with pleasure.

"That's my naughty little thing," he grunts, putting his hand between our bodies as he moves to rub my clit just the way I like.

"Only yours," I cry as a wave of pleasure crashes over me. His name leaves my lips in whispered pleas as my orgasm washes over me, taking over all my senses.

"Fuck, Cami," he moans into my neck, stilling as he finds his release.

We lie like that for a few moments, my hands running up and down his back as he presses kisses all over my neck and face. Once he pulls out, he uses my panties to clean me up, then helps me get dressed. After we're fully clothed and cleaned the best we can be in the middle of a field, we relax into one another once more, staring out at the clear blue sky.

"You asked me to tell you something." I clear my throat.

"Mhm," he hums peacefully.

"My life was meant to come straight out of a fairytale, but today's the first time it's ever felt like one."

Ryker crushes me against him, nuzzling his face against mine.

"If I believed in fairytales, you'd be in mine," he whispers.

In the silence that follows his confession, I can hear the faintest crack of my heart, the first fissure from the man I know is going to obliterate it beyond repair.

Chapter Thirty-One

Camille

One full week of this bodyguard-slash-private investigator tailing me from afar, and I'm already annoyed. It's reminiscent of the life I lived back in Lorsica, where I was constantly flanked and guarded. I understand why it's needed, yet I hate it all the same.

I don't see or hear from him, but knowing he's there makes me feel uneasy, even though the point is to make me feel at ease. At the same time, I prefer this than a life back at home without any freedom at all.

The gym is the one place I'm left alone after I told my brother that his guy is not to follow me in here. He grumbled about it but agreed, giving me what I wanted.

I take all my frustration out on the bag, throwing punch after punch until I'm dripping in sweat. Throwing a left hook, I huff in exasperation as anxious thoughts creep in and nestle themselves in my head.

What if my parents come here?
Another hook.
What will I do post-grad?

Another hook, followed by another as my frustrations boil.

I want Ryker to keep me forever despite knowing it's not what he wants.

My fists fly rapidly as I let it all out, my arms burning as I continue to hit the bag, tears spilling down my cheeks. I don't stop and keep going as all the emotions that have been like an undercurrent, threatening to pull me under, take over. I get rid of them, one hit at a time.

I'm not sure how long I'm doing it for until a hand rests on the small of my back. I jolt around and nearly punch Travis in the process. I stop mid-throw, my gloved hand mere inches from his jaw.

"Travis, what are you doing?" I breathe heavily, stepping back as I attempt to catch my breath. I didn't think there would be anyone here, seeing as it's ten o'clock at night.

"I came in for an extra cardio session even though running on the treadmill isn't my favorite kind of exercise, if you know what I mean." He chuckles as if I'm his friend who would dab him up after that joke.

I'm kind when we interact because of my position within the team, but we are not friends. Not even close. After the way he cornered me at Theo's party, I tend to steer clear of him when I can.

"Yeah," is all I say, unwrapping my gloves and dropping them to the floor.

"You okay?" Travis asks, taking a step toward me. "You seemed to be giving that bag a beating."

"Just getting a good workout in." I muster the best smile I can while I crouch down to collect my things and get out of here.

"I can tell you do it a lot. You look amazing," he drawls.

He's giving me an eerie feeling, the same one I felt *that* night in my hometown.

I glance up at the mirror and see his eyes glued to my ass as I throw my water bottle in my bag. It raises alarm bells in my head, my heartbeat ratcheting up as I quickly stand and walk away from him.

"Where are you going?" he calls after me, jogging to keep up as he walks with me out into the hallway toward the change rooms.

I ignore him, hoping he'll get the hint.

He doesn't.

Travis grips my bicep, holding me still. "Not so fast. We need to talk."

"About what?" I attempt to pull my arm free and fail. "Let go of me, *now*." I seethe, my voice firm and strong, much to my surprise since I'm scared as hell right now.

Travis clucks his tongue, a menacing laugh leaving his lips as he removes his hand. "I mean no harm. That is, unless you fail to give me what I want." He steps into my space, trailing a finger down my cheek.

I move my face out of his reach as adrenaline courses through me. Does he know my secret? "What do you want?" I hold my composure steady, despite wanting to crumble apart.

"What I want is simple. It's you, Camille." He smirks, holding up a finger. "Now, before you protest, I want you to watch this."

Travis pulls out his phone, tapping a few times before turning it toward me.

My stomach hollows once I see it, knowing exactly what this is. It's a video of Ryker and me in the locker room showers, a video of us having sex.

"Where did you get this?" My voice is tight with unshed tears.

I want to throw up, but I push it down as he shoves his phone back in his pocket.

"I happened to forget my necklace in my locker after the game, so I went back to get it, when I heard odd sounds coming from the shower. And you know how the rest goes.

"To top it off," he continues. "I have a secret about your

boyfriend, and I'll expose that along with this video if you don't cooperate."

"What are you talking about?"

A secret? I briefly wonder if he's bluffing, but then again how would I know? If it truly is a secret Ryker hasn't shared with me, then I have no idea whether he's telling the truth or not.

"Ryker was arrested for assault. He broke my friend's arm and ruined his baseball career. If you don't believe me, ask him. Or maybe he won't tell you, considering it doesn't look good on him if his little secret gets exposed just in time for the draft." He smirks, loving every minute of this power he currently holds.

Too bad he doesn't realize the power I have, and the connections *I* possess. While knowing he watched us makes me sick to my stomach and pissed the hell off, I can salvage this situation.

I'll have my brother's guy wipe Travis's entire phone and computer clean, eliminating any evidence he has of that video. As for Ryker's secret, that's something I don't know if I can protect.

I roll my eyes, attempting to walk away from him. "I don't do blackmail."

He grips my arm again, harder this time as he pulls me back, right to his chest.

"A sex tape won't bode well for his career, nor yours, sweetheart. I'd think twice about this." He swallows. "All you have to do is leave with me right now, or hell, we can do this right in the change room. I don't care. I'll fuck you better than he can, believe me."

That's it. I've had enough.

Using the adrenaline to my advantage, along with my training in self-defense, I shove my knee up hard, right into his groin. Travis keels over like I knew he would, so I use the angle to jab him right in the throat while giving him another swift kick in the groin.

He falls to the ground, crying out in pain, and I run away. I hear him call me names, but I don't stop until I'm outside, where I crouch over with my hands on my knees as I try to catch my breath.

It only takes a few seconds for the PI to be by my side. Despite not having seen him at all, I know it's him. "Camille, what happened? Are you okay?" the man asks, his voice deep and familiar.

I take him in before I respond, noticing the scar running through his eyebrow. I know exactly who he is.

Idris.

I should've known my brother would assign him to me. Idris was the top of our security at the palace. In his late fifties now, he looked out for us more times than I can count growing up. He'd been more of a father to us than our own, often taking us to our trainings, helping with homework, and even playing games with us when he could.

He left the palace when Quentin did, claiming he wanted to spend more time with family. The knowledge now that he meant Quentin makes me want to sob.

"We need to go," I tell him, worried Travis will come after me and cause a scene. "I'll tell you in the car."

Idris follows me to my car, his eyes alert as we do. I wait for him to check the car out, ensuring nothing's been tampered with before we get in. Once we're settled with Idris in the driver's seat as we drive back to my place, I tell him everything that occurred.

He pinches the bridge of his nose once I finish. "Camille."

"What? I defended myself, and I'm fine, okay? I didn't need someone to save me for once and that felt good. Really freaking good." I smile to myself as tears pool in my eyes. For so long, I've feared not being able to handle myself, and proving that I can protect myself makes me feel lighter than before.

It's healing a part of me that hadn't felt settled ever since the night of my graduation party. I'm not magically healed or anything, but it's reassuring to know that not only do I have people to look out for me, I have myself too.

Something I feared I'd never get back.

"That's good. I'm glad you were able to defend yourself, but I'm talking about the bigger issue here."

Oh right. The sex tape. Realizing I told this to a man I look up to as a father figure makes me want to crawl in a hole and hide.

"Can't we have your team hack into his electronics to delete it?"

"We can, but we don't know if he has a copy stored on a hard drive."

Fuck, I didn't think of that.

Nerves creep back in, eating at my fleeting proud moment. "So what do we do?" I ask.

"I'm going to call the team, get them started on hacking him immediately. Then we're going to have to go to his house, search the whole place to ensure there are no copies."

I nod along, hoping Travis isn't smart enough to have stored multiple copies. Although unlikely, it's not impossible. He's proving to be worse than I thought.

Then there's Ryker.

My chest aches when I think about telling him what happened tonight. He's going to be livid about the fact that Travis touched me, let alone the blackmail he's threatening us with. I want to call him, but Idris prevents me from doing so as he wants the video gone before Ryker does anything to set Travis off even more.

And knowing Ryker like I do, he'll want to destroy Travis.

Hours later, Idris and I sigh in unison on my couch once his team confirms that all traces of the video are gone. They were even able to see from the original video how many times it was copied, which told us we were in the clear once they deleted the evidence on his phone and the two copies he had on his laptop. After that, they did a sweep of his dorm for any other traces, coming up empty, which was a relief.

"Thank you so much," I tell Idris, grateful he's here. Had I known it was him this whole time, I'd have been a lot less negative about it.

"No problem. It's my job." He stands from the couch and heads to my fridge, where he grabs a beer. "Don't ever do something like that again. It's too risky. You're smarter than that. I know it to be true, because I raised you."

I sigh as embarrassment floods my body, knowing he knows I had sex in a locker room. "I know."

Wanting to change the topic, I ask, "What should we do about Ryker's secret, though?"

Idris shrugs, unsure for once. "Hard to say. I looked into it, and it is true. He was never charged, and it's not on public records since he was so young, but for a guy going into the major leagues, it could affect him."

My heart sinks because baseball is everything to Ryker. He'd be devastated if he didn't make it over something so trivial that shouldn't matter.

"Can't the PI team get rid of anything Travis says that makes it online?" I throw out an idea, trying to find anything that would help Ryker.

"We can, but if he goes directly to the agency and speaks with the manager, there's nothing we can do there. I don't think he has any contacts to do that, but you can never be sure." He sighs, running a hand through his graying hair. I'm sure I'm more than responsible for a majority of those growing up.

I blow out a frustrated breath.

"What I would suggest is that Ryker comes clean to whoever he signs with. Tell them it was a misunderstanding, an accident, as the report itself states. If he tries to hide it, it'll make it seem worse than it is."

I dabble with the idea in my head, realizing he's right. I'm not sure if Ryker will see it that way, but there's only one way to find out. I need to talk to him, tell him everything that happened tonight.

He has no idea that Travis knows his secret, and I have a feeling it's going to change things as we both know it.

Chapter Thirty-Two

Ryker

My phone ringing startles me out of sleep.

Who the fuck is calling me in the middle of the night?

I roll over and grab my phone from the nightstand, cracking one eye open, but when I see the name on the screen, both widely fly open.

"Cami, what's wrong?" My voice is breathless with panic.

"I'm so sorry to bug you this late, but I need you to come over. Something—"

"I'll be there in twenty, baby."

I cut her off because it doesn't matter why. If she needs me, I'll be there. Especially when she sounds as frantic as she did. Within twenty minutes, I'm there, knocking on her door. She opens it right away, stealing the breath from my lungs.

Camille's in sleep shorts and a tank top, but what really gets me is how fucking pretty she is. My arms reach out, and I pull her into me. I cradle her head while we sway, her body tucked safely into mine. It's my favorite place for her to be, right where I can keep her safe.

I kiss her hair and pull back so I can look into her eyes. "What happened?"

Her eyes cast downward as she gnaws on her bottom lip. "Maybe we should sit."

Dread fills every crevice of my body because I know I'm not going to like whatever it is she's about to say.

I nod, then pick her up, enjoying the squeal and giggle Camille emits as I carry her toward the couch and sit with her in my arms. Putting her in my arms is the only way I can trust myself to stay calm at whatever she's about to say. She soothes me, something I never knew I needed to feel.

"I want to preface this by saying I'm perfectly fine, not a scratch or an—"

"Who the fuck put their hands on you?" My voice is cold, while white-hot anger brews in my stomach.

Camille runs her fingers through my hair, pushing a strand behind my ear. "I'm okay," she reassures me, leaning down to give me a chaste kiss. "I was at the gym, hitting the bag because I needed to work some frustration out, when Travis approached me."

Travis is fucking dead to me. That motherfucker.

"He was making comments about my body, and I ignored him, but he didn't like it. So he followed me and grabbed my arm to make me stay and hear him out. Then he…" She inhales and exhales, her eyes apologetic. "He showed me a video he had, of us in the locker room showers."

Scratch that, Travis *is* fucking dead.

"How—"

"Let me finish, then you can go off, okay?"

I nod, and she continues. "He said he forgot something in his locker, which is why he came back and heard us. He was using the video as blackmail to try to get me to sleep with him."

My mind blanks as everything stills around me. He did *what*?

She explains what happened, then shrugs nonchalantly. "So I'm fine. He didn't hurt me. My brother's PI team handled it. The video's gone for good." Her voice is calm as her fingers rake through my hair.

"Cami." My voice cracks, so many differing emotions flowing through me at once.

Rage. Hurt. Protectiveness.

Travis not only watched us have sex, he recorded the damn thing. It's utterly disgusting, and I'm distraught that she had to go through that. Not only that, he tried to hurt what's mine, and it pisses me the fuck off.

Camille is *mine*. It doesn't matter that she shouldn't be because we're graduating in a month and who knows where we'll end up. Or that she could break my heart. Aurora's words are finally making their way to my core, changing the roots that were wilted and needed to go. Filling me with new possibilities.

I shake my head. "I'm so fucking sorry. I should've been more careful."

"We didn't think anyone would be there, and even if someone was, we wouldn't expect them to stop and record it. It's gone now. Don't blame yourself, please," she pleads, stroking my beard in a comforting way.

"And that motherfucker. I'm going to lose it if I see him again. How dare he put his hands on you?"

"Ryker, don't do that. He…he has something on you that he also threatened to expose if I didn't follow his orders." Her voice carries a twinge of worry as she bites on her lip.

"He told me a few weeks ago that he knew about it," I admit as my hands begin to trace circles on her back, needing to feel her in order to keep me calm.

"Why didn't you tell me?" she asks.

"It's not something I'm proud of. The whole thing was an

accident. We were fighting because he wouldn't leave Theo's sister alone, and when we fell, I accidentally fell on his arm at the wrong angle."

"You can share all the parts of you, Ryker. The good and bad ones. I want them all. Not that this was bad, because it's not. It was an accident, but you get my point, right?" She looks at me for confirmation and I give it with a nod.

"My brother's head of PI, Idris, whom I have a lot to tell you about, by the way, thinks you should talk to your agent and get ahead of this, in case Travis does tell people. His team is going to get rid of any articles about it, shall they arise, but the best course of action is for you to tell them, spin the story your way."

I blow out a breath as tension forms behind my neck. This is going to be a shitstorm, but I'd rather be ahead of it than in the midst of it. "You're right. Thank you for looking out for me. You didn't need to do that. I could've handled this on my own," I tell her.

Camille shakes her head, then rests her forehead against mine. "It's okay to have someone in your corner too, you know."

"I'm glad I have you, *Rocky*," I tease, lightening the mood.

"What does that mean?" she asks, seemingly confused.

My mouth gapes at that. "You've never seen *Rocky*?"

"Nope. I didn't grow up watching American television. I've been catching up the last four years, but I haven't seen everything yet."

"Rocky is a boxer, and since you kicked Travis's ass tonight, it felt fitting." I smirk, earning myself a wide smile from her.

It suddenly dawns on me that this was similar to what happened to her back home. "Are you okay?" I ask, and somehow she understands exactly what I'm asking.

"Yeah, I think it was healing for me in a way. To be able to protect myself when for so long I feared everyone around me.

I'm sure I'll still have nightmares from time to time, but it was liberating in a weird way." She grins, looking pleased with herself.

"That's my girl, but just know, I'm going to kick his ass too."

"Ryker, don't bother. He's not worth getting suspended or ticking him off to share stories to the media," she points out.

I groan, laying my head back on the couch. "I'll agree, but I'm not happy about it."

"Are we okay? I know we're just friends with benefits and this caused a lot of issues you probably didn't want to deal with," she stammers, eyes filled with uncertainty.

I sit up straight as my hand strokes her cheek, my thumb rubbing gently under her eye. Fuck, I could get lost in those eyes and never look for directions back. While I want to tell her we're far from just being friends with benefits, I don't think it's the right time after all that's happened tonight.

We both need clearer headspaces and enough energy to have that conversation. It's not something to breeze over. There's too much to consider to do that.

"You and me, we're always good, princess." I nudge my nose against her, breathing in her cotton candy scent.

Camille takes the lead, her lips pressing against mine. Our kiss starts off sweet as we take our time. Her hands rest on my neck while mine tighten on her hips, grinding her against my growing erection.

"Ryker." Her voice is breathy and needy, and it's all for me. That fact alone makes me grow harder, and gone are the sweet kisses.

Our teeth clash as our kiss turns more heated. Her thin and barely there sleep shorts don't do anything to hide how wet she is, and I can feel it on my sweats as she grinds that sweet little pussy all over me.

Our tongues enter a seductive dance as we suck and lavish

each other's mouths while our hips move, looking for any friction we can get.

"Take those shorts off, *now*," I growl.

Camille gets up and pulls down her shorts while I remove my sweats, freeing my aching cock. She returns to straddling my lap, resting her bare pussy on top of me, rubbing her arousal over me.

"Cami, fuck, I need to be inside of you." My breath hitches, overcome with need for her.

She reaches between us, lines up the head of my cock with her entrance, and slowly sinks down my length. We both let out a breathy moan when she bottoms out as we clutch onto each other. Her hands are on my shoulders while mine are on her hips, waiting for her to adjust and move.

After a beat, she lifts up, then sinks back down, making my thighs tighten as I try not to come already.

Being inside of Camille is an experience like no other, our connection making everything more intense. Add in how sexy it is when she's in control and on top? I stand no chance at lasting very long like this.

"Take those tits out, baby. Let me get a taste."

As Camille moves up and down on my cock, she lowers her tank top straps, exposing her breasts to me. I instantly lean forward and bite one of her nipples, earning a yelp. I chuckle then wrap my lips around the same one as I toy with her piercing, then soothe the sting as I suck and lick along her breast.

"Oh, Ryker," she moans, tightening around my cock.

"Be a good princess and come all over my cock," I urge her, rolling her other nipple between my fingers as I return to her breasts, sucking on the skin hard enough to leave a mark. My free hand travels between our bodies to her clit, rubbing it exactly how she likes.

Within seconds, she explodes, her pussy constricting

around my cock as she moans loudly. I pound up into her, loving how fucking tight she is. It sets me off, my own orgasm hitting me as I come inside of her.

We're both breathing heavily as we attempt to catch our breaths, with her head resting on my shoulder. I stroke her hair, knowing she loves it when I do that. The little contented hum she releases tells me so.

Camille lifts her head, then rises, not enough that I slip out of her, but enough for us to see my cum seeping out of her and around my cock. She looks down at where I'm staring, then moans once more as she sinks back down onto me and begins riding me.

I harden immediately, which is no easy feat, but somehow she manages it.

"That turns you on, seeing my cum drip out of you?" I groan, her tits bouncing with each movement.

"Yes, so much," she breathes, tightening around me already.

I stroke her clit again, feeling her thighs shake on either side of me as I do.

"Naughty little thing wants to be filled with my cum once again, doesn't she?"

She nods, unable to form words as she loses herself to the pleasure our bodies create together. It's fucking amazing, the best high I've ever felt in my life.

Within seconds, she goes off again, this time screaming my name as I clamp down on her nipple while she comes. Feeling her tighten and spasm around me is all it takes for me, and once again, I release inside her, relishing in the warmth of her around me.

This time, we get up and head for the shower where I clean her up, and then she does the same for me. By the time we get into bed, it's nearing early morning, and we snuggle against one another.

My fingers sift through her hair as I whisper, "Don't ever leave without telling me."

Ever since all of this went down with her family, I've had this intense fear of her just being gone one day. No explanation, no goodbye as she's whisked away back to her country.

Camille nuzzles her face against my chest, her body fitting perfectly against mine. "I won't, no bullshit."

We both chuckle softly, caressing each other as we drift off to sleep. She's safe and mine, something I don't want to change. Ever.

I'll do *anything* to keep her.

Chapter Thirty-Three

Ryker

I've never felt like my balls could shrivel up inside of me until now. Because sitting beside me is my agent, Ben Andrews.

He knows the game of baseball better than any agent out there and is respected by every single sports team for the talent he acquires for them.

I was more than grateful when he approached me at the end of my freshman year here at RLU, and that same sentiment still stands now as he sits beside me before our Zoom call with the Detroit Panthers' owner, Mark Suby.

I took Cami's advice and wanted to get ahead of this thing in case Travis decides to leak the story somehow.

Mark Suby appears on the screen, looking less like a dominating businessman and more like a friend you might be meeting up with on the golf course with his polo and baseball cap.

"Ryker and Ben, what a pleasure to speak with you today. What can I do for you? You know we still have a few more weeks before our final decision on the draft," he reminds us, his voice curt since we had to beg for this meeting because of how busy he is.

"We're aware of that," Ben speaks up. "We wanted to talk about something that needs to stay between us."

That attracts Mark's attention, and he sits up straighter on his side of the screen. "You have my word. What's going on?"

I take over, wanting the information to come from me. "When I was in high school, I got into a fight defending my friend's sister. It resulted in an accidental broken arm for the other person and I was arrested, but ended up never charged with anything. However, I did do community service, so it was never put on my record."

Mark remains quiet, as does Ben while I continue.

"I'm telling you this because someone is threatening to go to the press with the information, with hopes it'll deter anyone from drafting me. While I understand the severity of something like this and how it can affect your organization, I hope there's something we can do to overcome it. I was just a kid, and it was an acc—"

"I'm going to stop you right there." Mark holds up his hand, making my body freeze in fear. "If some punk thinks they're going to sell this story, then let them. There's no recorded proof, and we will work with our head of PR to put out a statement to address it. When we tell our own stories, it gives us the power back."

I let out a breath, my entire body relaxing as the tension fades away.

Ben knocks his shoulder into mine. "I told you, kid, everything will be fine. You did nothing wrong."

"Thank you so much, Mr. Suby. I appreciate it," I tell him, expressing my gratitude for his grace.

"Not a problem. Shit happens in life." He shrugs, then types away on his desktop computer. "I'm going to have a meeting with our PR department in a moment, and they will be in contact with you shortly. I know we haven't signed you yet, but I'm extending this service as a kindness. I don't want to see you lose out on a career in baseball because of some idiot who wants to tear other people down."

Ben and I chuckle at that and share our appreciation once again. Then our screen turns black.

I slump back in my chair as waves of emotions wash over me.

Relief. Thankfulness. Happiness.

Thank fucking God that is over with and went well. Now all I have to do is make a post explaining what happened with the help of their head of PR, if Travis decides to sell the story. I swear, if I knew it wouldn't upset Camille that I kicked the shit out of Travis, I'd have done it two times over already. He deserves it for ever thinking he could come after what's mine.

Yeah, *mine*. I'm done pretending like it's not true anymore, because she is.

"What do you want to watch?" I ask Camille, who's snuggled under the blankets in her bed. I'd bet anything that she's going to fall asleep within the first twenty minutes.

"*The Aristocats*," she offers, setting her tea cup on the bedside table.

I find the movie online and then throw the covers back and climb under with her.

Our bodies instantly move to be closer to one another's, my arm around her waist while she rests her head on my chest. My hand gently strokes her hair, playing with the strands as the famous castle appears on screen.

Camille lets out a contented sigh, snuggling in even closer.

"How was your day?" I ask softly.

"It was busy, but good. I spent the day going over interior decorating ideas for Jasmine's bakery with her, and then I had to edit a bunch of videos to post," she tells me, never failing to impress me with how hard she works. "How was yours?"

"I had the meeting with Mark Suby and it went well as you already know. After that, I went for a run and worked on some final assignments."

"Sooo was it good or…?" She trails off, looking for my final stamp of how my day was.

"It was okay, but it's better now." I tighten my hold on her, pressing my lips to her forehead for a small kiss.

We watch in silence as the movie begins, my hand still working through the silky strands of her long hair. As I predicted, within twenty minutes, she's fast asleep on my chest.

This is one of the highlights of our time together, when Camille falls asleep because then I get to look at her for as long as I want and wonder how fucking lucky am I for having gotten to know her.

I get to reacquaint myself with the beauty of her face, from the slope of her nose, to her full pink lips and the crease between her brows when she's dreaming.

Of all the nights we've spent together, she's only had two nightmares since that very first one in New Mexico.

As much as I'd like to believe that I'm the reason they've lessened, deep down, I hope it's because she's more confident in the fact that she's safe now. Not just because of me, and don't get me wrong, I wouldn't think twice about ending anyone who dared hurt her, but I think she feels safe within herself and her ability to keep herself protected.

Camille stirs on my chest, so my hand drifts from her hair to her back, rubbing soothing circles that will hopefully get her to drift back to sleep.

Her eyes peek open, a look of relief on her face when she looks up at me.

"What's wrong?" My voice is almost a whisper, so as not to startle her.

"Nothing, just a bad dream."

"Do you want to talk about it?" I hedge, continuing to rub the circles on her back.

"No, tell me a funny story instead. It'll help me." She rests her chin on her forearm, staring at me for an answer.

I raise an eyebrow. "Me? Funny?"

She rolls her eyes playfully. "You are when you want to be. I'm sure you have at least one funny story."

I rack my brain, because of course when someone asks you directly, nothing comes to mind. I now know why contestants on *Family Feud* choke on the fast money round.

Until finally, a memory flashes in my mind.

"When we were eighteen, Theo and I went to Mexico for my aunt's wedding. Theo is basically like my mom's second son because he was always around the house growing up. Anyway, since the legal drinking age is eighteen there, Theo drank for the first time."

"First time? He never drank illegally in high school?" She sounds surprised, her eyebrows furrowed.

"Theo's a rule follower, through and through. So he decided to let loose there. We were day drinking at the pool, and there was a dance contest."

"Let me guess, Theo lost?"

"No, actually, he's a great dancer. But because of the alcohol in his system, he didn't register that his swim trunks were falling off…and let's just say he flashed the entire pool, including my family."

"Noooo." She giggles against my chest, the vibration making me chuckle with her.

"Yes, and it gets better. In his rush of embarrassment, he

tried to pull them back up but lost his balance and fell into the bushes, ass up, flashing everyone, *everything*."

Camille's laughter fills my ears, the sound easily my favorite as tears begin to leak from her eyes. She wipes at them. "I feel so bad for him, but that is so funny."

"What was *your* first drunk experience?" I ask in turn, my interest piqued.

Camille looks away for a beat, then returns her gaze to mine, looking timid. "Well…I was only sixteen. Quentin and I stole the finest bottle of wine we could find from the cellar, and we drank it in the gardens, far away from prying eyes." She shakes her head, folding her lips together. "We snuck back into the kitchen, and this is where my obsession with hot sauce and popcorn began because I ate an entire bowl of it. I then proceeded to have way too many *gougères*, which is this delicious pastry that's made with choux dough. So, mix cheese with the hot sauce and wine, and let's just say I threw up all over Quentin. The sound woke a maid, who then went and told on me. So not only was I throwing up profusely, I was also getting reamed out by my parents."

"They sound real shitty," I mutter, annoyed at her parents for doing that rather than taking care of her.

"*C'est la vie*." She shrugs. "What about you? What was your first time like?"

"I thankfully don't have a story to tell really. Me and some buddies in high school got drunk at a party. I passed out on the couch. End of story."

"*Boooo*." Camille pouts, giving me a thumbs-down.

I grin, rolling my eyes before looking back to her. Our eyes lock amidst the easy conversation, and my fingers grasp her chin, lifting it up so I can gently press my lips to hers, suddenly needy for her.

Before I know it, we're rolling around under her covers, lips pressing on each other's bodies anywhere they can reach while our hands squeeze and caress. Camille pushes my sweats down and my cock easily slides into her as she wore nothing but a big T-shirt to bed.

We spend the rest of the night moving slowly together, no rush or urgency. We simply enjoy our bodies moving together, prolonging our releases the best we can to get our fill of one another.

When we come down after our highs, we snuggle in bed together and as we drift closer and closer to sleep, one thought dominates my mind.

I love this girl.

Chapter Thirty-Four

Camille

Don't throw up. Don't throw up. Don't throw up.

I repeat the mantra to myself as I walk down the hallway toward Coach Warren's office before the game today. He emailed me early this morning and told me we needed to meet, and I've been stressed ever since.

Did he somehow find out about what happened in the locker room? Did Travis say something or did we miss a copy?

The anxious thoughts don't stop. In fact, they triple when I sit across from him.

"Camille, thanks for coming to see me. I know you are usually busy filming the team, but we need to talk." His gruff voice fills the quiet space of his office.

We need to talk, are the worst four words I've heard in the English language. No matter what the context is, they make me feel like I've done something wrong.

"Of course. What did you want to talk about?" I ask, appearing calm and confident. If there's one thing I appreciate about my upbringing, it's all of the skills I was taught, one of them being to hide my true emotions when in an important situation.

"What you've done for the team is fantastic, absolutely wonderful. I haven't said it enough, and I apologize for that. The school's page about our team is a hit online and we have you to thank for that." He peers down at me through his glasses, his normally cold eyes shining with warmth.

I smile, feeling myself relax a bit. "Just doing my job."

The team's page is doing extremely well, gaining thousands of followers everyday. We broke one million last week, when previously they only had around ten thousand followers.

He grins. "Well, now it looks like this really could be your job. I had the pleasure of speaking to the Detroit Panthers' owner, Mark Suby, today. He wanted to know what I thought of our social media manager who's garnering hits left and right."

My mouth pops open as complete shock hits me. What did he just say?

I lean forward, skeptical to believe it. "Is this a joke?"

"Ms. Blanchette, I'm not a man who jokes," he says with utter seriousness as he too leans forward. "They wanted me to pass on their contact information in hopes that you all may discuss the prospect of working with them after graduation."

I think I might pass out from the way my heart starts beating erratically while the strongest rush of happiness washes over me. My dream job, and with my brother's team—wait a second. Did he orchestrate this?

"Camille?" Coach Warren prods, staring at me with trepidation.

"Sorry, that was a lot to take in. Of course I would love to further speak with them about this opportunity. Thank you." I beam while ignoring the need my legs feel to kick like an overly-excited toddler.

"Excellent, I will forward you their information. I'm sure you'll do great things for their team, but for now, focus on ours. We got a game to play." He raps his knuckles on the desk and stands.

"Yes, go Coyotes!" I cheer, walking out of his office on the highest cloud I've ever been on. Before I take off on that cloud, I need to make sure this isn't a result of my brother putting in a good word. If it is, I will not be happy with him.

I'm about to pull out my phone and do exactly that, but Idris's name fills my screen.

"Hello?" I ask, instantly on edge.

"Everything's fine. That's not why I'm calling. I want you to know the offer from Detroit is legit. You both have different last names and you also both stay out of the media. He doesn't tell anyone about you to respect your privacy, so there's no connection there. You did this all on your own, got it, kid?"

"How do you know that?" I inquire, not at all surprised he snooped in on my conversation.

"If they knew Q was your brother, they would've gone through him to hire you. Hell of a lot easier. I promise that you earned this all on your own. I'm proud of you, Cami." His voice chokes with emotion, making my eyes instantly pool with tears.

Idris is the closest thing I have to a father figure, and hearing that means everything to me. "Thank you, Idris," I whisper as happy tears overflow and release down my cheeks.

I wish I could tell Ryker, but he's getting ready for the game. It'll have to wait until after the game. He mentioned that the Panthers were one of the teams looking to sign him, and if fairytales do exist and the universe is a thing, then, universe, please let this be one.

Make him get drafted by the Panthers and allow us to live out the happily ever after that we both deserve.

Please.

Chapter Thirty-Five

Ryker

All week long, I've had to do my best to tamp down the rage that simmered in my blood every time I had to be near Travis. If it wasn't for Camille pleading with me not to say anything, I would've slammed my fist in his face by now.

He's purposely avoided me, barely looking my way unless needed. Whenever he did, I'd give him a menacing look that had him quickly averting his gaze.

I thought he'd have confronted me, yelled or something. But the silence from him has me suspecting that it freaked him out how suddenly the video was erased from everything with no explanation. He's scared and I thank fuck he is. That'll teach him to ever even think about bothering her again.

I pull my focus back to what's important right now, and that's the game happening today. We're playing the California Bulldogs, who we're currently tied with in our division, which means this game will determine who will be number one.

"Stretch your arm over your head for me," Mackenzie instructs as I lie on the table, getting warmed up for the game. I do as she says and she uses a massage gun on my deltoid, making sure I have peak mobility tonight.

There's one thing that might hinder my movements, seeing as my latest addition is only a week old. I knew it wouldn't heal in time, except I didn't think when I did it. I only thought about how this was the best way I could show Camille how much I've fallen for her.

How I want to make her mine, to keep her forever and never let go.

Once I left Camille's house the following morning after what happened, I went straight to the tattoo shop. I don't like Otto much, but he's a damn good artist and the only person available to do what I wanted.

A princess crown on top of the baseball that rests right against my heart. I wanted to show her that she was now my number one.

I can't wait to show her after the game tonight and ask her to be my girlfriend. Hell, we've always been acting like it since the very beginning. I don't think we were ever truly just friends with benefits.

I love Camille. It's a surety I feel down to the depth of my bones, fueling me from the inside out. And now all I have to do is tell her.

Minutes later, Mackenzie dismisses me and I return to my cubby to start my pregame routine. I'm about to select a song from my pregame playlist when I see a text from my mom.

Mama L

Good luck tonight, Paul and I are
cheering you on from Vancouver!

Attached is a photo of her and Paul, who is wearing a foam finger that reads "Ryker rocks." I have to admit, it's cheesy as hell, but also sweet in the way he supports me like I'm one of his own.

After selecting the song I was looking for, I go to pocket my phone when I get a new text, this time from Aurora.

I chuckle at that, feeling more support than I ever have.

And when the game starts, I look out into the stands above our dugout and see my people.

Theo's sitting next to Camille, with Jasmine on his other side. I usually make Cami sit in the dugout since the incident, but Theo promised he'd make sure no flyouts got near her.

My chest swells with love, making me smile brightly as I wave at them. It feels like I just hit a grandslam when I allow the joy to take over for once. It's freeing.

Camille smiles sweetly, then blows me a kiss. I pretend to catch it and place it over my heart, earning a blush.

I cannot wait to tell her how goddamn in love with her I am.

Chapter Thirty-Six

Camille

I'm beginning to wonder if my happily ever after *will* include Ryker after all. Something shifted between us since that day at the lavender field. While we were always friendly and flirty, it's turned into more.

It's the way Ryker looks at me with the same adoration as someone watching fireworks for the first time. The way he smiles in between our kisses now, when he used to only scowl at me. Or how every time we're intimate, my body feels more at peace than ever before.

My cheeks heat up when he catches the kiss I just blew him, making me sink further into my seat.

"You two don't seem like just friends to me," Jasmine comments, making my eyes avert to her instead of the man who owns my heart.

"What do you mean? We're besties," I defend, sitting up straighter.

Theo chuckles, leaning over to say, "Bullshit. Ry guy just put his glove over his heart while he looked at you as if you were hanging the stars in the sky. There is nothing *friendly* about that."

My cheeks burn even more as butterflies dance in my belly because he's right. Before I get too giddy and mentally plan our wedding, I play it cool while shrugging my shoulders. "Maybe."

Jasmine leans toward us. "Maybe, my ass! That man is in love with you. This is so exciting. We can go on triple couple dates and—" she starts, but Theo interrupts her.

"Oh, so now y'all are in love and good old Theo gets the boot? I see how it is." He shakes his head, crossing his arms over his chest.

We both laugh at his pouting. I know he's been hooked on Marcela since he first laid eyes on her, but with her recent breakup, I don't think she'll be open to anything anytime soon.

We made a group chat with us four girls, and we've been checking in with her. She, Jasmine, and I have plans to go out for dinner next week. I meant it when I said that she now has us and she'll never be alone.

"Not at all, Theo. Single or not, you're with us for life," Jasmine says, leaning her head on his shoulder.

"Uhm, Jay bay bay, I love you and all but please take your head off my shoulder. I would love to see my senior year and if Elio sees this somehow, I'm not sure I will."

"He's just a little possessive when warranted, but it's you. It's fine," she tells him while digging in her purse. "You just reminded me I should text him and see how it's going. He's working with my dad today."

"I still can't believe I'm friends with Elio fucking Mazzo," Theo swoons, never missing the opportunity to express how much he loves him.

I shake my head as I laugh, and it hits me all of a sudden. I feel like I'm finally where I'm meant to be. Not only do I have a group of friends that feel like family and a man I'm in love with, but I also got the job offer I've been dreaming of.

I have yet to email them as I've been busy with social media tasks before the game, but as soon as I get home tonight, that's my plan. I cannot wait to tell Ryker.

Hope for the future I've been dreaming about since I was a kid begins to bloom in my chest, leaving me with the cheesiest smile on my face as we settle in for the game.

There's a full crowd for tonight's game against RLU's top rival and they're fighting for first place. I have various cameras set up in strategic spots to catch the best angles all night. That way I can sit with my friends and enjoy the game.

"It's going to be weird without you two not here next year," Theo comments as the game gets underway.

"It's going to be weird not being a student. I mean, what is that even like?" Jasmine adds. "And I'll be running a business? Yikes."

"I thought you were excited, Minnie?" I ask while dipping my soft pretzel into hot sauce.

"I am, but it's also nerve-wracking. I want to do well, and the pressure feels immense at times. Thank God for Elio. He's been helping me stay calm and organized." She sips her water, a small smile on her lips.

She's so in love, and I know the feeling because I am too.

"You'll be great. I can't wait to be the first customer," I tell her.

"Nope, I'll be camping out the night before so I'll be the first," Theo protests.

I'm about to argue with him for fun when my phone vibrates in my pocket. I don't even look to see who it is, answering with a finger to my other ear in order to hear over the cheering of the crowd. "Hello?"

"Maribel," my father's commanding, smooth voice hits me like a ton of bricks.

"Before you hang up, I need you to hear me out," he pleads, sounding frantic. It puts me on edge because he sounds genuinely nervous.

"Give me a minute," I tell him, then signal to Jasmine and Theo that I'm stepping aside to take a call.

As soon as I'm outside the stadium, Idris is right beside me. "Put him on speaker," he mouths.

I do as he says then say, "What is it?"

"Tell Idris I say hello."

My blood runs cold, while Idris begins tapping away at his phone.

"How did you know?"

"I am the king, Maribel. You should know better. We may not have spoken to you in years, but we've always known where you were."

My gut sinks at that. "You also haven't reached out to me in years. Why now?"

"We wanted to let you live. I know you thought we were hard on you, but we love you. We made sure you were safe from afar but never wanted to interfere," he says, something akin to surprise filling me.

"What do you want?" I ask, needing to get to the point.

My father sighs, and I imagine him pulling a hand down his face. He always did that when he was frustrated. I haven't seen him in years, and I wonder if gray sits where chocolate brown hair used to be.

"*Tu dois te marier.*"

Sorry, what? I blink and blink again, losing focus of what's in front of me. I grip onto Idris as I try to form words. "*Attends, quoi?*"

"Our country hasn't been doing well…and we need to join forces with our neighboring isle, Calis. The only way that is going to happen is if you marry the prime minister's son, Jacques."

My ears ring while my blood runs cold, a sense of dread consuming me. I knew this would happen, where one day he would guilt me back home. If there's one thing I don't want more than going back to the life of royal affairs, it's to see my country fall apart. I may not like being a princess, but I've never had an issue with my country itself.

"I plead with you, Maribel, come back and marry Jacques. *C'est la seule chose qui peut nous sauver, sauver notre peuple.*"

"There has to be another way," I cry, tears soaking my cheeks. "Partner with a different country. Ask Q for money—"

"Your brother chose to leave us. I will not ask him for a thing," my father spits, hatred coating every word.

"But he would do it. You know he would," I try to convince him.

"You're coming home to get married. End of story." His tone is final.

Idris takes the phone from my hand. "What if she doesn't, Your Highness?"

"Well, then that boyfriend of hers will never play baseball again."

I yank my phone back, my voice icy as I threaten, "Don't you dare even think of hurting him."

"You know violence is not my thing, dear. I'd simply make a few phone calls and ensure he's never drafted. Not even by a minor league."

"We'll think about it and get b—" Idris starts, but I cut him off. "When?"

Idris mouths, "What are you doing?"

I ignore him and listen to my father's answer. "You're set to be married in two days. I'd like you here as soon as possible."

"I'll be on the next flight out." My voice is devoid of emotion, numb as I hang up on him.

Idris sets his hands on my shoulders, shaking me. "Cami, what are you thinking?"

"There's nothing we can do, Idris. He's won." My tears are now free-falling down my face.

"I'd like to make sure everything he said is true. It'll take some time to hack into their systems again, so just give me a day."

I shake my head. "We don't have that time. If I'm not there within the next twelve hours, who knows what he'll do."

"I don't like this." He began to pace. "Let's call your brother and figure out a plan, okay?"

I nod, but my mind is set. I know what I need to do. Let's just say it won't be the first time I give Idris the runaround.

"Okay, but can I finish watching the game first?" I ask.

"We need to get back to your place. My team needs a debrief and we need to get started as soon as possible," he stresses, his jaw clenched tightly with each word.

"You go ahead then. I'll stay here."

"Do you think I'm clueless, Camille? I know what you're doing."

More tears wet my cheek, my breath unsteady as I speak, "I'm not doing anything. I need to talk to Ryker in case this is all true...I need to say goodbye." My voice cracks, my chest aching at the thought. "I'll have him bring me home."

Idris looks conflicted, his dark brown eyes searing a path right through me. "Fine," he relents. "But it's not a goodbye. We're getting you out of this."

I nod, unable to say much more.

"I'm having the team meet at your place. I told them I'd be there in fifteen. Text me if anything else happens, okay?"

"I will." I half smile, but it doesn't reach my eyes. I make my way back when he leaves with one name running in my mind.

Ryker.

The thought of saying goodbye to him is like a weight on my chest. I can't do it, but I have to protect him. I love Ryker more than anything or anyone in this world, and in order to make sure he's happy, I have to sacrifice my own happiness.

He won't be able to keep me forever, like I imagined in our happily ever after, but I'll cherish what we had for the rest of my life, no matter how painful it'll be to hold on to the memories.

I text Jasmine as soon as Idris leaves and tell her to meet me by the concession stand. I can see her once I round the corner, right where I asked her to be. My chest caves in once more, because I'll be losing her too.

"Cami." Jasmine's brows pinch as she rushes toward me and envelops me in her arms. "What's wrong?"

I wrap my arms around her, squeezing her tightly. "I have to go home." I sniffle.

Jasmine pulls back slowly, her eyes pooling with tears. "Why do I feel like you won't come back?"

I shake my head as another tear slipped through. "I don't know if I am."

"What's going on?" she asks, pulling me off to the side so no onlookers can watch.

"My dad called me, and I have to get married to someone in a neighboring island in order to save my country or else he'll ruin Ryker's life, as if the guilt from our country going under wouldn't be enough," I tell her.

Her mouth pops open. "This isn't real life." She huffs. "This just doesn't happen. How is this happening?"

"I don't know, but I can't test my father. My brother's security team is looking into the validity of everything he said, but it'll take hours. I don't have that kind of time." I stand taller, gathering what little confidence I have left to see this through.

"This isn't fucking fair," she cries, pulling me in for another hug.

I shake against her, our sobs mingling together. "I know, but I need you to do me a favor."

She pulls back, looking at me with sadness. "Anything."

"I need you not to tell anyone where I'm going. My brother's team wants me to wait here until they figure it out. But I'm going to head to the airport now. The sooner I get there and assess what is going on, the more help I can be to figure out what I can do to get out of it," I explain. "And I need you to tell Ryker. I…I can't say goodbye to him. Tell him I love him and that hopefully I'll be back for him if he wants."

I know it's going to hurt him if I leave without giving him a reason why. He specifically asked me to never do that, but he'd convince me to stay, and I need to be out of here sooner than later.

"So there's hope you'll be back?" Jasmine brightens a little.

"I can't promise anything, Minnie. But I'm going to try my best. You can count on that." I pull her into another hug, hoping this won't be the last time I see her.

Once we part, I walk down the hall, beginning my journey back to Lorsica.

With hopes that I'll be back where home truly is.

Here.

Chapter Thirty-Seven
Ryker

Something feels wrong.

Ever since the second inning, Camille has been missing. Then Jasmine left minutes ago and when she returned, Cami wasn't with her. I'm already pissed the fuck off because we're losing. I'm personally having a great game, but I'm about to ruin it if I can't get my mind off my girl.

Where is she?

Rationally, I think to myself that she's probably doing something for social media, but a deeper part of me feels like something's not right.

I curse as we jog out to the field to play defense, my eyes scanning the stadium again in the hopes of seeing her, with no luck.

Yanking my ball cap down, I force myself to focus back on the play at hand. The captain for the opposing team is up, and he's arguably the best hitter on their team. From my peripheral, I see Cuddy jogging backward, preparing for this guy to bomb it outfield.

Our pitcher winds up, whipping a fast ball down to the plate, and the batter swings, hitting a foul ball right past me. I groan in frustration because I should've caught it and got us an easy out. If my focus were where it needed to be, I would have dove toward it and attempted to make the play.

To make matters worse, he crushes the next pitch, hitting a home run. The desire to whip my glove on the dirt is strong, but I hold it together, knowing I'm being watched at all times with the draft coming up.

We manage to end the inning without letting anyone else score, and I jog to the dugout with my head hanging low. Not only are we losing, but I can't focus and I'm stressed the fuck out about Camille.

"Have you seen Cami?" I ask Noah as he downs some water.

He shakes his head. "Nope. Isn't she in the stands?"

"No, she's been missing for a while now," I tell him, fear itching its way up my spine.

"I'm sure she's around here somewhere. You know how busy she is during games," he reasons, but his words don't help.

What if she's just like *him*? Leaving me with no goodbye or intention to see me again. Anxiety creeps in, thousands of what-ifs swimming in my head until I feel like I'm drowning.

My hand shakes as I find my coffee cup, a smile finding my lips when I look at the tongue design in my coffee. She told me it was because she came on my tongue three times last night.

My smile fades when I remember that I have no idea where she is right now.

Fuck this.

I jog out of the dugout with my glove still on and hop the fence, right into the stands. Fans are staring, cheering and making a commotion of it, but I don't pay them any attention.

I beeline right for Jasmine and Theo, needing to get to the bottom of this. Jasmine stands up once I reach them, and it's then I notice how red and puffy her eyes are. My stomach bottoms out.

Something bad happened. I fucking knew it.

If someone even breathed on Camille the wrong way, there's going to be hell to pay.

"Where is she?" I seethe, my chest heaving up and down erratically.

Theo stands up between us, a solemn look on his face, which is highly unusual for him. It only makes me that much more pissed off.

"Let's talk somewhere more private," he says, motioning for us to head outside the gate to the parking lot.

I'm about to make the move when a hand is placed on my shoulder. I turn around to see Coach Warren staring at me. "What in the hell are you doing, son?"

"Cami's gone…I need to find out where she is," I answer honestly, feeling like my skin is crawling with dread.

Coach looks between the three of us, and I'm not sure what makes him comply, but he does. "Go, Lewis. But your ass better be at our game tomorrow," he orders, clapping me on the shoulder before returning to the dugout.

Once we're outside the stadium, I turn to Jasmine, needing answers. "Talk," I bite out, much harsher than I want.

Theo places a hand on my chest, drawing my attention to him. "Look, I know you're pissed, but you need to watch how you talk to her."

I take a deep breath, then nod. "I'm sorry, Jasmine. I'm freaking the fuck out, and you don't deserve that."

"It's okay, Ryker." She gives me a small smile, but it's gone just as fast. "Before I talk, I'd like to say Theo is aware of the situation because I couldn't stop crying when I got back to my seat."

"I won't say a word," Theo swears, a hand over his heart.

"Jasmine, spill it. I'm losing it," I urge her.

With a deep breath, she peers up at me with an apologetic look on her face. "Her dad called her during the game, and she was gone for a bit but then texted me to meet her in the concession area. When I did, she was in tears," she explains. "She told me that her dad is forcing her back home to be married in two days in order to save their country. If she doesn't go, he'd ensure you never stepped foot on a baseball field again. She lied to her bodyguard, Idris, who told her to wait so they could look into how legit this is, but she didn't want to risk anything happening to you. She already left."

What. The. Fuck.

Married?

My heart stings in my chest, an ache so forceful it nearly sends me to the ground at the image of her in a white dress for some fucking guy who isn't *me*. I know she thinks she's protecting me, but hell, I'd rather never play a baseball game again than lose her.

The thought is shocking, yet somehow makes perfect sense. There is no happy ending without her.

Jasmine's full-on crying now, her voice shaky. "She told me to tell you this. She hopes she can make it back here to you and that she lo—"

"Don't." I hold up my gloved hand for her to stop. I don't want the first time Camille tells me she loves me to be through her friend. I plan on hearing it from her, because that girl is fucking mine and I'll do anything to make sure of it.

"What are we going to do?" Jasmine cries, just as Elio comes running up to us, concern etched on his face.

"*Dolcezza*," he calls out, and Jasmine runs toward him, burying herself in his chest as he runs a hand up and down her back.

"I texted him. I knew she'd need him," Theo explains.

I debate on texting Camille, but everything is raw right now. I need to figure out what the hell is happening before I do that.

"What's going on?" Elio asks, looking at the two of us.

Theo gives Elio the rundown, while he continues soothing Jasmine the best he can.

"Jesus fuck, does her brother know?" Elio asks.

"I'm not sure," I answer.

"I'm going to call him. Either he knows or we need to tell him," Elio says, pulling out his phone.

Elio speaks to Quentin in French, leaving us out of the loop. Once he hangs up, I'm on him instantly. "What did he say?"

"He's back at Cami's place with the security team, trying to hack into her dad's system, but it's taking longer than usual. King De Beaumont must've caught on to them and upped his firewall," he says. "And Q wants you to go there, Ryker. Wait till they find out more before *anyone* does anything."

"That could take too long. I'm not letting her marry whoever her father wants her to marry," I scoff, feeling myself grow impatient with the reminder that she's boarding a plane back home.

Theo claps his hands together. "I have an idea."

"Well, let's hear it," I snap.

"Millie Moo can't get married if she's already married, right?" His lips twist, smirking as if he's a genius.

"She's not, though," I point out.

"What I think he's saying is that we should take my jet to Lorsica so that you can marry Camille before they make her. But only if you're ready for that kind of commitment and to face the possibility of her dad fucking with your career after ruining his plans," Elio interjects.

"Do you hear yourself right now? I'm only twenty-two and who in her country would even marry us?" I ramble, feeling all sorts of emotions. Fear, nerves…and excitement all merging into one at the prospect of truly making her mine forever.

"Ryker." Elio's calm voice draws me to him. "Do you love her?"

"Yes."

"Do you want someone else to marry her?"

"No," I growl, pissed off at the fucking images he's painting.

"Then if she's it for you, and I know that girl is wild about you, what's holding you back? Go get your girl," he encourages, wrapping his arm around Jasmine, who's looking at him with pure admiration.

"I doubt there would be any minister or town hall official that would marry the princess of their country to someone else and face the wrath of their king," I tell them.

Theo steps forward, a cocky smirk on his face. "Didn't I ever tell you I'm an ordained minister? I could marry y'all."

We're all speechless for a moment, deciphering what he said. It doesn't surprise me, but it does at the same time.

"How did you become an ordained minister?" Jasmine asks with a puzzled look on her face.

"I always wanted a situation like this to happen, so I got it just in case. Thank God I did. I'm so hyped I get to marry Ry guy and my Millie Moo!" he exclaims, all too happy.

"That's if he says yes," Elio chimes in, and suddenly, they're all looking at me for an answer.

"What if she says no?" My voice is barely above a whisper.

"She's gone for you, Ryker. I don't see her saying no," Jasmine says softly. "But if she does, at least you can say you tried. It's always better to know than to wonder about what-ifs."

My gut churns with nerves at the prospect of asking her to marry me and her saying no. We're young and we've never talked about becoming more, always skating around the truth because we agreed to just be friends.

And hell, I don't blame Camille for never telling me if she has feelings because I'm such a grumpy asshole who's always said he doesn't have space for love in his life.

But now? She's filled my entire world with possibilities I've never seen before.

Love. Family. *More.*

She's it for me. I can go without baseball if I have to, but I won't go without *my* girl.

"How fast can we get there?"

Theo's, Jasmine's, and Elio's faces light up at my words, smiles on their lips at the confirmation that we are going to get our girl back.

"Let's fucking go get my besties married!" Theo's hand clamps down my shoulders, shaking me.

I laugh and shrug him off just as Noah and Cuddy jog out the gate.

"Ryker, are you coming back to play the game?" Cuddy asks, and Noah slaps him on the back of the neck.

"What he means to say is, is Camille okay?" Noah corrects him, looking at me with genuine concern. I love that she's got my entire team wrapped around her finger, that they care and love her like she's one of us.

I can't tell them everything, not without asking Camille if it's okay.

"We need to go get her. She went back home and it's a messy situation," I somewhat lie, concealing her secrets without fully lying. "But we have to leave now, so no. I won't be back for the game. Tell Coach I'm sorry, but this is important."

Noah smiles, pulling me into a hug. "I told you there was more to life than baseball. Proud of you, Ry."

"Thanks, man." I hug him back.

"Go bring our girl home. I need to keep my fans happy and she helps with that." Cuddy chuckles, fist-bumping me before jogging back to the stadium with Noah.

I turn to face my friends, ready to get on the road. "I need my passport..." I trail off, suddenly feeling unprepared for this.

"Get in my car. We're going to get everyone's passports. We're leaving in two hours. My jet will be ready by then. I know it's a bit long, but it's the best choice we have at entering the country undetected by avoiding the mainland airport," Elio informs us as we walk to his car.

"Why is it going to take so long? Theo asks.

"For a domestic flight, it'd be shorter, but my crew needs more time to prep to fly over water into a different continent," Elio explains while opening the car door for Jasmine.

Once we're in, it hits me that I don't have a ring for her. Nothing about this wedding will be traditional, but I need to have something to put on her finger from me.

I pick at the seam on my weathered glove as I think it over, trying to come up with an idea. My fingers tug on the black leather laces while memories of teaching Cami how to throw and catch a baseball come to my mind.

Let's just hope she says yes.

Chapter Thirty-Eight

Camille

Being back in Lorsica is weird.

I know how to speak countless languages, and that is still the only word I can come up with. *Weird.*

Everything still looks the same, but while it seems as though nothing's changed, I have.

The last time I was here, I was scared, unsure of who I wanted to be. But now, I know who I am. I'm no longer afraid. I created a life in Colorado with friends and a man I love, and even got my dream job in the process.

Well, I *was* creating that life until I was forced back here.

Once I landed, I was rushed into the palace's SUV, covered with bodyguards to avoid photos taken by paparazzi. Before I even made it to the palace, my father's right-hand man informed me that I had scheduled appointments to "freshen up" before I could see my parents.

And so it began, the slow, unwanted shedding of who I really am. Gone were my ashy blonde hair, brightly-painted nails, and ripped jeans. They were replaced with dark brown hair, white nails, and a cream pantsuit.

They even took away my phone so I wouldn't be able to get into contact with anyone.

My stomach twists as our car winds along the curved path toward the castle, and it sinks once that wrought iron gate is in front of us. The driver flashes his pass, and the silver gates leading to hell part before us.

My leg bounces incessantly as the lush garden catches my eye, leading us right to the back entrance of the gray-colored brick manor I used to call home.

"Princess," one of my guards says and I flinch at the name, having grown accustomed to only hearing it from Ryker's deep voice. "The king and queen are expecting you in the drawing room for tea." The guard places a hand on my back and guides me inside.

I yank it off me, causing his eyes to widen as he takes a step back. The itch to run as soon as the door closes behind us becomes strong, especially when the high ceilings, pale blue walls, and white linoleum floors come into view.

Muscle memory is a wild thing because my legs take me exactly where I need to go, while my mind is barely able to take it all in.

"Princess Maribel," the guard announces my presence as he opens the door, the name making my knees tremble.

I curtsy, then flick my eyes up to my parents for the first time in four years.

King and Queen De Beaumont.

They appear older than the last time I saw them. My father now has a beard that's a mix of gray and brown, while my mother's hair is the same mix. There are also worry lines I've never seen before, the sight making me wonder what's been going on since I left.

I'm at a loss for words, my lips parting then closing. But my parents ignore my lack of greeting.

"Maribel!" my mother says in disbelief, a hand to her chest as she takes me in.

My father waves me over to the couch, motioning for me to sit across from them. "Daughter, come sit. We have much to talk about in so little time."

There's no *wow, it's nice to finally see you, how are you?* Or *what are you taking in school? What have you been up to in the last four years?*

I'd say I'm shocked, but this is exactly why I left. It's always business with them. Part of me wonders if they weren't royalty, would things be different?

That's not to say we have no good memories together, because we do, but they're few and far between.

"What would you like to discuss?" I ask, noting how I sound different to myself.

My father takes a sip of tea, eyeing me like he's happy with the transformation of my "American" appearance.

"You look amazing, dear." My mother fills in the silence, always the one to avoid conflict with compliments.

"It's not really my style, but thanks," I tell her bluntly. If they thought I was coming back without a voice, they were so very wrong.

"It is how Jacques wants you. He likes the old Camille best, the sophisticated one who will be ready to become his wife and bear his children. Not the wild girl you were in America," my father retaliates, making bile rise in my throat.

Bear his *children*? There's not a universe in which that man is touching me. I don't care if I'm legally his wife. He can find a mistress for all I care. I'm just here to protect my country and my man.

"I don't quite care what Jacques likes," I mutter, earning a glare from my father.

"Oh, I am so happy my little girl is finally getting married.

I've dreamed of planning your wedding since you were born." My mother gleams, interrupting the tension as she sets her teacup on the table.

"The seamstress will be here in twenty minutes to alter the dress I've picked out for you. After that, you have meetings with our head of public relations to figure out how to announce your arrival to the country, and then you need a good night's sleep. Tomorrow at eleven a.m. is the big day. The wedding will be here in the great hall. You should take a peek at it when you get the chance," she prattles on, losing me with every word she says.

I can't believe I'm doing this.

Tears want to burst from deep within me, but there's no time for crying apparently.

"Where are my brothers?" I interrupt her because if I am home, that would be the one positive to all of this.

"Simon and Antoine are meeting with Jacques to make sure the wedding contract is all set. Mathéo is at a fundraiser event. You'll see them all tomorrow at the wedding," my father supplies. "I must go now. I have a meeting to attend to. Thank you for returning. Your country will thank you for it." His words pull on my heartstrings, knowing exactly where to hit me the hardest.

"Now that he's gone, let us talk, just ladies." My mother scoots closer, leaning toward me over the table. "Do you know what happens between a lady and a man once they're wedded?"

Is she serious right now?

A laugh bubbles out of my throat because of course my mother never gave me that *talk* growing up. I had the conversation with my maid. The staff here taught me more than either of my parents did.

"I'm not a virgin, Mother, don't you worry." *And I'm not screwing Jacques either*, I add mentally.

My mother coughs at my comment, dabbing her lips with

a napkin as her cheeks pinken. "The dress I got you is lovely. It's a traditional silk gown w—"

"I don't care, Mother," I shout, startling her. "I don't want any of this. The dress, Jacques, or to look like this. I'm here for my country and to protect the person I love. Let's get that settled right now."

She straightens in her seat, the tucking of her bottom lip beneath her teeth telling me she's not happy.

"I don't know where we went wrong raising such an ungrateful child. You should be shouting from the rooftops about this. Jacques is a good man, far better than you deserve after what you've done to us."

Her hateful words are like a slap across my face, stinging as they seep into me. Except they don't fill me with sadness, rather anger. But I won't give her that either. She doesn't deserve any part of me.

Instead, I stand and smooth my blazer down. "It's great to be home." I give her my fakest smile and curtsy. "I'll be in my room. Tell the seamstress to meet me there."

I leave with that, not sparing her a second glance as I slam the door and run to my old room on the second floor.

My hand claps on the silver handle once I get there, pushing the double doors open. My old room comes into view. Pale gray walls, white porcelain floors, a four-poster bed with white sheets and white pillows. My white vanity and a shelf of classic books I've never touched in my life but my mother insisted needed to be there still stand in the corner.

I close the door behind me and walk to the shelf, pick up a book by Charlotte Brontë, and whip it against the wall. I do the same with another classic, throwing every single book at the wall until they lie in a heap on the ground.

I don't realize I'm crying until a tear drips down my chin.

My knees finally give out, and I slowly sink to the cold floor, curling up into a ball as sobs rack my body. With my eyes closed, I think of Ryker, but it only makes me cry harder. I wonder how he reacted… or maybe he didn't even care? Maybe he's glad I left, making our agreement that much easier to end.

I crawl my way to my bed and under the covers. I say a silent prayer to the universe that Idris finds a loophole, that something, anything will get me out of this mess. And if you're not too busy, universe, I'd like my man back too.

That's whose arms I pretend to be in, safe and content as I drift off to sleep. Only for my own blood-curdling scream to wake me up moments later. Except in this nightmare, it was my own parents locking me in a cage.

Chapter Thirty-Nine

Ryker

The twelve-hour plane ride to Lorsica felt like twenty. Theo tried to keep our spirits up with his jokes, but none of us were in the mood for it. We're all tense with what's to come.

There's no chance in hell we'll be able to get anywhere near the palace, which means we need to break her out in the middle of the night. Or at least try to, because we have absolutely no idea how to do it.

"Why don't we just go to the palace and ask if we can see her, that we're friends from school?" Theo asks as we set our bags down in the hotel we're staying at.

"Jesus," Elio mutters, scrubbing a hand down his face. "She's a princess, remember? A member of the royal family. We can't just roll up to the palace and ask to see her. Chances are her security team has us all red flagged too."

"I don't see y'all coming up with a better idea," Theo points out while turning the TV on.

A picture of Camille fills the screen, except it doesn't look like my girl. This version of her has darker hair, fancy clothes, and a smile that doesn't meet her eyes.

"Turn it up," Jasmine instructs.

Theo does as she says, but a French voice fills our ears.

"Tell us what they're saying." I look at Elio.

"I will, now shh," he orders me, listening quietly as various pictures fill the screen. Most of them are of Camille, some of the palace, and then there's a blond guy who has the most punchable face I've ever seen.

Somehow I know without the translation that this is the guy she's supposed to marry. Not on my fucking watch.

We wait quietly while Elio listens, and my stomach churns with each passing minute, feeling like the more time we waste, the more I lose *her*.

Elio turns the TV off, then moves to face us. "The wedding is at eleven a.m. tomorrow at the palace. She's to be married to Jacques Auclair, the son of the Prime Minister of Calis."

Fuck.

"We're too late." I worry, sitting on the edge of the bed.

Jasmine turns to me, a fire in her eyes. "Hey, we did not come all this way to be scared off by timelines. We're here, and we'll do this. I'm not leaving without her."

It's exactly what I needed to hear, her determination filling me with a burning desire to take my girl home. "Neither am I." I stand, feeling more confident than I was just seconds ago.

A piercing ring interrupts the moment, all of us looking at Elio as he pulls his phone out of his pocket. "It's her brother," he tells us as he puts him on speaker. "Quentin, how's it going?"

"Not fucking good. My sister ran back home to our father, disobeying Idris's orders to stay put until we figured this shit out. Which is still taking a hell of a lot longer than we anticipated or wanted. To top it off, my dad destroyed her phone," he groans, clearly stressed by the situation.

"I know it's a shit show, but we're here in Lorsica. I'm trying to help my girlfriend and your sister's boyfriend to get her back," Elio admits.

"And your sister's best friend, Theo," Theo shouts, earning eye rolls left and right.

"Sorry about that," Elio murmurs.

"Wait, what? You're in Lorsica? What are you planning to do? You do know there's no way you're going to get anywhere near her or that wedding, right?" Quentin half laughs, half scoffs in disbelief.

I grab the phone from Elio, deciding to speak directly to Quentin. "Then tell me what I can do, because I'm not letting your sister marry anyone but me."

"Presuming she wants to marry you, that is," Theo jokes, but no one laughs.

"That could buy us the time we need to prove my dad is lying about everything," Quentin says as if a light bulb went off in his head. "If you could prevent the wedding from happening, at least we can avoid that disaster and work on defusing the one that will come after. Which includes my father trying to ruin your life."

"I know, and I don't care. All I care about is her. He can destroy me all he wants. I'm not letting him destroy her," I tell him with absolute certainty.

"Give us something. What can we do to get her out of there? You broke her out of there once. Do it again," Jasmine speaks up, and Elio wraps his hand around hers with a gentle squeeze.

Quentin chuckles. "Never thought I'd have to break my baby sister out of a country again but—wait, that's it!"

"What?" we all ask in unison, waiting with bated breath.

"My brother Mathéo, he's like me and Camille. While he never left the palace for good, he has a heart of gold. I think I can trust him to take Camille to a secret spot to meet with you guys."

"You think, or you know?" I ask. "We don't want to risk

losing our advantage of being here by involving him, only to have him rat us out."

Call me skeptical, but I don't trust easily.

He's quiet for a moment, then with clarity says, "I *know*. I'm going to call him right now, then I'll give you a call back."

Quentin hangs up, and I say a silent prayer that he's right.

"So *if* this doesn't work… Y'all ever seen *Wedding Crashers*? I can start on our background stories as soon as possible," Theo offers, always trying to lighten the mood.

Jasmine's smile is faint. "This is going to work, but yes, Theo, that can be plan B."

We fall into our own thing while we wait. Theo's on his phone, Jasmine sits on Elio's lap in the chair by the desk in our room, while I sit here and think of Camille.

Of her long champagne silky hair, of those big light blue eyes that I could spend hours staring into, and her smile that feels like that first warm day after a long winter.

Fuck, I've missed her and it's barely been a full day.

There's not a fucking chance I would let her go for good.

A few hours later, Quentin gives us a plan that he ensures will work.

Mathéo apparently had no idea about any of this until he saw Camille all over the news. That information lit a fire in all of us because it meant that her dad was bullshitting this whole save the country crap just to get her back under his reign.

The plan is to have Mathéo take Cami for a drive tonight, asking for some sibling time since it's been so long. He'll take her to a small waterfall about twenty minutes from the palace, a place they used to go to as kids, I guess.

What she doesn't know is that I'll be there, along with

Jasmine, Elio, and Theo. Then I'll ask Camille to be my wife, and hopefully she agrees to a happily ever after with me.

I double-check my pocket, ensuring my makeshift ring is there like I've done every ten minutes since we've landed.

It's fucking game time.

Operation *Get My Girl Back* is officially in action.

Chapter Forty

Camille

Sleep evades me as I toss and turn in a bed that doesn't feel like my own, despite having slept in it for most of my life.

I slam my fists down on my comforter in irritation. Not only has this been the longest day with the time difference, but I'm also mentally exhausted.

Within twelve hours, I'll be married to a man I've never even met before.

I debate running away, but then I picture Ryker. I see him never making his dreams come true, and the gut-wrenching pain that accompanies that picture is one of the things that keeps me from bolting. The other being that I don't want my country to fall apart because I know how much wealth this partnership with Calis will bring Lorsica.

A knock on my bedroom door has me sitting up in bed, my breaths heavy as I wonder who's on the other side at this time of night. Lorsica is the place that *does* sleep. It's rare you find anyone here up past eleven.

Swinging my legs over, my feet pad quietly across the cold floor to grab my lavender silk robe. My pajamas are decent, a tank top and shorts, but the chill in the air has me wanting to wrap up in the comfort of my robe. With every step I take toward the door, my heart pounds loudly in my ears, more so once I have my hand on the knob.

I breathe in deeply, channel the strength I know I can muster, and open the door. "Mathéo!" I whisper-yell as my eyes instantly fill with tears at seeing the youngest of my brothers, only two years older than me, for the first time in years.

He hasn't changed much. Wavy brown hair, green eyes, and skin that's tanner than the rest of us from all the time he spends volunteering outdoors, looking the same as he did four years ago.

"Maribel," he whispers, his eyes bright and wet with emotion.

I pull him into me, and we hold on to each other, basking in the connection. I step back and motion for him to enter my room, locking the door behind him.

"What are you doing here?" I ask, unsure what his take is on all of this.

"Taking over Q's job of busting you out of this place." His lopsided grin appears. "Not for good sadly, but I thought we could go for a drive. Go to our spot."

He means the waterfall. It's where he, Q, and I used to sneak away to as kids when Simon and Antoine, my other two brothers, annoyed us. Which was seventy-five percent of the time.

While sadness fills my chest that he can't somehow get me out of this situation, I am thrilled about the temporary relief. "How will this work? What if we get caught?"

Mathéo chuckles, always the easygoing and laid-back one. I don't think he knows what anxiety even feels like. "My little hellraiser of a sister is worried about getting caught? Since when?" I laugh at that, and he continues, "Do you trust me?"

"Of course. You're my brother."

And I do. We may not have seen each other in years, but

I've never once had a problem with Mathéo. In fact, he's the purest of us all. He constantly spends his time giving back to our community and is the sweetest person I've ever met.

He motions his head toward my door, while putting a finger to his lips.

"Then follow me, Cami."

Warmth fills my chest at the fact that he called me Cami, acknowledging the new life I've created for myself and the most authentic version of me.

Mathéo pops his head out the door, checking to see if the hallway is clear. He then motions me to follow him. We quietly tiptoe down the hallway until we reach a large art piece on the wall, stopping in front of it.

"Mathéo, why are we stopping?" I whisper.

Mathéo just grins and pulls on the frame, revealing a hidden door.

"Are you serious? How did I never know about this? I could've escaped so much more easily all those years ago!"

He puts a finger over his mouth, reminding me to be silent as we quietly make our way through the dark corridor, using his phone for light to guide our way. Within minutes, we reach another door, which opens up to the courtyard on the back side of the palace where his car is parked.

We quickly get in and as we drive down the curved path to the gate, I can't help but ask, "What about the gate? Won't security see us?"

"I may or may not have turned off the gate cameras before I came to your room," he admits, looking sheepish.

He's never done a bad thing in his life, so I can imagine he feels a bit guilty.

"Thank you, Mathéo. I needed this breather." I sink into the seat, feeling the tension leave my body the farther we get away from there.

His grin is wide as he looks over at me, then focuses back on the road. "Just so you know, I never hated you for leaving. I only wish you had let me in on the secret."

My own guilt creeps in at his admission. "I'm sorry. It truthfully happened so fast and you were gone that whole year. I didn't want to bother you."

"You can always come to me. You're family," he affirms. "We're good, just do me a favor and say yes, okay?"

"To what?" I tilt my head in confusion.

"You'll see."

Chapter Forty-One

Camille

Mathéo's car winds down the country road, the palace long gone from our rearview mirrors. With each mile behind us, I feel lighter yet slightly nervous.

What does he want me to say yes to? To marrying Jacques tomorrow?

He should know by now that once I set my mind to do something, I do it. No matter how much it's going to kill me.

Minutes later, we veer off the path onto the grass and park behind the large olive tree where we used to park our bikes. It seems like it was just a few years ago when we did this as kids, but in reality, it's been close to almost a decade.

"I wish I had changed because walking around nature in slippers isn't super ideal," I complain as I slam the door shut.

"And yet it's probably the only clothes you have that suit you," Mathéo comments as he leads us down the stony path toward the entrance to a lush forest that contains our secret waterfall.

It's quiet and dark here, the perfect escape I needed. The moonlight shines above us, casting a silvery glow on the stones as we let them guide the way.

We catch up on the twenty-minute walk to our spot, filling each other in on our lives that we missed over the past four years. He recently returned home at the beginning of this year but is already planning his next humanitarian trip.

"What about you, Cami?" Mathéo asks, holding a branch back as he lets me walk ahead of him on the path.

A mixture of happiness and pain fills my chest as images of the life I was building comes to mind. "You know how when you're a kid and you make up this dream life? Well, I was finally living mine." My voice catches in my throat. "I fell in love, I had a great group of friends, and the job I've always wanted. I got to live life the way *I* deemed fit. I learned how to live on my own, figured out how to cook for myself, and what I liked or didn't like to do. I know that sounds so simple, but growing up the way we did, those are things I never would've had the chance to experience had I stayed."

"Let's backpedal a little bit. Tell me about this falling in love thing you speak of?" Mathéo grins.

We're a minute away from the small clearing, and I use that time to gather my thoughts.

"His name is Ryker, and he's a baseball player."

"Of course he is." He laughs.

I chuckle and continue. "He's entirely my opposite, but in the best way possible. I've never felt that way with someone, ever. Ryker can come off as an asshole, and he can be, but with me, he's different. He's my Ryker the biker." A sad smile attempts to lift my lips but fails because talking about him is making my heart want to jump out of my chest and never return to the pain it's feeling.

Mathéo turns and steps in front of me, blocking my view of the waterfall I know is a few feet behind him now. I can hear the waves crashing softly in the distance, but all I can focus on is the excited grin on Mathéo's face.

What is going on?

"He sounds great. Think you can introduce him to me?"

I'm about to tell him it's not possible, when he steps to the side and my eyes instantly zero in on the tall, tattooed man with long hair standing in front of the pond that the waterfall goes into.

Ryker.

He's here. I don't think. I only run, and I don't stop until I'm in the safety of his arms.

My body shakes against his, my tears soaking his neck as I grip him tight while he holds me just as tightly. "I'm s-s-orry," I mumble through my tears.

"*Shh,*" he whispers, his hand cradling the back of my head as he holds me close.

"You asked me to never leave without telling you and I did. I—"

Ryker silences me with his lips crashing against mine in the most passionate kiss I've ever felt in my life. My tears are probably staining his face, but he doesn't seem to mind as his hand grips my jaw and deepens the kiss.

Feeling his lips against mine after fearing I might never again makes me shiver and I pour everything I have into the kiss. All the love, longing, and appreciation I have for him, for what we share together.

Mathéo coughs somewhere behind us, reminding me that he's indeed still here and watching this, most likely uncomfortably. We both pull apart, breathless, and stare into one another's eyes, shock painted in his irises as if he can't believe I'm really here. I could say the same about him.

"How are you here?" I ask as he sets me down, but keeps an arm around me.

"I knew something was wrong when I couldn't see you anywhere." His voice is tortured as he relives the memory, which only makes me cry more. "So I went to the stands to ask Jasmine and Theo, who told me everything. And from there, we decided to come and get our girl back."

"We?" I repeat, unsure what he means until I hear, "Millie Moo!"

I whip around to see Theo, Jasmine, and Elio emerging from the trees.

I move to go toward them, but Jasmine holds up her hand, "Wait."

"What's going on?" I ask Ryker, turning back to face him in confusion. That's when I see an emotion I never thought I'd see in him. *Fear.* "Hey," I murmur quietly, only for Ryker to hear. "What's wrong? No bullshit."

"I fell in love with a girl I told myself I couldn't have more with, for reasons that don't matter anymore. And now, I would give it all up, because I would still have everything I need with her." His stormy blue eyes soften as he gently caresses my cheek. "I love you, Camille."

His deep voice mixed with those sweet words has my entire body melting into a puddle of overwhelming joy. My hand reaches up to stroke his beard, and Ryker leans into the touch, covering my hand with his own as his eyes never once leave mine.

This man who I never thought would even look my way, loves me.

I'd kick my feet and giggle if it were possible, but for now, I'll settle with pressing my lips softly against his. When I pull back with both of my hands on his face, I smile and repeat the words back to him. "I love you, Ryker." My lips curve into a smile, but it fades when I remember why we're all here in the first place. "But I'm getting married tomorrow."

"You can't get married if you already are."

Everything around us fades as I say, "Ryker..." My throat bobs, clogged with emotions. "You can't. My father, he'll ruin your life and I won't let that happen, not to mention the fate of my country relies on me showing up tomorrow even though every fiber of my being is loathing each second I get closer to having to do it."

He shakes his head as he tucks a hair behind my ear before stepping back and pulling up his black shirt. "You didn't hear me, Cami."

My heart rate picks up at the sight of his chiseled abs and tattoos, despite being unsure what he's doing—wait.

Atop of the baseball he has tattooed near his heart lies a crown.

"Why is there a crown there?" My voice trembles from all the differing emotions coursing through me.

"I got this a few days ago with the intention of showing it to you to prove that you are my number one in life. Then I was going to ask you to be my official girlfriend," he explains while my fingers gently trail along the outside of the tattoo, careful not to touch it.

For once, I'm at a loss for words. Ryker pulls his shirt back down, then speaks up again, "I'd never play a game of baseball again if I knew I'd get to have you by my side for the rest of my life. I love baseball, and it would suck if I lost it, but I'd find other things to fill that void. Losing you, though? There's nothing that could replace the spot in my heart that was made just for you."

I suck in a breath while, *shocker*, more tears cascade down my cheeks.

"As for the country part, your brother and Idris are working on proving that your father is lying. And if it's true, your dad can figure it out. It's not your responsibility to bear, but I know you love the people here, so I'll work with you to figure out a solution. Anything except you walking down that fucking aisle tomorrow toward a man who's not me." Ryker's eyes darken, a hint of danger radiating off him at the bite in his words.

He has a point. What if this is all a ploy to get me back

here and I marry Jacques for nothing? If it's not a ploy, I'm sure there is something else we can do to help Lorsica. I've been consumed with so many emotions in the last day that I haven't even considered the countless other solutions that could solve this that wouldn't involve me walking down the aisle.

"Ryker, what are you saying?" I whisper as butterflies erupt in my stomach at the idea he's hinting at.

Slowly, he lowers to one knee in front of me. My hand flies to my mouth, while he holds the other.

"Camille, there's not a day that I don't think about meeting you at the gala and how much it pissed me off."

"This is not how you start a proposal," Theo interjects from behind me.

Jasmine shushes him.

Ryker shakes his head, but continues. "It pissed me off because I wanted you, but knew you were too good for me to keep. I thought I'd shake it off, but you planted yourself in my soul with no plans on leaving."

I marvel at hearing it. Even though he's said something about this in passing, I've never heard all of the details.

"I tried to keep my distance, especially once you started working with the team, but you want to know when I realized how fucked I was? The day I taught you how to throw a baseball, and you danced around in a circle with the biggest smile on your face."

"Why?" I somehow manage to ask through my tears.

"Because it was then that I realized how badly I wanted to wake up to that exact smile each and every day, how much I wanted to bask in the bliss you radiate each time you light up like that."

"Is that why you stormed away all grumpy-y?" I hiccup as I wipe under my eyes.

"Shh, this is my proposal." He grins, leaning down to press a kiss to the hand he's holding, while reaching in his pocket for…a lace from a baseball glove?

"Camille, I love you *so* fucking much. Will you please do me the honor of being my wife?" Ryker's eyes shine with love as he holds up the black leather to me. "I know this isn't the ring you deserve, but it's all I could do on short notice." He blushes, which makes my heart squeeze in my chest.

We may be young, yet I've never been more sure of something in my entire life. Ryker's it for me, and why not get started on our happily ever after as soon as possible?

"I love it and you beyond any words I could conjure. I never imagined I'd live a fairytale life, clearly." I chuckle, wiping at my eyes with my free hand. "But you've given me the love little girls dream about, the one I've secretly always hoped for." I smile widely and freely as I nod up and down. "Yes, a thousand times, yes."

Ryker ties the lace around my finger, then stands to lift me into his arms as he kisses me.

I break the kiss. "Who's going to marry us?" I question, looking nervously at Ryker because there is not a church in the country that would dare betray the king.

"That would be me," Theo shouts, causing us to turn toward him. "Say *bonjour* to your ordained minister." He grins, pointing to himself.

"Do I even want to know?" I murmur.

"Nope." Ryker shakes his head, taking my hand in his as we walk toward our friends and my brother.

We're an intertwined mess of congratulations between the six of us, and when Jasmine hugs me, we both cry harder.

"I'm so happy to see you," I tell her. "I can't believe you came all this way for me."

Jasmine tilts her head slightly in Elio's direction. "That would be thanks to Elio and his private jet, but even without it, I would have come."

"Thank you, all of you." I raise my voice, ceasing all side conversations between the boys.

Elio motions us along. "Let's get this wedding done. We don't know when or if someone will come looking for you."

Ryker hands me a bouquet of flowers. "Here, I picked these for you. Figured if anything, you'd like to have a bouquet of some sorts."

I marvel at the mix of wildflowers wrapped together with grass, much like the ones he tattooed on me. I'm the luckiest girl in the world, despite not feeling like it less than an hour ago.

You never know when life is going to surprise you, and isn't that the beauty of it all?

I thank him with a quick kiss, and then within minutes, Theo is standing between us, Elio and my brother by Ryker's side while Jasmine is on mine.

"Wait!" Jasmine squeaks as she pulls out her phone. I'm about to ask her what she's doing until I hear the tune of a FaceTime call and two familiar faces fill the screen.

"Did she say yes?" Aurora yells.

"Ask her yourself," Jasmine says, flipping the camera toward us.

Aurora's hand flies to her mouth while Cameron smiles. "I can't believe I'm missing my brother's wedding," Aurora pouts. "You owe me a do-over!"

"Stay on the line and be a part of it," Ryker offers, and I'm so proud of him for opening up his tiny circle to now include Aurora in his life.

"Why is she wearing pajamas?" Cameron whispers, probably thinking he was quieter than he actually was.

"You mean you don't like my purple robe and pajamas?" I tease him, striking a pose with my robe hanging dramatically off my shoulders.

Everyone laughs and Theo clears his throat for us to return to the task at hand.

"I stand here today…"

I'm getting my fairytale ending.

Chapter Forty-Two

Ryker

Camille is officially my wife.

God, there's nothing better than those two words now that they're attached to her. Camille *Lewis* is mine. Mine to protect, mine to love, mine to cherish. And I'll do it no matter the obstacles, I remind myself as we walk through a side door to the palace with Mathéo leading the way.

After the ceremony, Theo, Jasmine, and Elio chose to let us deal with things inside on our own, but are waiting in our getaway car so that once we're done, we can get out of here as soon as possible.

As Mathéo warned us, the guards are on us instantly.

Mathéo holds his hand up, ceasing their impending steps to no doubt remove me from the premises. "Stop. Touch either of them and you'll lose your job."

The guards halt, their eyes all fixated on me and my hand that's holding Camille's with no intention of letting go.

"Move," a booming voice projects from behind the barricade of guards, creating an open path between them, and I instantly know who it is.

King Antoine De Beaumont.

Rage simmers beneath my skin at the sight of him, for all that he's done to Camille.

He stomps toward us with purpose, darkness filling his eyes when they lock onto mine. I smirk back, not giving him the angry outburst I know he's expecting from me.

The king stops in front of us, while who I'm assuming is her mother comes jogging toward us.

"What do you think you're doing here?" he says through gritted teeth.

"Taking back what's mine." My voice is sardonic, and he hates it if the reddening of his face is any indication.

He rips Camille's hand out of mine and pulls her toward him.

I move just as quickly, gripping his wrist hard and yanking it off hers and stepping between them. "Get your hand off my *wife*," I grit out, my jaw clenching as anger threatens to take over.

The guards are on us instantly to protect their king, and I pull Camille into me in a protective stance, but Mathéo stops them again.

"Back off. He won't hurt my father. He's protecting the princess," Mathéo huffs, stepping between his dad and me.

Queen Marie's hand flies to her chest as she looks between the two of us. "Wife? What is the meaning of this?"

"She's not your anything. She will be married in less than twelve hours to someone else," her father informs me, utterly clueless.

Camille smirks, reaching into the pocket of her robe to retrieve the paper we signed that Theo printed off for us prior to the ceremony. "Actually, I'm not. You can't be married when you already are to someone else."

Mathéo takes it from her, holding it up so that her parents can read the fine print.

Her mother's face pales while her dad's explodes with fury.

"I am the king!" he shouts. "I can have you down that aisle if I so please."

"You can't. It was a legitimate wedding with a registered minister and witnesses. There's nothing you can do," Mathéo explains while he hands the paper back to Camille, who tucks it safely in her pocket.

"I will ruin you," her father seethes, looking at me. "Say goodbye to baseball, because you'll never play a game again. I'll make sure no organization would dare sign you on."

I shrug, tightening my hold on Camille. "Go ahead. This right here is the only thing I need."

He balks at that, squinting his eyes as he tries to figure out what game we're playing here. He then turns his anger to Camille. "What about Lorsica? Are you going to let your people suffer? You knew how important this merger was for us!"

"Speak to her like that again and I'll make sure it's the last time you ever speak to her at all," I threaten him, ready to do whatever it takes to keep her safe.

"Stop," a voice yells from behind us, and we all turn to see Idris storming through the palace.

"Idris," Camille whispers, her eyes wide with shock.

"You never listen, do you?" he says quietly to her as he passes us. He turns his attention to the king as he stops and stares him down.

"I should have you thrown in jail. My best employee quits to secretly work for my son, then protects my daughter whom he knows I've been looking for?" The king's voice drips with disdain as he faces off with Idris.

"Wait, I thought you said you knew where I was this whole time," Camille calls her father out.

"A lie, like everything else he said," Idris confirms as he looks over his shoulder at us, then back toward the king. "Isn't that right, Your *Highness*?"

Fear passes through the king's face so briefly I nearly miss it, but it's in that split second of truth that I know he's been lying this whole time.

"How dare you call your king a liar?"

"Because you are. We have concrete evidence that you only recently found out where Camille was. Most importantly, you lied about needing her to marry to save our country."

Silence falls upon us as we wait with bated breath to see what happens next.

"I wanted my daughter back." He tries to appear genuinely distraught as he looks at Camille. "And the country is indeed struggling. That wasn't a lie," her father defends, proving it truly wasn't about missing his daughter, looking more and more like a coward as the seconds tick by.

That's when Idris drops a bomb no one saw coming. "Ah, but she's not the solution, not when this country is facing struggles because of *your* gambling problem."

Her mother gasps. "Tell me that's not true."

Her father falls silent, answering her without saying it outright.

"That's what I thought," Idris says. "So you won't be blackmailing Camille into anything. If you dare to try, I'll be breaking it to the press that you're gambling your citizens' money away. Your only option here is to let her go and leave her alone for good while you do something to figure out how to save the country you are indebted to."

The queen begins to rub at her temples, seemingly overwhelmed by the news, while the king quietly seethes as he glares at Idris, knowing he's lost.

"My wife and I are leaving., I suggest you don't try to stop us," I warn, gently tugging on Camille's hand as we exit through the side door.

"I hope you figure it out, my *king,* because it won't be us who will save you," Idris calls out before he too follows us out, along with Mathéo.

"I can't believe he'd do this," Mathéo murmurs as we approach the SUV with our friends inside.

Camille sighs, turning to her brother. "I can. My heart breaks for these people, but I don't know what we can do. I'll do anything except sacrifice my own happiness. It's far too precious to gamble."

"I wouldn't want you to, sis," he tells her earnestly. "I'll figure something out. I've always loved helping. No better time to demonstrate that than now."

"We'll all help you. Q. We're family." I extend my hand out to him, and he takes it instantly, giving me a firm but welcoming grip.

"I'm glad she has you. Take care of her for me." Mathéo places his hand in mine, giving it a firm hold then releasing it.

"You can always count on that," I tell him, but my eyes are on her.

"Our team will do some more digging, see what we can find and how we can help," Idris cuts into the conversation. "And you." He faces Camille. "I should've expected you to run, especially when I told you to stay."

Camille sags against me for comfort I'm more than willing to provide as I wrap my arm around her shoulder. "I'm sorry, but I didn't see any other way and I wasn't risking anything happening to Ryker."

"As soon as we found the information, I hopped on the next flight out. It of course helped that I knew Ryker would be saving you from going through with the marriage, but I still needed to get here to make sure your father didn't manipulate you any further," Idris explains, looking exhausted from the days of nonstop investigation.

Camille's eyes water, nose sniffling with unshed tears. "Thank you, Idris, for being the dad I never had."

Idris cracks a smile, his head shaking. "Thanks for being the child I never knew I wanted. And for never listening, making the experience of parenting that much more real."

We all chuckle at that, and I feel gratitude toward Idris more than I ever have. Knowing there's someone who cares about Camille and has her back like this is everything she deserves.

"I should get back in there and do some damage control. We'll talk soon," Mathéo says, then hugs all of us, lingering with Camille as they whisper to each other in French.

He leaves, and we all climb into the getaway car where we explain everything that happened inside to our friends.

"Wow, Ry guy, you told off a royal member? That's ballsy, even for you." Theo chuckles from the very back seat as Elio drives down the path to the gate.

"Yeah, well, when he put his hands on my wife, I didn't give a fuck who he was," I grumble while my fingers gently trace circles on her thigh.

"Shut up!" Jasmine turns from the front passenger seat. "You're a wife now. I'm so jealous."

I don't miss the look Elio gives her, and I'm sure he'll be saying those words much sooner than Jasmine might know.

"I sure am." Camille looks up at me and it makes my heart skip in my chest because she's beautiful and mine to keep. Forever.

I lean into her, my breath hitting her ear as I speak.

"Just so you know, I would've asked you to marry me even if Idris told us about the blackmail first."

"Really?"

"You leaving made me realize I never want to be without you," I admit, kissing her cheeks that pinken from my words.

"*Moi aussi, mon amour.*"

"Pussy? Baby, we can't talk about that right now," I groan, already halfway hard thinking about it as I kiss her neck.

Camille shoves me playfully. "I said *aussi*, as in *me too, my love*."

"I love that y'all are in love and what not, but do you think we could tone down the PDA just a tad? I got Jelio holding hands up front and Rami nearly making love in front of me," Theo pipes up.

"Jelio? Rami?" I shoot him an annoyed glare.

"Yeah, your couple names. Cameron and Aurora are Cora," he says all too happily.

"And yours and Marcela's would be…?" Cami asks.

His enthusiasm fades as he sits back in his seat. "That's not happening. She's taking a break from dating after everything that happened, and I think she sees me only as a friend right now."

"Maybe you should move on, find someone else to have fun with." Idris shrugs beside Theo.

"Maybe," Theo mumbles back, staring out the window.

I don't think Theo is the type to do that, because once he has his mind set on something, he doesn't waver from it. Which means if he has his sight set on Marcela, I wouldn't be shocked if he waited for her…

Well, for forever.

Chapter Forty-Three

Camille

"You're what?" Coach Warren coughs, looking between the two of us with an unreadable look on his face.

"Married, Coach." Ryker doesn't shy away from Coach Warren. Instead, he proudly holds my hand in front of him.

After we spent the day sleeping and consummating our marriage yesterday, we knew we needed to come back to Colorado as soon as possible before word got out. We also needed to talk to his mom.

To say I'm a bundle of nerves and excitement is an understatement.

I know people will judge us because of how young we are, but what they don't know is how deep and real our love is. It's not something that can be explained with fancy words or excessive gestures. Although intangible, I've never had the privilege of holding something so precious before.

Ryker gives my hand a gentle squeeze as we wait for Coach's response. His hardened gaze flicks between the two of us for a moment before the corner of his lips turn up in the slightest.

"Congratulations." He stands, shaking my hand and then Ryker's.

"You're not mad?" Ryker asks warily.

Coach shakes his head as she settles back in his brown leather chair. "Mad? Why would I be mad when two people who love each other decide to commit to that love?"

"Because of your speech at the beginning of the season about needing to be focused and all that," Ryker reminds him.

Coach waves him off. "As your coach, I need to play that role, make sure I got the best guys on my team. But as someone who cares about you, I'm happy for you. So long as you still win me a championship and don't interfere with Camille's job."

"It won't, Coach, I promise," I speak up, giving him my most reassuring smile.

"Did you talk to Suby yet?" Coach looks at me, then at his computer, always multitasking.

Ryker looks at me, confused as ever. "*Mark* Suby? The owner of the Detroit Panthers?"

"I was going to tell you, but then everything happened…" I trail off, a mixture of happy and sad memories hitting me all at once. "Anyways, he reached out to Coach Warren because they're interested in hiring me to run their social media. I haven't had a chance to talk to them yet."

Ryker's face lights up at my words. "Baby, are you serious? That's fucking awesome. I'm so proud of you." He smiles before kissing my forehead.

"All right, none of that in here, son," Coach grumbles.

"Thank you." I tilt my head up at my husband, and the fact that I can say that about him is beyond my wildest dreams.

Ryker was a fantasy to me, a fairytale I never thought would happen, but Ryker's shown me that they're not just for movies. They can happen to anyone, especially when you least expect it.

"Camille, I'm so glad you could meet with us today," Mark Suby's voice emanates through my laptop. "I have here the head of HR and our social media department to sit it on for today."

As soon as we left Coach's office, Ryker suggested that I email Suby to set up a meeting as soon as possible to avoid losing out on the opportunity. He emailed me back right away, so we rushed back to my apartment and changed my tank top into a blouse for the video chat.

"Hi, everyone, I'm beyond excited to be speaking with you all." My voice is confident, yet calm.

He sits up in his chair, hands folded on the desk he's sitting at. "As are we. Look, I'm going to cut right to the chase because I'm a busy guy. We want you to come work for us. There's room for growth in your career, travel opportunities, and benefits along with a salary I don't think you will be disappointed in. So what do you think?"

I do my best to take it all in and remain composed because I'm currently freaking out on the inside. "I think this sounds like an amazing opportunity," I start and look up, over my screen, at Ryker, who's giving me a thumbs-up. It was our code if the offer sounded good. "I would love to accept the position and begin as soon as graduation is over."

"Excellent, we're lucky to have you on the team. Welcome to the Panthers, Camille. I'll have HR send over the contract as soon as possible."

"I have to tell you something," I blurt, startling even myself with my outburst.

He gives me the floor to speak. "Go ahead."

"My brother, Quentin, is one of your pitchers. It's a long story, but I really hope that won't affect things going forward." My voice threatens to shake for fear of ruining this, but I control it.

"Really? That's amazing. We had no idea. Hell, I would've asked him for your number to contact you instead of going through the damn school." He chuckles, and it makes me smile in relief. "It's no problem. We don't have a policy that says siblings can't work together."

With a deep breath, I bring up the next potential issue. "I also recently married Ryker Lewis, who I know is a top prospect for you in the draft this year," I add, noticing the look of shock on Mark's face.

"Wow, congratulations. We also don't have a fraternization policy because I believe my players' personal lives are just that, personal. As long as it doesn't affect their performance on the field."

"Thank you, and that's really great to hear, because I am beyond excited to get started on my dream position."

"Not a problem, Camille. Tell your husband that I plan on getting in contact with his agent within the next week. He's had an exceptional season," he remarks, and I don't miss the way Ryker lights up at the praise behind my screen.

"That he has. Thank you so much, Mr. Suby." I beam, waving as we end the call and slam my laptop closed. I jump up from my spot at the dinner table and right into Ryker's open arms.

He spins me around as I wrap my legs around his waist. "Congrats, princess," he says, squeezing me tighter.

I pull back, seeing his eyes shine with love and happiness like never before. "Back at you, Ryker the biker."

He grins, eyebrow raised. "Soon to be coworkers, huh?"

"It's looking like it. Is that something you're okay with?" I find the need to ask because we've yet to talk about this.

"Am I okay with it? I get to see my wife at work everyday, live together in the same city, and not have to miss you when I'm out of town on away games? Yeah, you could say I'm more than okay with it."

I'm imagining our future begin to form right before me, and it's everything I've ever wanted. I kiss his cheek, then his lips, where our mouths linger for a beat.

He sets me down with a pat on my ass, guiding me toward the front door with my hand in his.

"As much as I'd like to fuck you right now, we need to go tell my mom that we're husband and wife."

I've never even met his mom before, and now, I'm her daughter-in-law. My stomach churns with worry at the thought, but then I tell myself that if she's the person responsible for raising the man I love, she's more than likely just as amazing.

Chapter Forty-Four

Ryker

One thing that will never get old is seeing Camille dismount my bike, take her helmet off, and allow her long hair to blow in the wind as she shakes it out. Her hair is still chocolate brown because there hasn't been time for her to get it dyed back, but I don't care what color her hair is, so long as she's happy with it.

She's the sexiest woman in the world either way, and she's all mine.

"What are we doing at the tattoo shop?" Camille asks, her head tilted in confusion.

I take my own helmet off, dismount, and store them away before answering her. "I have an idea, but if you don't like it, be honest," I tell her, looking down into her eyes.

She peers up at me, curiosity in her gaze. "Okay, what is it?"

"You don't have to do it with me, but I'd like to get your initials tattooed on the inside of my ring finger instead of wearing an actual ring. I'll get you a ring because I want everyone to know you're taken, forever," I grumble the last part, my possessive side bearing its ugly head.

Camille's plush pink lips part, then lift into her bright smile. "Ryker, that's so sweet. I love that, so long as you're sure about it."

"More than I've ever been about a tattoo, except for the crown. That also ranks up there." I grin, loving the way she blushes as I say it.

"I want the same on mine. While I would like a ring one day, I'd love to have your initials on me."

God, I love this girl so fucking much.

"Then let's go." I grab her hand in mine and lead us through the back door. The shop's closed on Sundays, which means we have it to ourselves.

It only takes about an hour in total, and when we put our ring fingers next to one another, mine has *CL* on it and hers has *RL*.

Camille admires our fingers until I wrap them both to keep them clean. "I love it."

"You ready?" I ask her, referring to meeting my mom.

"I'm nervous, but excited to meet the person who raised the man I love," she admits, wrapping her arms around my neck as she steps into me.

I lean down and take her lips in a sweet kiss. "She's going to love you, just like I do."

"I don't think I've ever thanked you," Camille says when I pull back.

"For what?" I inquire while my arms wrap around her waist.

"For loving me the way you do. It makes me feel safe, cherished, and whole. I can be myself with you and know you'll always love me for me, not for what I can do for you. Most of all, thank you for allowing me to love you because it's been the greatest thing I've experienced yet." Her eyes mist with tears, and I don't hold back the same emotions that are flooding me as my own eyes dampen.

I answer her with a searing kiss, letting my love for her be felt with the way my mouth moves with hers. Moments later, we pull back, both panting and needy for each other.

"And we're just at the beginning, with forever to go," I rasp, undoing the button of her jeans while pulling on the zipper.

Camille mumbles incoherently, her eyes glazed with desire as she does the same to my pants, yanking my jeans down and freeing my hard cock. I do the same with her jeans and panties, discarding them on the ground.

Camille inclines her head toward the leather chair in the middle of the room. "Sit."

I do as she says and hold my hand out to her. "Come sit on my cock, *wife*."

Camille takes my hand and lifts her leg over my hips, straddling me. The feel of her bare, dripping cunt against me is almost enough to make me lose control right there.

"Are you not sore?" I ask her because all we did yesterday was lie in bed either fucking or sleeping. If she didn't have an IUD, she'd be pregnant for sure.

She grinds against me and lets out the sweetest moan of pleasure. "I am, but I need this."

"Take whatever you need."

"I'll come twice, and then you can come. Sounds good, *husband*?"

I smirk, darting my tongue out to flick her nipple. "Make it three times, princess."

And I make sure of just that, because I'll always take care of my wife.

Chapter Forty-Five

Camille

Meeting my mother-in-law with her son's cum still seeping out of me is not the most ideal of situations, yet here we are. At least I look presentable on the outside with my white skinny jeans, a lavender baby doll top, and my white Chucks, my hair draping over my shoulder in waves.

"Bear!" his mom exclaims, bounding down the steps to pull Ryker into a hug.

Once they part, Ryker turns toward me. "Mom, I have someone I'd like you to meet. This is Camille, Camille Lewis. My wife."

Something is off because his mom doesn't seem shocked in the slightest. She simply smiles widely and claps her hands together. "This is so lovely," she says, then pulls me into a hug. "Welcome to the family, honey. I can't wait to get to know you more. Come, let's have a drink on the back porch."

We agree and follow her to the backyard gate. Once we pass the wooded frame, there's an eruption of voices yelling, "Surprise!"

Standing in his mom's backyard is everyone we love. Theo, Jasmine, Elio, Aurora, Cameron, Marcela, Noah, Cuddy, Aurora's dad and brother, Quentin, Idris, and even Mathéo is here.

"Is this okay?" Ryker says low enough only for me to hear.

I turn to face him, shocked and overjoyed. "You planned this?"

He nods. "We may not have gotten married the traditional way, but I wanted to celebrate with our friends and family. A make-up reception of sorts."

"It's perfect. Thank you." I quickly hug him, then we turn to our friends, exchanging hugs as we make our way around.

Everyone mingles as music plays through a speaker, and it's then I notice the makeshift dance floor on the patio deck, the cake on a table to the side waiting to be cut by us, a minibar being run by Nate, and a photobooth for us to take pictures.

It's perfect and I don't think I could be any happier.

I never wanted the Cinderella kind of wedding, so I'm beyond ecstatic with the simplistic and casual setting this is.

Before I can greet anyone, I'm dragged away by the girls to get changed into something a little more appropriate. I marvel at the dress they picked for me, unable to take my eyes away from it in the full-length mirror. The white silk full-length gown clings to my body. It has a cowl neck and bows holding the straps together at the top.

It's simple, yet perfectly me.

"Ryker isn't going to be able to keep his hands off you," Jasmine teases, fanning herself as she stares at me.

I shake my head with a wide smile. "Thank you so much for all of this. It's truly perfect. I couldn't ask for better friends."

Aurora, Jasmine, and Marcela stand before me, looking absolutely beautiful in their matching strapless silk gowns in their favorite colors. Mint green for Aurora, orange for Jasmine, and pink for Marcela.

Aurora grins. "My brother is one lucky man."

"You look gorgeous, Cami." Marcela smiles shyly while Jasmine wraps an arm around her. Marcela easily became one of us, like she's always been a part of our little group.

The four of us embrace in a group hug, but Jasmine doesn't let it go on too long. "All right, let's get this bride ready to go. Marcela, I need you to do her hair, and, Aurora, you need to do her makeup."

"And what will you be doing?" I quirk a brow at her.

She holds up her phone and begins doing just that as we finish getting ready. "Take photos for memories and enjoy this moment."

Once we're done getting ready, nerves churn in my gut as we descend the stairs and make our way to the glass doors that will take us onto the patio deck. While everything is still very much casual, the change in outfit has me slightly on edge to see Ryker's reaction to me in it.

In a good way.

The girls exit first, and from my position, I watch as Cameron's eyes light up, then Elio's, then Theo's as Marcela is the last to go.

With a deep breath, I exit through the open door, the music and noise halting as everyone turns to stare at me. I've spoken at charity events and even parliament meetings, but I have never been as nervous as I currently am.

Until my eyes find Ryker's and in an instant, it all goes away.

His lips part, his eyes roaming over every inch of me, and I swear I can see a sheen of sweat on his forehead.

I stop right in front of him and press my palm against his heart to find it racing. "Ryker? You okay?"

"Goddamn, baby," he chokes out, placing his hand over mine. "You're so beautiful."

My cheeks lift at his words, my smile vibrant. "Thank you, as are you."

Ryker changed as well, now sporting a black long-sleeved button-up, with the sleeves rolled up because he's trying to kill me, I suppose, and black jeans.

"As much as I want to keep you to myself, we need to go make our rounds." He puts his hand out, and I take it as we begin to make our way to our friends and family, as husband and wife.

Ryker and I are just finishing catching up with Noah and Cuddy when Aurora and Cameron walk up to us.

"Welcome to the family, officially!" Aurora squeals, pulling me into a hug.

"Thank you, sis." I beam, happy I can finally utter those words since I only have brothers.

"I'm still upset you didn't want to redo the whole wedding, but I'll get over it eventually." She chuckles while Cam looks down at her with heart eyes if I've ever seen them.

"How are things going with work?" Ryker asks Cam, pulling our quiet friend into the conversation.

He grins, his dimples showing. "Really good. My latest game is just about ready for the testing phase, so I'm quite excited about that."

"And Team USA, superstar?" Ryker looks at his soon-to-be stepsister.

"It's hard work, but I love every second of it. Only one more year to go until the Olympics. It'll be in Paris, and you two have to come," she exclaims.

"Of course we'll be there," I reassure her, ready to cheer her on anywhere in the world.

That's what family does.

Jasmine and Elio walk up to our group, sharing their congratulations, but before they can say anything else, Theo enters the conversation. "All right, who wants to place a bet on the next couple to be engaged?" He claps Cameron on the shoulder, who shrugs him off.

"Well, we know it's not you," Elio retorts.

"Be nice." Jasmine tries her best to sound serious, but her smile gives her away.

"You excited for senior year?" I ask Theo, taking the attention away from his love life.

"Hell yeah. Our team is looking stronger than ever, and I think we could finally win that championship."

"Let's hope so. The football team is the only athletic program that hasn't won a title since the school's conception," Ryker responds.

"Don't remind me." Theo sighs while looking around the yard for who we all know is Marcela.

I find myself looking too, knowing she's very shy and introverted and must feel uncomfortable being here. I spot her sitting on the bench under the oak tree, reading on her Kindle.

I excuse myself from the group and make my way over to her, then sit down beside her. "Whatcha reading?" I nudge her with my shoulder.

Her honey eyes flick up to me, a blush covering her cheeks. "I'm sorry. I hope you don't think I'm being rude by reading. It's just, I don't know many people and—"

"You're not being rude. You're taking care of yourself by taking a break. I appreciate you coming, I know how hard parties are for you," I tell her earnestly.

"Thank you, and I'm reading a fantasy book about dragons and their riders." She smiles shyly, pulling a brown wave behind her ear.

"Sounds like fun. I've been wanting to get into reading." I smile at her. "We could maybe grab coffee one day, then go to the bookstore and you could give me some suggestions?"

Marcela perks up at the idea. "That sounds like a dream day. Let's do it."

I nod as a comfortable silence falls between us.

"The love you and Ryker share is really special," Marcela comments, breaking the quiet lull.

I look over at where my husband is sitting with our friends and I feel so lucky I get to call him mine. "It is."

"It reminds me of the love I see in my books, but I never knew it could actually be real," she murmurs, her eyes casting downward.

The reminder of her shitty ex is a punch to the gut, because how could someone not love this girl and make her feel that true love is only in fiction?

It's with that thought that I make a silent wish to the universe that one day Marcela gets the love she's been reading about.

The wedding party has been nothing short of amazing, and I'm just about to sit with Ryker for a break when Quentin storms past me with Mathéo hot on his heels. Ryker and I exchange a glance and immediately follow after them.

"Q, what's going on?" I huff as we catch up to them.

Quentin stops, his body heaving up and down as he looks up at the sky with his back to me, then slowly turns to face us. Mathéo stands beside him, with a growing smirk on his face, making me less worried and more intrigued.

"Do tell, brother." Mathéo grins.

Quentin shakes his head. "It could be nothing."

"What could 'it' even be?" I stress the word it, needing to know what they're referring to.

"You know the girl Quentin's slept with? Well, there's a good chance she's pregnant," Mathéo explains, making my mouth pop open in shock.

"What?! How?" I shriek, knowing what a disaster this could be.

Mathéo gives Ryker a quick side-eye. "I think you know how, Camille."

"Gross, not what I meant. Q, why does he think that?" I turn my attention to my other brother, who seems distraught.

"Mathéo is over exaggerating. All he did is ask me how she's doing, and I said that she's been sick for a week with the flu, but I haven't been able to see her because of everything that happened."

"Ah, ah," Mathéo cuts in. "This is where I pointed out that the flu doesn't last for a week."

We're all quiet for a minute as Mathéo's words sink in. It's not a definite answer, but it also is a possibility.

"What are you going to do?" Ryker asks Quentin.

Quentin shakes his head, looking at the ground. "For once, I don't know."

"There you two are!" Jasmine shouts, making her way over to us. "We've been looking for the newlyweds to cut the cake."

My brother gives me a look, one I know from years of being his sister means not to say a word.

I link my arm through Ryker's. "Let's go."

As we walk together, my mind races with how Quentin's life could be changing, forever. If this girl—who is his enemy's little sister *and* works for his team—*is* pregnant, I have no idea how that can all coexist without imploding.

But if there's one person who does what he needs to do for his loved ones, it's Q.

Jasmine leads us to the three-tier cake, topped with a plastic heart and baseball. "This is the best I could do on short notice, so in order to save time, I got the toppers from the dollar store. I hope that's okay," she admits, handing Ryker a large knife.

"More than okay. Thank you for this," I tell her, smiling as Ryker pulls me in front of him.

With our hands interlocked, we cut the first slice of cake. While it may seem small, it feels significant. As if it's the official start of us diving into our life together.

After handing out pieces to friends and family, Ryker and I make our way to the bench under the tree, sharing a piece of the vanilla sprinkle cake together under the slowly-setting sun.

My eyes light up at the decadent-looking piece on my lap. "This looks so good."

Ryker drags a finger in the icing, then holds it up to me. "Try it."

I quickly dart my eyes around, making sure everyone's milling about and not focused on us. Once we're in the clear, I quickly suck the icing off his finger.

A moan gets trapped in my throat. "*Mmm*, this is so good."

"Jesus, this was bad idea," Ryker grunts, shifting on the bench beside me. "Here I thought I'd try to be a cute, doting husband."

I quirk a brow at that. "No, you didn't. Don't lie."

Ryker only laughs, then takes a bite for himself, his eyes rolling as he swallows. "Fuck, that is good."

We finish the piece in comfortable silence, watching as Cameron feeds Aurora a bite, who then goes to return the favor but squishes it on his nose. Elio has Jasmine's feet in his lap, giving them a massage, while she eats and talks to Marcela next to her.

Then there's Theo, standing on a chair. "All right, y'all," Theo yells, cupping his hands around his mouth to enhance his already loud voice. "Shift your eyes to the dance floor. It's time for Mr. and Mrs. Lewis to share their very first dance."

I think Ryker's about to protest, but when the slow, sweet melody of "Crazy Love" pours out of the speaker, his eyes dart to mine, a knowing smile on his lips. It's the song that played when he tattooed me, one we both loved then, but now has an even bigger meaning.

"You asked me then if the song meant anything to me, and I said no," he says as he stands and takes my hand in his own, lifting me up as well.

"And now?"

"It reminds me of you, of *us*." He smiles, the wide and bright one he keeps just for me. It makes my entire body buzz from the sight of something so beautiful.

"I love you, Ryker." My voice cracks with affection while my eyelashes fight for their life to hold back my tears. I've done far too much of that in the last week.

He smirks, referencing the song as he begins to pull us onto the dance floor. "And I love you, like crazy."

We sway slowly on the makeshift dance floor while his arms band behind my back, hugging me close to him. My head rests on his shoulder, along with my hand, and he holds my other hand.

"Do you want kids?" I blurt out, unable to control the random question.

Ryker stills against me and I lift my head from his shoulder. "I'm not pregnant. Don't worry," I assure him. "We've never had that talk, so I'm curious."

He breathes a visible sigh of relief, then gently guides my head back to his shoulder, and his hand stays there, playing with my hair as he speaks. "I always thought I didn't because I never saw room for love in my life. But now, I want the extra rooms. I want as many rooms of love as possible."

I laugh against his shoulder while we continue to sway. "Slow down there, Ryker the biker, I am not birthing a bunch of babies. I was thinking one or two."

"Whatever you want, princess." His voice is low and sweet in my ear.

"You know, your life is turning out like a Disney movie,

oddly enough. You saved the princess from distress, married her, and are keeping her forever," I point out.

Ryker's deep laughter rumbles against my chest, making my own spill out of me.

"And I wouldn't have it any other way."

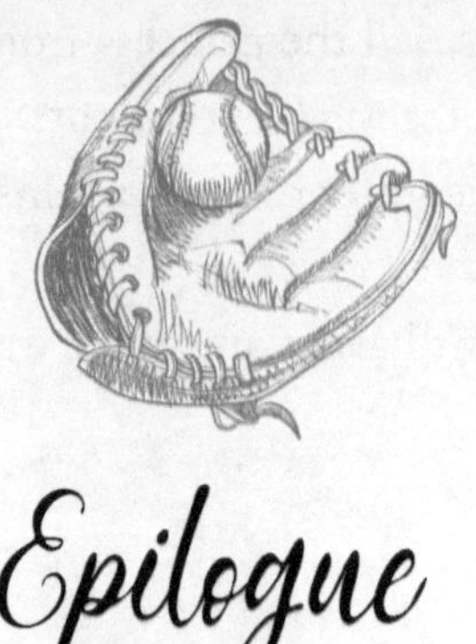

Epilogue

Ryker

My knee bounces anxiously on my mother's couch, my hand gripping Camille's thigh to keep me grounded. The MLB draft starts today, and while I know the Detroit Panthers will be selecting me as their first-round draft pick, it does nothing to erase my nerves.

I was excited as hell to begin my career in major league baseball, don't get me wrong, but there was something to be said about the difference between knowing your dream is going to happen and it *actually* happening.

What if I don't live up to the demands? What if I choke on my first year?

While getting signed was the first step, performing was the next. I had a long road ahead of me of hard work to make my dream happen.

"Hey," a soft voice muses from beside me, drawing my focus to her.

My wife.

Fuck, those words never get old.

"What's wrong?" she prods, resting her hand on my bouncing knee, easing the action.

I inhale deeply, the smell of my mom's infamous popcorn wafting in the air, then exhale. "I'm so fucking happy this is happening…but also terrified. It's a big change. What if I'm not ready for it?" I voice my innermost thoughts, something that's come easier and easier since falling in love with her.

Camille pulls my face to look at her, making my heart lurch forward at the sight of her. "That's okay, completely normal to feel that way. You think you're the only guy in this draft scared shitless? Behind all these smiles and success stories, you can bet that each one is worried," she reassures me with her bright smile. "Besides, you'll always have me cheering you on no matter what."

That right there is exactly what I needed to hear to soothe the incessant worries in my mind. It was the same thing she whispered to me during our championship game this year, when our team was down by one, and I was up to bat in the bottom of the last inning. We ended up winning the title, bringing a trophy home to RLU.

My lips press chastely against hers, our foreheads touching as I whisper, "Thank you, baby."

What she doesn't know is that drafting isn't the only thing contributing to my nerves. I finally got her the ring she deserves, and I plan to give it to her once this is all said and done. We may already be married, but fuck, I hope she likes this ring.

It was custom-made, a round diamond surrounded by smaller diamonds in the shape of petals, mirroring a flower. She loves flowers so much that I thought this would be perfect for her.

My mom returns to the couch and sets two bowls of popcorn on the coffee table in front of us. "I cannot believe it, Bear. You're about to be drafted into the MLB." Her voice shakes with emotion.

"Please don't cry, Mom," I urge her, not needing to add this to my emotional wheelhouse today.

"I know. I'm incredibly proud of you, that's all." She smiles, her words filling me with warmth. My mom shifts her focus to Camille, handing her a bowl of popcorn. "Ryker told me you like it hot, so I made this one extra spicy."

"Thank you so much," she says appreciatively.

We settle in with our snacks, watching as the commentators begin the 2024 MLB draft. The commissioner of the MLB steps up to the podium, calm as ever as he leans against the wood, staring right into the camera. He doesn't bother to read the paper on top of the podium or give a mini-speech before he gets to business. He is a waste no time kind of man, and it shows.

"The Detroit Panthers, with the first pick in the first round of the 2024 MLB draft select… Ryker Lewis, from Rock Land University, Colorado."

My mom jumps off the couch, shouting and clapping. Camille stands and attempts to pull me off the couch, so I let her. They both pull me into a hug, shouting their congratulations into my ears, and wrap me in their love.

To think I never wanted anything to do with love. Funny how things change.

My mom is the first to let go, knowing what I plan to do next.

Camille wraps her arms around my neck, crying into it. "I'm so happy for you, Ry. I can't wait to start our lives together in Detroit. After we watch Aurora crush it at the Olympics next week, that is."

I untangle myself from her, noting the confusion in her eyes as I drop down to one knee for the second time.

She tilts her head to the side, eyes wide like I've lost my mind. "What are you doing?"

I pull the black box from my pocket, then pop it open as I hold the ring up to her. "Starting our lives out the right way by giving you the ring you deserve, so that everyone knows you're mine."

Both of Camille's hands fly to cover her agape mouth, while tears cascade down her cheeks.

"Oh, Ryker, it's so beautiful." She sniffles. "Is that a flower?"

"Yeah, it is, but wait till it's on." I grin, coming to a stand as I take her hand in mine, and slide the ring onto her finger, gliding it over my initials on the side of her finger.

A wave of possessiveness rocks me so hard I nearly keel over. Seeing my ring and my name on her finger is giving me ideas I shouldn't be having while my mom's in the room.

"I love it so much. It's perfect. You're perfect." She sobs, her eyes in awe as the ring glitters from the sunlight drifting in through the windows. "I love you."

"I love you." I seal my words with a kiss, pulling back sooner than I'd like because again, my mom is in the room. "And I'll spend every day of our lives making sure you feel it."

She beams, her hand entwining with mine. "How lucky am I that I get to keep you forever?"

I smile, something only she can make me do. "Not as lucky as me because I get to keep you."

THE END

Want more of Camille and Ryker?
Head to my website *carliejean.ca* to get a bonus epilogue.

What's next?
The last installment in the RLU series,
Theo and Marcela's story comes out in the Fall of 2024.

Acknowledgements

To make a writer speechless, or writer-less in this case is truly a great accomplishment on your part my readers. Because that's what I am. Utterly shocked and beyond grateful for how much love and support you've shown me over this first year as an author. I couldn't be where I am today without you all, and I am forever grateful for what you readers have done for me. To be living out my dream of writing romance novels is wild, and I have you all to thank for it.

To my family for being so supportive, and for also not actually reading these books, thank you. To my boyfriend for being my biggest fan and giving me the love I've read and dreamt about, thank you for being you and giving me so much inspiration. To my friends who cheer me on throughout this journey, thank you.

To my editing team - Salma, Emily, and Isabella - thank you for all of your hard work and efforts to shape this book into what it is today. I truly couldn't do it without you all. Thank you for being amazing people to work with, it's always the best time despite me feeling dumb half the time for the things that you notice are missing or don't make sense. I appreciate you all immensely!

To my beta readers, Kylie, Summer, Lucile, Jordyn, and Jennine thank you for all your love and excitement for Keep Me. The comments in the document filled me with a confidence I've yet to have before publishing a book, and I am forever grateful for that. The way you all loved these characters meant the world to me. Thank you for the comments and ideas that pushed this story upward, making it the best that it can be. I appreciate you all.

To my cover designer Cat, for always knocking these covers out of the park. Pun intended. You are the absolute best to work with, and your creativity is simply unmatched. Thank you for being a ray of sunshine in my life, I am so glad to call you a friend.

To Shaye and Lindsey at GoodGirls PR, thank you for hyping up and loving this book as much as I do. You ladies are not only amazing to work with, but amazing people who deserve the very best.

To Nada at Qamber, you always blow me away with how amazing your services are. Not only is the work you produce of the greatest quality, but it is done promptly and to top it off, you are a joy to work with. I look forward to many more books with you!

About the Author

Carlie is a romance author who loves all things swoon, sunshine, and spice. She lives in Canada. She has two brothers, and a dog named Milo. Some of her favourite things are sunsets, warm weather and iced matcha lattes. She loves to watch and play a variety of sports, which is where her obsession with sports romances originated. When she's not teaching, she loves reading, writing, going for walks, and traveling.

SOCIALS

Check out my website and socials for
in-depth book information, what I'm currently
writing, and bonus materials!
www.carliejean.ca

@carliejeanwrites on TikTok and Instagram.

www.ingramcontent.com/pod-product-compliance
Lightning Source LLC
Chambersburg PA
CBHW030940120726
47906CB00002B/656